STORY

Gwen Hernandez

Happy reading!

Gwen Hern

www.gwenhernandez.com

First edition: February 2014

Cover design by Kim Killion.

This book was written and formatted in Scrivener.

For my husband.

You're the reason I believe in love and "happily ever after."

❋ ❋ ❋

# ACKNOWLEDGMENTS

I owe thanks to so many who helped me bring *Blind Fury* to life.

Absolutely first is my husband and my two boys for their unwavering support.

Thanks to my mom who taught me to love reading, and to my dad who didn't even blink when I told him my books had sex in them.

To my good friend, Michele Bridgeforth, my first fan and ardent cheerleader. And many thanks to her husband, Brandon, who's been letting me bug him with law enforcement and gun questions for years now. If I got anything wrong, don't blame him. He tried.

Piper Rome was kind enough to share insights from a scary car ride. Thanks!

I also owe Laura Hayden for encouraging me to write my favorite kind of book: romantic suspense.

I wouldn't be here without the love, support, and cheering of all of my Kiss & Thrill sisters: Sharon Wray, Krista Hall, Rachel Grant, Lena Diaz, Manda Collins, Diana Belchase, Carey Baldwin, and Sarah Andre. Special thanks to Rachel and Sarah —along with my friend Maura Troy—for their early reads and fabulous feedback!

My editor Angela Polidoro made this book so much better, pushing me to stretch myself, my characters, and the story to a new level. I owe Ava Miles for connecting us, and for just being her wonderful self.

Thanks to Kimberly Killion for a better cover than I could ever envision on my own.

And, finally, to my golden retriever, sweet Zoe. For putting up with forgotten walks and late meals, and for hanging out near my favorite writing chair.

# CHAPTER ONE

IN THE LAND OF DUST and sand, things got messy when it rained. Mick Fury's boots made sucking sounds in the mud left behind by a morning shower as he strode along the graffiti-covered blast wall that ran the perimeter of Kandahar Airfield.

He kept pace with Rob Ryan, ignoring the kerosene scent of jet fuel assaulting his nose as they headed to meet up with their Claymore Security teammates. They were scheduled to train local police recruits in tactical shooting techniques today. A worthy exercise if the trainees stayed alive long enough to use their new skills. Unfortunately, cops in Afghanistan were one of the Taliban's favorite targets.

Rob waggled a large rip-proof envelope addressed to his sister in Virginia. "Let me drop this in the mail on our way."

They detoured to the makeshift post office. "Did I forget Jenna's birthday or something?" Mick asked.

"Have you ever remembered it?" Rob ribbed him.

Actually, he had. Every year. November twenty-fifth.

"No," Rob said when he didn't answer. "It's just some

notes and stuff that I don't have room for in my bag."

"So you're really not coming back?" A lead weight settled on Mick's chest. He and Rob had been best friends and teammates for twelve years. They'd had each other's backs through boot camp, pararescue training, and now at Claymore. If Rob left in two weeks like he planned, then Mick would be left here with only his friend Dan Molina and a bunch of assholes, the kind who thrived in an industry where the rules of civilization didn't apply.

The brotherhood he'd experienced in the Air Force—putting the members of the team above all else—had been hard to find in the world of private security contracting. Any one of them could walk away at any time, and some of the guys were outright criminals who'd never be allowed to carry a gun in the States.

"I'm really not coming back," Rob said, stuffing the envelope into a slot in the shipping containers that masqueraded as a post office. "And you shouldn't either."

It was an old argument. The constant stress, the poor management, and the barren surroundings chafed like a tight shoe. But there was no substitute for the adrenaline rush. There was something about cheating death that made him feel alive like nothing else could.

"What else can I do?" Mick asked. "Every time we go home, I'm happy for about two weeks. And then it all starts to seem so pointless, so boring." And quiet. There was nothing worse than being left alone with his thoughts. At least here in this hellhole he knew without a doubt that he was good for something.

Rob shoved his hands in his front pockets and rubbed a heel in the mud while they waited for the others to show up. "You think I don't feel the same way? But every time I leave, the look in Jenna's eyes nearly rips my heart out. I can't do that to her anymore."

Mick knew that look. Had memorized it long ago, along with everything else about the one woman who was off limits to him…and not just because Rob had threatened to permanently end his sex life if he tried anything.

He couldn't toy with the heart of a woman who'd suffered so much already. Jenna was the kind of girl you married and took home to Mom. Not Mick's usual type. She was smart and sweet, hardly a seductress. But somehow he couldn't get her pale, almost-gray eyes and schoolgirl freckles out of his head.

"What will you do?" he asked Rob, bringing himself back to the ugly reality of Afghanistan. "I can't see you settling down to a desk job and a white picket fence."

Rob laughed, but the humor didn't reach his eyes. "Screw that. I was talking to Dan, and he knows a guy who's a flight medic for one of those MedEvac helicopters. They also do search and rescue missions. I'll have to go to school first, but it'll be worth it. It will be like being in the PJs again, but without anyone shooting at you."

"Then where's the thrill?" Mick asked, not entirely joking. He plastered on his trademark carefree smile and tapped his rifle. He never should have left pararescue, but the money he'd been offered to join Claymore had been impossible to resist.

His friend shook his head. "Just think about it, okay?"

"Sure." He'd think about it. In fact, he already thought about it almost daily. Jesus, why couldn't he be normal? When he was here, he wanted to go home—drive his new Camaro, flirt with girls, party with his friends; and when he was back in Virginia he could hardly stand it. The tedium and pettiness of Stateside life was suffocating. At least things made sense here.

His job was to survive. Simple as that.

"Hey." Rob grabbed Mick's arm as a large armored vehicle rumbled past, leaving deep grooves in the mud. "Promise me one thing." He looked way too serious for Mick's taste. Even more serious than usual.

"What's that?"

"If something happens to me, you'll leave Claymore and take care of Jenna."

Oh, hell no. They were not going to have this conversation. Not right before going outside the wire. He bounced his eyebrows at Rob and forced a smile. "Take care of her, huh?"

"Yeah, and that includes protecting her from guys like you." Rob ran a hand through his close-cropped hair. "Come on, man. I mean it. I'll feel better knowing that she wouldn't be left alone."

"We've been here for two years. Why are you asking me this now?" Mick wrinkled his nose as the wind shifted, bringing with it the pungent odor of the sewage treatment plant—aka The Poo Pond. "Did something happen?"

Rob glanced around and shook his head with feigned indifference that didn't fool Mick for a second. "No, I'm just being, you know, superstitious now that I've given my notice. If I don't leave any loose ends, then nothing will happen."

He was full of crap, but Mick let it go. "Dude, you don't even have to ask. She's the closest thing I have to a sister of my own." Except for the very un-brotherly thoughts he had about her. "But you're the one who's going to be there for her, so it doesn't matter. You're going to go home, find a job, get a dog, and meet a girl. In another year, I won't recognize you. You'll probably even own a minivan." Mick pulled a face, like he couldn't imagine a worse fate.

Rob's shoulders visibly relaxed and the line between his

eyebrows softened. What the hell was going on with him? He'd never been this tightly wound before.

"Thanks. I owe you one."

Mick consulted his palm as if it were a notebook, and pretended to cross something out. "By my calculations, that makes us even." He grinned. "Hell, if I'd known you were this easy to get square with, I would have offered months ago."

Rob finally laughed, and the knot in Mick's chest loosened.

"Hey, ladies. You ready to run the gauntlet?" Three of their crew trudged toward them, nine millimeters in their thigh holsters and M4s strapped to their chest rigs, always at the ready. Dressed in khaki pants and polo shirts, they looked like an army of muscle-bound frat boys.

Mick and Rob fit right in.

"As long as you brought your diapers this time, Beavis," Mick called out, using the nickname the man had earned for his rat-like resemblance to the animated character. "I don't want shit to get all over the seats if we take fire."

Beavis flipped him off and they walked toward their armored vehicles to meet up with the rest of the group for the briefing.

Just another day in paradise.

An hour later, Mick dropped to his knees in the mud next to Rob. "No, no, no!" He tore at his friend's mangled body armor and sticky, wet shirt and—oh God, *no*. He spread his hands over the ragged mess that used to be his friend's chest, as if he could hold him together by magic. His skills as a medic were of no use to him with an injury this bad… All he could do was try to stop the alarming flow of blood. "Damn it, Rob, hang on for me. You're going home, remember?

Come on, *come on.*"

Fucking Murphy and his law. Rob should have known better than to announce that he was going home right before they went outside the wire. Everyone knew a convoy was an easy target for roadside bombs and insurgent attacks.

Today, they'd managed to find both.

*This can't be happening.* Mick adjusted his position and pressed harder. Rob couldn't die; he was one of the good ones. Jenna needed her brother.

*Mick* needed him.

"Jenna," Rob whispered, clutching weakly at Mick's arm. His look said he knew he wouldn't make it.

Mick blinked against the burn of hot tears and nodded. "Don't worry. I'll watch out for her until you're on your feet again. Just stay with me." But the blood wouldn't fucking stop. It bubbled through his fingers, warm and sticky and relentless.

Rob closed his eyes and mumbled.

Mick leaned close to hear him over the noise of engines, men shouting, and the buzzing in his ears left by the ricochet of gunfire. "What's that?"

"Don't tell her."

Sharp smoke stung his nose as Mick surveyed the carnage surrounding them. The barren ground was covered with lifeless figures slicked with mud and blood. He closed his eyes briefly to block out the images, but like so many other horrors he'd witnessed, the scene would haunt him forever.

No way in hell would he ever want to talk about it. Keeping this horrific moment from Jenna was an easy promise to make. "Never."

Jenna Ryan couldn't remember the last time she'd been so full of hope. She used her running shirt to wipe the sweat from her face and filled a glass with cold water from the door of her refrigerator. According to the clock on the microwave, she didn't need to leave for two more hours. Even then she'd probably be early for her interview, but it was always better to play it safe with traffic in the D.C. area.

She perched on the arm of the sofa in her living room and drank the icy water, letting the scent of vanilla from her favorite plug-in air freshener calm her jumpy nerves as her body cooled. Her lips curved into a smile when she looked at one of the pictures on the fireplace mantle. Dressed in desert camouflage and holding large rifles in front of an armored truck, her brother Rob and his best friend Mick stared down at her.

Rob was going to be so happy for her if she got this new database analyst job. It wasn't the self-employment route he'd been pushing her to try, but Travers & West would be a huge improvement over her current employer. And interviewing for a new job was just about all the stress she could handle until he was home safe.

An hour later, showered and dressed, she reviewed her resumé one more time and practiced her answers to potential interview questions. After three years of putting up with the jerks at Quicksilver Defense Systems—QDS for short—she wanted to be as prepared as possible for the job that could be her ticket out.

Travers & West had a reputation for treating its employees well, offering flexible hours and performance-based bonuses. What a nice change that would be. And if she got the job, Rob could quit worrying about her and focus on himself.

And they both needed *that*.

Her cell phone rang as she was loading her breakfast dishes in the dishwasher.

"Are you ready?" Jenna's best friend, Tara Fujimoto, asked in her high-pitched voice.

"Yep. As long as I don't pass out from nerves. But I'm feeling better after Rob's call yesterday." He and Mick had called to wish her luck, knowing she would need encouragement.

"And did you talk to Mick too?"

"Yes." Jenna couldn't keep the exasperation out of her voice. As usual, he'd made a point of talking to her before Rob ended the call. Mick had told her once that he needed a little bit of normal every once in a while. He didn't have a sister to call, so he borrowed Jenna.

"I think he likes you," Tara said.

"As a surrogate sister, maybe." If she tried hard enough, she could convince herself that she saw him as a brother. The man hiding beneath the reckless playboy facade had always tempted her, but she couldn't risk her already fragile heart.

Tara snorted. "Hardly."

"How Mick Fury thinks of me is irrelevant. I'd never get involved with a guy who goes through women like I go through tissues."

"Don't you mean he *blows* through them?" Tara chuckled.

Jenna groaned. "Can we talk about something else? Like the fact that Rob is finally coming home?"

Tara went silent for a beat, no doubt trying to rein in a sarcastic comment. "For how long?"

"For good." The words danced on Jenna's tongue and she found herself bouncing on her toes like a little girl at Christmas waiting to open her gifts.

"That's great," Tara said evenly.

"I think he really means it this time." Jenna leaned against the cool countertop. Somehow she would find a way to make him happier, a way to convince him to stay. "He was talking about going back to school and adopting a rescue dog. It sounds like he's given it a lot of thought."

"Well, good. Maybe that will make up for having Carl on your case all the time."

Jenna covered her ears. "Ack, no. I don't want to talk about my boss right before my interview. Besides, if things go well, Carl will be history." Though if he found out she'd used a personal day to go on a job interview, she might be history at QDS whether the interview went well or not.

"You're right. You're going to be great today and we'll never have to talk about that jerk again." Tara giggled. "Let's talk about Mick instead."

"Tara!"

Her friend gave a dramatic sigh. "Fine. I'm glad you're looking for a new job, even though it'll be lonely here without you around. But are you sure you wouldn't be happier working for yourself? From what I hear, programmers are in high demand. Finding work should be a piece of cake."

A pipe dream. Wishful thinking. "You sound like Rob. He even offered to front me the money when he gets back." No matter how much the private security company he worked for paid him, she didn't want to take him up on the offer. She couldn't risk losing the money. Not when he'd literally dodged bullets to earn it.

"Do it," Tara said, her voice filling with excitement. "You're hard-working, conscientious, and super smart. You'll make a killing."

Jenna's chest squeezed. Easy for her friend to say. "I appreciate the pep talk, but you're forgetting the part where I'd have to be my own salesperson." Her nose wrinkled at the thought. *Nightmare.* "Besides, if I lost all of Rob's money, I'd never be able to forgive myself."

"Sometimes you need to take a risk," Tara said.

"I think a job interview is enough risk for one day."

"All right, I'll back off. I have to run to a meeting, but good luck today. Call me when you're done."

"Thanks, I will."

Jenna hung up, and walked over to the gilt-edged mirror in the foyer, smoothing the collar on her blue button-down shirt as she looked at her reflection. In the silk top and crisp slacks she exuded power and confidence. Still, she'd rather be wearing jeans and a sweatshirt. If she ever got up the nerve to work for herself, she'd be able to spend the day in her drawstring cotton pants and the fuzzy purple slippers that Rob had bought her for Christmas.

Maybe one day. For now, she'd settle for a new job. If she nailed this interview, today could rank up there with getting her driver's license, college graduation, and her first kiss.

At ten o'clock, she went through her red leather tote bag —a splurge in her campaign to break out of her too-sensible tan and black rut—one last time. Resumé. Cell phone. Wallet. Everything was in place, ready to go. Just as it had been last night. And an hour ago. And ten minutes ago.

She didn't need to leave for another fifteen minutes, but she'd rather arrive early and sit in the parking lot than be stressed out over traffic. She picked up a book and tucked it into her bag. Keys in hand, she checked her reflection in the mirror one more time, smoothing the blonde waves that had come loose from her hair clip.

Sliding the tote over her shoulder, she reached for the front door just as her cell phone rang. Shoot. It was the number of the phone Rob used to call her from Afghanistan. Reluctant to miss the call, she shut the door and answered.

Mick's smooth voice greeted her from the other side of the world, and her stomach dipped.

"Hey, I'd love to talk," she said, "but I'm leaving for my

interview. Will you be around in a few hours?"

"Jenna, this can't wait."

His use of her given name stopped her dead. He'd been calling her Jay for as long as she could remember. "What's wrong?" She and Mick never discussed anything important. The only thing they had in common was—

A sick feeling settled in her chest and she took a step back, as if she could put distance between herself and what he was going to say. "No."

"I'm sorry," he said, his voice rough and scratchy on the long distance line. "Rob's…" Mick cleared his throat. "He's gone."

Her body went cold. "Gone?"

"We got into a firefight while on a convoy this morning, and Rob was hit." He hesitated. "He died at the scene."

Her throat tightened and she let out a strangled sound of grief.

Mick blew out a long, shaky breath. "I'm so sorry, honey. I wish I could be there right now, but it's going to take me a couple of days to get back. Someone from Claymore will be coming to see you, but I didn't want you to hear the news from a stranger."

"Thank you," she managed, her voice barely a whisper.

Mick urged her to call Tara for support and signed off. Jenna stared at the phone in her hand without really seeing it.

*He died at the scene.* The words swirled through her brain and brought her whole world crashing down. "No, no, no." Little black spots danced in front of her eyes, and her stomach threatened to return her breakfast.

Rob was done with private security. No more Afghanistan. He was coming home in two weeks. He *couldn't* be dead.

Her legs must have given out because suddenly she was

on her hands and knees, staring at the wood floor. "Not Rob, too," she said on a sob, pressing her forehead into the hard, cold surface. It wasn't fair. She'd lost too much already. And now her brother, her protector, her only remaining family, was gone.

Irreversibly, irrevocably gone.

In the biggest picture on the mantle, her family of five was laughing on the beach during a Christmas trip to Hilton Head thirteen years ago. She'd been twelve, Jimmy ten, and Rob seventeen. Now she was the only one left. A reckless driver had seen to that. Her parents had died instantly, but Jimmy had hung on in a coma for six months before finally letting go. Rob had been fresh out of the Air Force with plans to go to school, but Jimmy's medical bills were staggering. So Rob had gone to work for Claymore instead.

Tears splashed onto the shiny wood between her hands, beading up on the buffed surface. If it were possible for a person's heart to burst from too much grief, she'd be joining Rob any second. She wanted to curl into a ball and hide in the dark where she could cry her guts out.

Instead, she stayed glued to the floor until her legs went numb and she was out of tears.

God, she had to get a grip. With a deep breath, she wiped her eyes and stood on shaky legs. Her knees were sore, her toes tingling. She leaned against the front door and snatched up her tote bag from the floor where she must have dropped it. *The interview.*

Somehow she managed to hold it together long enough to call Travers & West. The secretary clucked in sympathy at her reason for canceling, but explained that she couldn't reschedule. They had plenty of applicants and would probably fill the job tomorrow. Jenna didn't have the energy to push the issue.

She slammed the phone down on the kitchen counter and stumbled down the stairs to her one-car garage. The tiny space was stacked to the rafters with boxes labeled in neat print. Soon Rob's things would join them, and her entire family would be reduced to belongings packed lovingly into cardboard. Some people went to a cemetery to commune with their lost loved ones. Jenna hung out in her garage with the boxes. Maybe she was crazy, but it helped.

"It's too much!" she shouted into the whitewashed room as tears threatened again.

Had she wronged someone in a past life? Done something heinous as a child that she'd blocked out? Maybe the Ryan family had picked up a curse somewhere along the way. She laughed—an unbalanced sound—and smoothed her hand across a box of travel souvenirs.

Jimmy's Swiss Army knife from Lucerne, a set of blue and white Delft plates from Holland, an obi—a Japanese kimono sash—her mother had picked up in Tokyo. Bits and pieces of the Ryans' short lives, wrapped in paper and taped up because while she had no place for all the things left behind, she couldn't bear to let them go.

She wiped her eyes and slumped against the wall. She'd give anything to have Rob walk through that door with a hundred-watt smile and lift her into a bear hug. In fact, a hug would be really great right about now.

Tara would be there in an instant if she called, no question, but Jenna wasn't ready to share her pain yet. Instead, she sat there among her boxes until her joints turned stiff.

Finally, she stood and dusted herself off before turning out the lights, and slowly made her way back upstairs. She'd call her friend later. Right now, there was only one thing that could make her feel better. She changed back into her workout clothes and set off for a nearby trail.

Maybe if she ran hard enough, she could outrun the pain.


"What did you find?" Ghost asked the imbecile on the other end of the line as he stared through the floor-to-ceiling window at the sun setting over the Potomac River.

"Nothing more than the documents I took off Ryan's body. Fury got to his things before I could."

"And you're sure Ryan had more evidence?" He squeezed the phone until it dug sharply into his palm. Between these idiots and the asshole who'd discovered them, everything was at risk. The contracts, the money, the company. *Everything.*

"Yes, sir," Beavis said. "Rizzo saw him taking pictures."

"*Fuck.*" He had just over a week to clean up this mess or everything that he'd worked so hard to accomplish would crumble between his fingers like a clod of dirt.

"I thought we might be able to get to his bag on the plane back to the States, but Fury kept it with him, and there were too many people around."

Ghost sucked in a deep breath. A good leader didn't lose his cool. "There's too much at stake for this to get out." He rubbed his forehead. *Goddammit.* None of this shit was supposed to follow them to the States. "Find any evidence and destroy it before he and the girl figure out what they have."

"Yes, sir."

"And if they get in the way…"

"I'll take care of it, sir."

Ghost slammed his phone on the desk. *You'd damn well better.*

# CHAPTER TWO

EARLY THURSDAY AFTERNOON, JENNA WAS wallowing in bed when the doorbell rang. She'd been trying to nap, but was instead staring at the stripes of midday sun that painted the ceiling, thinking about Rob. Tara's head appeared around the bedroom doorjamb a minute later. "Mick's here. I'm going to run a few errands. Do you need anything?"

*Yes.* She needed Rob and the rest of her family back. She needed something in her life worth living for, because as it stood now, she couldn't think of one compelling reason to get out of bed.

Jenna sighed. Leave it to Mick to drop in without calling first. He was a master at hijacking other people's schedules. Rob had called him spontaneous, but she wasn't feeling that generous.

Not that she had anything on her schedule.

She sat up and shook her head at Tara. "I can't think of anything." The poor woman probably needed a break. Tara had been helping her with the funeral arrangements and forcing food down her throat for the last three days.

"Okay. I'll be back in a couple hours." Tara gave her a quick smile and disappeared down the hall.

Jenna glanced in the mirror above the blue dresser her mom had painted for her twelfth birthday. She looked like crap. After taking a shower, she'd dressed in sweats and corralled her curls into a ponytail, leaving her pale face bare of makeup. She hadn't been expecting a visitor. Though in all honesty, she wouldn't have had the energy to primp even if she'd known he was going to show up today.

Bracing herself, she descended the stairs and found Mick standing on the threshold between the foyer and the living room, holding Rob's mobility bag in one hand. His lean, six-foot-two frame filled the space, and she kept her distance so she wouldn't have to tilt her head up to meet his brilliant blue eyes. "When did you get back?" she asked.

"We landed a couple hours ago." Gone was his ever-present grin. A crease cut a groove between his eyebrows and his jaw was clenched tight. Shadows under his eyes and the slope of his shoulders spoke of fatigue. He took in her outfit, his gaze spreading a warm tingle of awareness across her skin.

She tugged nervously at her bulky top. "I would have cleaned up a little if I'd known you were coming."

"That's why I didn't call." He dropped the bag, walked over, and wrapped her in his arms, his familiar scent of soap and something spicy kicking her heart into high gear.

Seeing him in person made Rob's death real, and she couldn't stop her tears. Mick held her as she sobbed against him, pounding his hard chest with her fists, angry at him for giving her the bad news, angry that he was there to watch her fall apart.

Angry that he was alive and Rob wasn't.

"I'm so sorry." He absorbed her punches and squeezed

her tightly, whispering in her ear, "I know, honey. I know."

Appalled by her outburst, she pushed back and wiped her face, turning away so she wouldn't have to look at him when she finally got the nerve to pose her question. "How did it happen?" she asked, her voice thick. Good idea or not, she needed to know.

He took a deep breath and blew it out slowly before answering. "Our lead vehicle hit an IED. While Dan and Rob and I tended to the wounded, the team became engaged in gunfire with a group of locals. Rob took a hit."

"What about his body armor?" He'd promised to wear it no matter how heavy or hot it made him. He'd promised.

Mick gave a pained expression and ran a hand through his sandy-blond hair. "It wasn't enough to protect him."

So not small arms fire? Clearly, Mick was trying to soften the blow as much as possible by giving her a sanitized version of the incident. The media and Claymore's official representative had been equally vague, as had the State Department's investigator. She knew all the tricks after being on the receiving end of bad news so many times. In fact, she should be an expert at getting it by now. But some things didn't get easier with experience.

"Why are you being so ambiguous?"

"Because it's easier than telling you the messy details. It's hard enough remembering them," he responded, his voice rough and low.

She gave him a closer look and was surprised by the sight of his red-rimmed eyes. Had he been crying? It hadn't occurred to her that he might be seeking comfort as much as giving it, but Rob had been his best friend. Here she was wrapped up in her own sorrow, not even thinking about what others had lost. Especially Mick. "I'm sorry. This has to be hard on you too."

"I'll survive. We both will," he said with a conviction and a seriousness she'd never seen in him before. He had always been so glib, ever ready with a quick joke when things got too heavy. Today he wasn't hiding behind his slick charm.

Would she survive? Possibly. Right now she wasn't so sure.

Her eyes on the floor, the fireplace, the chair—anywhere but his face—she said, "Thank you for coming." Then she risked another glance at his eyes. "Will you be at the funeral tomorrow?"

He gave her an odd look. "Of course I'll be there."

She nodded and clasped her arms across her chest. What a dumb thing to ask. But being around him had always lowered her IQ by at least ten points.

"You don't have to do all this by yourself, you know."

"I know." She focused on the wall behind him. "I'm not. Tara's been helping." And thank God for her. Without her, Jenna would be completely lost.

"I'd like to help too." He stuffed his hands into his pockets, apparently taking his cue from her unwelcoming posture. "Call me if you need anything."

"Yeah, sure." If he was smart, he wouldn't expect a call, but she nodded as she walked him to the door. He leaned in closer, as if for a hug, but she couldn't let him touch her again, not when the feel of his arms was still imprinted on her skin.

There was another time, a few years ago, when he'd been this close. The memory was still as vivid as the man before her. He'd been helping her and Rob move into this very house, and her brother had gone out to pick up lunch.

Jenna was cutting open a box, but the blade slipped and sliced her palm instead. Mick heard her gasp and practically dropped the chair he was carrying in his haste to reach her side.

"Jesus, Jay," he said as blood dripped from her hand. He covered her palm with his own and led her to the tiny bathroom where he rinsed her wound and placed a wad of folded toilet paper over it.

They sat there for several minutes while he pressed her hand between both of his, his expression fierce as he waited for the bleeding to stop. They'd never touched before, not really, and her stomach fluttered at the feel of his rough skin against her own.

He glanced up with the most serious expression she'd ever seen on his face, the look in his ocean blue eyes making her heart race. "You scared me there for a minute. I saw the blood…"

Heat crept up her neck and into her cheeks. At that moment she had wanted him to kiss her more than she'd ever wanted anything in her life. He didn't.

And now he stood in front of her, that same serious expression back on his handsome face, offering the solace she so desperately needed. But he was too tempting, and she was too vulnerable.

She gave him her best effort at a smile and positioned herself behind the open door as he stepped through. "Thanks for stopping by."

He hesitated on the stoop as if waiting for a sign from her, but then nodded and jogged down the stairs toward his car.

Jenna shut the door and plastered her back to the cool metal. She was messed up enough without adding the complication of Mick. But he was her last link to Rob, and God help her, she liked having him around.

Three hours later, Mick looked through the windshield of his car and squinted against the reflection of the evening sun off the window of the Manassas tattoo parlor he'd just left. Gripping the steering wheel, he was shaky and nervous, like a chain smoker who'd gone too long without a hit.

He had spent the last three days stuck in transport with the rest of his team—they'd all been sent home for an indefinite leave after the incident—and in spite of that transition time, the change from war zone to suburbia was disorienting. Home was both foreign and familiar.

People here went about their lives, ignorant of the daily fight for survival that went on in so many parts of the world. Oblivious to how petty and meaningless their struggle to keep up with the Jones family was. He rubbed the dashboard of his Camaro. *Hypocrite.*

But not really, because he'd bought this baby for speed, not looks.

Mostly.

He slammed the car into gear and peeled out of the parking lot with a satisfying squeal, keeping to a reasonable speed on the freeway. The car strained like a tiger on a leash, eager to be set free, until he passed Haymarket, an outer-ring suburb for those willing to suffer long commutes for larger, newer homes and manicured lawns.

Then Mick dropped the hammer, opened up the throttle, and unleashed the horses under the hood. In seconds, the endorphins flooded in, his hands steadied, and his brain calmed. His pulse thrummed with the engine, and just like that, he could finally breathe again.

God, he was such a wreck. Only a madman would need to go a hundred miles an hour to relax.

A sign for food and gas flashed by and he slowed to a crawl—seventy—to exit. An empty bagel shop beckoned and he parked behind the building, hidden from the main road.

He beat his forehead against the steering wheel a few times before sitting back in the seat, eyes closed.

The soft tick of the cooling engine disrupted the otherwise silent interior.

He'd promised to watch out for Jenna—whatever the hell that meant—but she didn't want him around. Probably didn't need him either. And when he was with her, she tested his restraint on every level. He could sense a wildness beneath her prim exterior that made him want to pin her to the wall and peel back her carefully crafted veneer of control. Nothing turned him on more than the idea of that tightly reined woman letting loose.

Maybe Rob had secretly hated him, because asking him to protect—but not touch—Jenna was like asking a starving man to box up a steak for someone else.

He'd also promised to quit Claymore and stay in the States, but after being home for just two days, he was already restless. There was too much time to think here. And all the promises he'd made collided in his brain until his head felt ready to explode.

Rob, Jenna, bullets, blood.

There was only one way to stop the voices and images flashing in his head. Both disappointed and relieved by his decision, Mick started the engine up again and went looking for a bar.

After letting Tara drag her out for Indian food, Jenna returned to her empty house. The oppressive silence lay over her like a blanket. The rooms would never again be filled with Rob's deep laughter or his exhaustive musings on everything from the Peloponnesian War to veganism.

He'd been gone more often than not over the past few years, but she'd always held onto the hope that he'd return.

After all, without hope, what was left?

Moving with leaden limbs, she dragged Rob's bag over to the sofa. Damn, the thing had to weigh fifty pounds. How had Mick hefted it like it was a kid's backpack? She opened the duffle and removed each item, sorting everything into piles on the coffee table. One to donate, one to decide about later, and one to go into a box in her garage along with the rest of the Ryan family's belongings.

Tara would probably be shocked that she was already beginning to mark her brother's clothes for charity, but the activity soothed her, giving her a way to occupy her mind and hands.

Underneath Rob's clothes, Mick had packed the few personal items he'd found. A twin of the family photo on her mantle, a cheap cell phone, Rob's toiletry bag, a pack of cinnamon gum, a large handgun, a rifle. Jenna stared at the guns, covering her mouth with her hand as images of Rob getting shot played through her head like a bad movie. How had it happened? Had he done something stupid or just been colossally unlucky?

The questions kept piling up, but she was short on answers.

Hastily shoving the weapons into the keep pile, burying them under a sweatshirt she remembered buying for Rob, she made a mental note to ask Mick if he wanted them. Rob had taught her how to handle and shoot all of his weapons, but that didn't mean she wanted anything to do with them now.

Returning her focus to the near-empty bag, she picked out Rob's digital camera. Unable to help herself, she turned it on, curious to see the photos her brother had taken in his last days. All she got was a message that there was no memory card.

She checked the slot, which—sure enough—was empty.

Weird. She removed the remaining few items from the bag—a flashlight, a pair of rubber flip-flops, and a tattered *Sports Illustrated* swimsuit issue—but didn't find the tiny card. Maybe Mick would know something about it. She could ask him tomorrow after the funeral.

She added the camera to the keep pile, then put the donations in an old shopping bag and set them by the front door. Another bag of items went into the garage until she could get a box for them, and the things she wasn't ready to decide on went upstairs into Rob's bedroom closet.

Emotionally wrung out, Jenna tried to relax in front of the television, but she couldn't pay attention to anything. She finally gave up trying and got ready for bed.

A few hours later, she lay shivering under her blue down comforter, the room bright with moonlight that had snuck in around the edges of blinds. She stared at a popped drywall nail on the ceiling. If Rob were still alive, he would have fixed it when he got home.

She pounded the pillow. How long would it take her to stop having those thoughts? Each one pierced her through with fresh pain.

The drumming of her cell phone against the nightstand startled away her impending funk, and she rolled on her side to answer it.

"Hey there, Jay," Mick said, his voice thick and muffled.

She glanced at the glowing red numbers on her alarm clock. Eleven-thirty. "Hi," she said cautiously. What the hell was he up to?

"Listen, sweetheart, the bartender here says I can't drive. Unfortunately, he's right." The slur in his speech was more evident now. "I know it's a bit late, but do you think you could pick me up?"

As if she could say no. The only thing that surprised her

was that he hadn't found a bar bunny to go home with instead. A smarter woman—one who sought to protect her heart—would tell him to take a taxi. But Mick was hurting, and she couldn't bring herself to pawn him off on a stranger. "Where are you?" she asked with a resigned sigh.

Forty minutes later she walked into an Irish pub about fifteen miles west of her townhome in Fairfax. The place was clean and relatively quiet, with dark paneled walls and a large wooden bar that dominated the center of the room. Muted flat-panel TVs broadcast various sports events, and maybe fifteen people sat in little knots, hunched over their beers.

Mick was at the back corner of the bar facing the door, his hands wrapped around a soda. Hopefully just a Coke, sans rum. A pretty brunette who was perched on the neighboring stool held his attention, and Jenna couldn't stop a little arrow of jealousy from lodging in her gut.

Fortified with a deep breath, she marched around the bar. "Do you still need a ride, or have you found a better option?"

"Jay." He grinned at her and her traitorous heart danced. "Thanks for coming, babe."

Gripping the bar, he slid carefully off the stool, pulled out his wallet, and threw a few twenties on the counter. Then he turned to the brunette, who was pouting at him, another victim of a Mick drive-by. "Good luck with that boyfriend of yours, Katie."

"Yeah, thanks," she said, the note of disappointment in her voice making it all too clear that she'd expected Mick to help her get over the boyfriend.

Oblivious, he hooked his arm around Jenna's shoulders and pulled her toward the door. He could walk, but not very well. If he fell, they were both in trouble because he was way too big for her to help him up. She'd never seen him this sloppy drunk before, not even at one of Rob's parties.

She wrangled him into her old Volvo and got behind the wheel. He leaned over, his warm breath feathering her neck. "You smell good," he said.

She shoved him away. "You smell like a brewery. Stay on your side." Focusing on the road would be hard enough with him in the car, but if he kept breathing on her—beer breath or not—she'd probably crash. And that thought was enough to break the spell.

Without looking at him, she pulled out of the parking lot. She followed the road to the freeway entrance, unable to decide if she was mad, disgusted, or sympathetic. Maybe all three.

"I'm sorry for being such an asshole," he said, his playfulness gone. "I'm supposed to be taking care of *you*, not the other way around."

She glanced at his handsome face, all angles and shadows in the dim glow from the dashboard. Where had he gotten that idea? "Why? I'm a grown woman."

"No mistaking that," he said, speaking so quietly she wasn't sure she'd heard him correctly. Then louder, "I promised Rob I'd watch out for you if anything happened to him."

Her throat tightened with the all-too-familiar need to shed tears, but she blinked them back. Rob had always been an overprotective brother, even before their parents and Jimmy died. Not that he'd stuck around to keep watch over her in person. He'd had his own demons to battle.

But he shouldn't have pawned her off on Mick. She didn't want to be anyone's obligation.

"He should have made you promise to take care of yourself. I don't need a protector. In fact, I absolve you of all duty to me," she said, wiggling her fingers at him as if performing a spell. "After the funeral tomorrow, you don't ever have to see me again."

"Is that what you want?" he asked, his gaze hot on her face.

Was it? No. What she really wanted was to take him home and show him that she wasn't the straight-laced schoolmarm he thought she was. Not on the inside. Her blood ran just as hot as any of those floozies who kept him company.

The problem was she wanted romance and love, not a roll in the sack and a note on her pillow. And she was never going to get her chance at forever if Mick was always there in the background, making every other man pale in comparison.

Still, when Mick wasn't in the room, she always found herself wishing he were there. How dumb was that?

If she could be sure he was out of her life for good, maybe she could finally meet a nice, stable man who didn't throw himself in harm's way just to feel alive. A man who could be happy with one woman. A man who stayed around longer than three weeks.

It ripped her heart in two to say it, but she forced the words out.

"Yes, that's what I want."


Mick tried to stay awake for the ride home, but the hum of the vehicle's engine and the sweet fragrance of Jenna had a drugging effect. He succumbed to the sandman before they reached the freeway.

The thud of a car door brought him out of it, followed by Jenna's irritated voice. "You're going to have to walk. I can't carry you."

He half-slid, half-fell out of the car, letting the door prop him up. Jesus, he was an idiot. She already thought he was an unreliable, womanizing mercenary—all true—but her opinion still mattered, and he was making a complete ass of himself.

Why the hell had he called her?

Because he'd wanted to see her. Simple as that.

"I'm sorry I'm such a pain in the butt. You have enough on your plate right now without having to deal with me."

She gave him a look that said, "Gee, you think?" and propped herself under his shoulder to help steady him. At which point he realized they weren't outside his high-rise condominium in Fairfax. "Why are we at your house? I thought you wanted to get rid of me."

They made it up the eight or so stairs to her front door, where she left him clutching the railing as she unlocked the door. "Because if you drown in your own vomit, I'd have to go to another funeral."

He might be drunk off his ass, but he was pretty sure she was pissed. Or maybe disappointed. Which made two of them. Yeah, way to go with the whole protector thing. She was right. He could barely take care of himself. What had Rob been thinking?

She got them inside, where he cut a wobbly path to the guest bathroom to relieve himself. When he emerged, she was straightening a dishtowel that hung over the door handle of the oven.

"So Rob wasn't kidding about your cleaning obsession," he said. The place was freaking spotless. At midnight. On a Thursday. When she wasn't expecting anyone.

"It's not an obsession. I just find clutter annoying. But it's not like one person makes much mess anyway," she said, using a fingernail to scratch at something on the granite counter.

He snorted. "You haven't seen my condo." Actually, it wasn't too bad, mainly because he didn't own anything. It was just his place to sleep when he was home. More storage unit than living space, it only featured the essentials. Jenna, though, had gone beyond the basics and made a home. Pictures on the walls—each one perfectly level and aligned with the others—houseplants, colorful pillows on the couch and armchairs, and a shelf full of books. It even smelled good, like vanilla. Or maybe cookies.

"I was thinking you could sleep in Rob's room. Would that be weird?" she asked as she filled a glass of water from the spigot in the refrigerator door.

He grinned and waggled his eyebrows. "You mean as opposed to yours?" The instant the words left his mouth, he regretted them. Goddamn alcohol. Her face reddened, but she wasn't blushing. He'd finally pushed her over the edge. He stepped forward with his hand out. "I'm sorry, Jay. I didn't mean to—"

Abruptly, she scooted past him. "Let's get you settled. Tomorrow's going to be a long day, and I could use some sleep."

*Hell.* He followed her up the stairs, gripping the railing to keep from tumbling backwards. His head wasn't spinning quite as fast, but he didn't trust his feet just yet. It had been a long time since he'd been in Rob's room. Sometime last year when he'd crashed on the floor after a wild night. It should have been odd or upsetting to be in there, but somehow it wasn't. It felt like home.

"Here's the trashcan, just in case." Jenna set the small container on the floor next to the queen bed, which was neatly made up with blue-and-white striped sheets and a red bedspread. She'd probably started preparing the room for Rob's return within minutes of finding out he was coming home.

"I'm not going to puke," he said. Unfortunately, he had enough experience to know. He sat on the firm mattress and felt the pull of fatigue.

"Okay, whatever. But sleep on your stomach for me. Just to be safe." She set the glass of water on the nightstand. "And try to drink this so you don't get dehydrated."

She turned away, but he grabbed her hand and pulled her closer before she could leave. Her skin was soft and cool, and he had the urge to warm her up. "Thanks," he said. Their eyes locked and something tugged low in his belly. And lower.

What was it about this woman that crossed his wires so badly? The brunette at the bar had been smokin' hot, but his response had been lukewarm at best. He wanted Jenna. He just couldn't have her. That realization had propelled him through a few more beers before the bartender finally cut him off.

He reached up and pushed a lock of golden hair out of Jenna's eyes, barely aware of what he was doing. Her lips were soft and pink, and they parted slightly when he stroked her cheek with his thumb. "You're beautiful. I should have told you before."

With a slight twist and a step back, she forced him to release her. "You're drunk. Why do guys always get horny when they're drunk?"

"That doesn't mean it's not true." His hands still tingled with the feel of her skin.

"Don't. I didn't bring you here for a good time. I brought you here so you wouldn't do something stupid."

*Too late.*

Her rejection stung, but not as much as the shame of his lack of control. Hiding his self-loathing behind a practiced smile, he leaned back on his elbows. "Can't blame a guy for trying."

Not even trying to hide her disgust, Jenna shook her head and walked out. "Good night, Mick."

*Good night.* As if such a thing were possible.

Somehow he must have managed to fall asleep though, because when he woke up hours later, it felt like someone was running a jackhammer inside his head. Every time he changed position it pounded harder against his skull. But at least he was no longer stuck in the running loop of Rob's death that had plagued him every night since the firefight. Coming to slowly, he realized someone was knocking on the door.

"Damn," he muttered. "Just a sec."

He rolled out of the bed—Rob's bed instead of his own, because, oh yeah, he was an ass—and pulled on his jeans before opening the door. Jenna stood in the hall, freshly scrubbed and smelling like flowers, dressed in black slacks and a satiny gray shirt. Perfect mourning wear. And somehow sexy in spite of it.

Her eyes widened at the sight of his naked torso and her cheeks flamed. Fixing her gaze on the bandage on his biceps where he'd gotten some more ink added to his tribal tattoo, she asked, "What did you get this time?"

"Just made the old one more elaborate." He'd needed something to hurt, something to distract him from the pain in his head.

She stared at him for a second. "Well, if you want to pick up your car before the service, we need to get going."

*Damn.* According to his watch it was already after noon. He rubbed his face vigorously, trying to get his mental shit in gear. "Yeah, give me five minutes."

Eight minutes later, they were on I-66 westbound, Mick feeling like more of a heel with every mile. Next time he would definitely call a cab. Though, if he were smart, there wouldn't *be* a next time. The thing was, drinking killed brain cells, and when you didn't want what was in your brain anymore, sometimes that seemed like a good thing.

"When you packed Rob's things, did you see a memory

card anywhere?" Jenna said, bringing him out of his downward spiral.

"What kind?"

"For his camera. When I was going through his things yesterday, I noticed that the card was missing."

He shook his head. "I don't remember anything like that."

She adjusted her rearview mirror and frowned.

Mick checked the side mirror. What was she looking at?

"Do you think that blue Toyota is following us?" she asked after another moment.

Using the vanity mirror in the visor, he spotted a Camry driving in the middle lane several cars behind them. He couldn't make out the license plate, but he'd recognize the general shape of the numbers if he saw it again. It didn't hurt that it was a Virginia specialty plate with the seal of the commonwealth in the center. Not unusual, but not exactly standard either. Plus, there was a tattered military base sticker on the front windshield.

"What makes you ask?" He faced forward, but kept the car in his line of sight, his eyes hidden behind dark glasses.

She shrugged. "Nothing specific, just a feeling. It's not the only car that's been with us for several miles. I'm probably being stupid."

"Get off at the next exit. We'll find out. You should always trust your instincts."

Like an actor straight out of a driver's ed video, she checked her mirrors and blind spot, put on her blinker, and pulled into the right lane, blinker still ticking. "Now what?"

Mick scanned the upcoming intersection and the large strip mall on the corner. "Pull into that burger joint's drive-through. I'm starving, so we can get some food. That way it won't look like we're trying to flush him out."

The Camry followed them, but then turned left at the

light. They continued straight before turning into the restaurant's parking lot.

"So I was wrong," she said.

"Not necessarily. Order me a number one and we'll see if he comes back."

She gave him a you've-got-to-be-kidding look.

"Please." His stomach rumbled helpfully. "See?"

Once they were on the freeway again, Mick dug into his food. "Want a fry?" he offered.

Jenna wrinkled her nose and shook her head, checking the rearview mirror for the twentieth time in a minute.

"Seriously? How can you resist?" He held it under her nose.

She pushed his hand away impatiently. "They're dripping in oil."

"But they're so good." He took a bite of crispy potato and almost moaned. Nothing soothed a hangover like fatty foods. "It's okay to splurge every now and then. There's a fine line between being healthy and obsessive, you know. Don't be afraid to enjoy life a little."

"I enjoy life just fine," she said, defensiveness creeping into her voice, "but that doesn't mean I have to do it your way."

"If you did it my way, honey, you'd be on your back right now."

Mick froze. *Fuck.* One of these days he really needed to learn to control his mouth. He held his breath and waited. He wouldn't put it past Jenna to leave him on the side of the road. He wouldn't blame her either.

"Huh," she said as if puzzled, her eyes never leaving the freeway. "I was thinking it would be more fun on top."

His jaw dropped. Then he laughed. *Da-yumn.* Not in a million years would he have expected that from her. He was still trying to figure out how to respond when she grabbed his arm and squeezed hard.

"He's back."

Jenna glanced at the Camry in her rearview mirror again and briefly wondered if she was dreaming. Maybe this whole horrible week had been a particularly detailed nightmare. Maybe Rob was still alive, and Mick was not sitting next to her swinging back and forth between unrepentant playboy, hungover loser, and determined protector.

And maybe someone wasn't following them. As gratifying as it was to be right, she would have preferred not to be. She'd played leapfrog with other travelers on long drives before, but this was different, and she no longer wanted to let Mick out of the car.

"Do you think he's following me or you?"

Mick's jaw clenched. "No clue." He was back in warrior mode. "I guess we're about to find out." They were moments away from the pub where she'd picked him up the night before.

"What do I do if he follows me?" she asked, holding the steering wheel in a death grip.

He glanced at her. "It'll be fine. Do you have your cell phone?"

"Of course."

Mick laid out the plan while she drove. Five minutes later, she was parked next to his Camaro in the lot of the now-closed pub. The building looked a lot shabbier in daytime with its peeling wood siding and all the weeds growing through the cracks on the edge of the asphalt. After Mick hopped out, she waited as his car rumbled to life with a throaty growl. Then, as agreed, she drove toward home while he detoured to a nearby shopping center.

For the first few miles, she didn't see the car, but as she approached Manassas, a different vehicle caught her attention. This time, it was a gray Taurus. She couldn't say what made it stand out—just that it was always there, hovering about the same distance away.

*You should always trust your instincts,* Mick had said.

She checked her mirror. The Taurus hung back in the pack, one lane over. Testing, she exited onto Sudley Road and fell into the busy traffic along the suburb's main business route. The gray sedan followed her, careful to stay several cars behind. Her heart went into overdrive. Now what?

Her cell phone rang and she jumped in her seat, giving herself a second to calm down before answering. The last thing she needed was to crash.

"It's Mick. The guy's following me."

She slid into the next left-turn lane and waited for the green arrow. When the Taurus passed her, she breathed a sigh of relief. Still, she kept an eye on it as it pulled into another left-turn lane two hundred yards ahead.

Paranoid much? God. This was a busy street with stores, restaurants, and offices lined up for miles. She had to be overreacting. Sure, it was odd that someone was following Mick, but she couldn't even imagine who would want to follow her.

"Jenna?"

"Yeah, I'm here." She got the light and made her way to the gas station on the corner. "What are you going to do?"

"Let him follow me," he said. "Maybe he just wants a date."

"Not funny." How could he joke at a time like this? "Where are you going?"

"My condo. Chances are, he knows where I live anyway. And if he thinks I've spotted him, he'll get sneakier. At least this way I can keep track of him. Go home and I'll pick you up in an hour."

For the funeral. "You don't have to drive me. I can handle it."

"Let me do this, Jay."

She huffed out a breath, not in the mood for an argument. "Fine. I'll see you in an hour."

"Hey."

"What?" she asked, immediately regretting the snap in her voice.

"If something happens and I don't show, call Kurt Steele," he said, referring to a former pararescueman friend of his and Rob's who now ran his own security company.

All of the air rushed from her lungs as she parked next to a gas pump. She swallowed and found her voice. "Be careful."

"Always." He ended the call.

She sat in her car until she felt steady enough to get out, then entered the station's minimart. The bell on the door chimed as she pocketed her phone, jangling her taut nerves. Three boys walked in, followed by a woman with a baby and a middle-aged man dressed like a biker. None of them showed any interest in her as she picked out a soda.

Her mind was on overdrive as she paid and made her way to her car. How had Rob and Mick survived being constantly on edge for so long, always wondering if they had a target on their backs? She'd been dealing with it for less than thirty minutes and she was a wreck. Her hands shook, and she saw a threat in every person she passed.

*Calm down. Deep breath.* Cripes, she was seriously losing it.

After several attempts to put the key in the ignition, she got her car started and rolled toward home with the windows down for fresh air. One of her favorite songs came on the radio and she turned up the volume, singing loudly to blow off steam. It was a beautiful May day, sunny and cloudless. Green fuzz softened the stark gray of the towering trees that lined the freeway, most of them still bare from winter. It was a horrible day for a funeral.

As if there were ever a good day for one.

She sang louder, pouring her anger and fear and hurt into every note, determined to hold back the tears that had been springing forth at a moment's notice all week. Wind poured through the car, the rushing air and engine noises wrapping her in a cocoon that almost defused her pain.

As she neared home, her pulse slowed and her shoulder muscles eased. Tomorrow it would all be over. She could go back to her miserable little life, pull back into her shell, and hide in the security of her boring, predictable existence.

It sucked, but at least it was familiar and safe.

She reveled in the thought for an entire minute, right up until she exited the freeway and spotted the gray Taurus five cars back.

# CHAPTER THREE

"OKAY, I'M HERE. HEAD HOME now," Mick said before ending the call. He thumped the steering wheel in frustration as he slowly drove through Jenna's subdivision. She had called him twenty minutes ago to tell him that she'd picked up a tail too. He had to give her props for noticing; the girl had good instincts.

He'd told her to run another errand—groceries or something—until he could get to her house. Though he still didn't want to alert their shadows that they were onto them, the idea of her going home alone didn't sit well with him.

The neighborhood was quiet, just an old man walking his dog and a chubby brunette pushing a baby stroller. Mick parked across from Jenna's three-story townhome, behind a grassy mound, and watched for surveillance. His tail hadn't followed him into the subdivision, but Mick wouldn't put it past the guy to circle back. Who could be following them? And why both of them?

He could understand if Claymore wanted to keep an eye on him after the incident. The company couldn't afford any leaks about what had happened. But as much as he hated keeping secrets for that outfit, they needn't worry. He had his own reasons to stay silent.

But it made no sense for them to follow Jenna unless they were just keeping tabs on her because she was close to him.

Within a minute, her boxy white station wagon turned the corner and pulled into her driveway. He met her on the sidewalk, already wishing he could get out of the suit and tie he'd hurriedly changed into at home. The tie was choking him, but at least he'd left the jacket at home. It was warm, even without it.

"Let me run these inside," she said, hefting a couple of cloth grocery bags.

He nodded, grabbing one of the bags before she could protest, and followed her up the stairs. "I'd feel better if you parked your car in the garage. And not just because of the surveillance."

"I can't. It's full of…stuff."

He'd never had a reason to go into the garage, but he'd expected it would be spotless like the rest of her house. Maybe it was the one place she was willing to allow a mess.

She fumbled with the keys, but finally got the front door open.

The first thing he noticed as they entered was the smell. It wasn't the clean, fresh scent he associated with her place. Then Jenna stopped in her tracks, her grocery bag sliding limply from her hand. He skidded into her, wrapping an arm around her waist to keep them both from falling. "What the hell?" His stiff dress shoes crunched on something hard and jagged that glittered in the light.

Shards of mirrored glass littered the foyer. He looked up, stunned by the scene before him.

Everything had been destroyed.

The pictures she'd taken hours to hang in perfect alignment lay shattered on the hearth. Her books were scattered across the floor, their pages torn and spines broken. Every seat in the living room had been gutted, and the overstuffed furniture hulked like wounded soldiers with their insides spilling out.

"Get out," he said, setting down the bag he was holding and pulling her toward the door. "We'll call the police on the way to the service."

For one who worshipped order, the disarray—and the timing—had to be devastating. Her carefully arranged sanctuary was now a war zone.

Jenna wrenched free and raced to the fireplace before he could stop her. She stooped down and flipped over a silver frame. The glass was cracked, but whoever was responsible for this destruction had gone out of his way to hurt her. Broken glass wasn't enough. He'd punctured the photo repeatedly, obliterating the smiling faces of the Ryan family.

She dropped it like a hot coal and backed away, her eyes wide with fear. A sob escaped her lips and Mick met her halfway, dragging her out the door, his blood boiling with rage.

"Wait." She twisted in his grasp. "I need to check the garage."

"Later," he said, holding her tightly against him as they descended the stairs.

Whether she liked it or not, she was stuck with him until he figured out what was going on. Because one thing was for damn sure.

He was not going to lose another Ryan.

The afternoon sun hung brightly over the cemetery, but a cool breeze cut the heat, rustling the branches of the ancient oaks and maples that watched over the dead. Dozens of Rob's friends and acquaintances, dressed in somber colors, were arranged in neat rows facing the gravesite.

Sitting in a  folding chair that had sunk unevenly into the damp grass, Jenna was trying to control her emotions. As if burying her brother wasn't enough, she couldn't stop picturing the destruction in her house or remembering the way she and Mick had been followed that morning. She glanced around the crowd, eyes hidden behind dark sunglasses, looking for…what?

Was someone trying to test her to see how much she could take before she snapped?

If so, they were pretty close to finding out. She was drained to the core, but she still had to face the service and the receiving line. Thank goodness for Mick. She hadn't realized he could be such a rock, such a source of strength and calm.

When the service started, he took her hand and gently squeezed it. Needing all the help she could get, Jenna didn't pull away. Even though Rob hadn't been active-duty at the time of his death, she'd been gratified to learn that he still qualified for a military funeral. It was one small thing she could do to honor his sacrifice.

She somehow managed to keep her tears at bay during the service, right up until a fresh-faced airman knelt before her and placed a folded flag in her trembling hands. "On behalf of the President of the United States, the Department of the Air Force, and a grateful nation, we offer this flag for the faithful and dedicated service of Staff Sergeant Robert James Ryan."

That's when she lost control. Not when the five-man team fired three shots that made Mick flinch next to her every time. Not when the bugler played *Taps*. The short statement delivered by the earnest young man in uniform was what broke through her defenses, what made her heart finally admit what her brain had known for days.

Rob was dead.

He'd never walk through the front door again with his goofy grin and booming voice or stumble through that same door after a late night out picking up girls with Mick. Or get married and have children. Or tease her when she organized the pantry.

After just thirty years on this earth, his life was over.

On Jenna's other side, Tara sniffed and wiped her eyes. Jenna did the same and took a deep breath, blinking back the rest of the flood. No more. *No more.* Her hands balled into fists with her effort to regain control of herself.

The airman stood and saluted slowly before walking away, and the rest of the service passed in a blur, thank God. Then, flanked by Tara and Mick, Jenna stood under a massive, gnarled oak to receive the mourners who stopped to offer sympathy. There were even more people in attendance than she'd expected, but she shouldn't have been surprised. Rob had been well liked. He was so different from her, picking up new friends everywhere he went, while she only had a few close friends and had never been comfortable opening up to others. He had possessed a certain quality, an easy charisma that had drawn in both men and women. There was some comfort in knowing that he would be remembered by so many.

Jenna hardly knew any of the other mourners, but she recognized several from her brother's welcome home parties. There were pararescuemen—known as PJs—who had served or trained with Rob in the Air Force, contractors from Claymore Security, which was based in nearby Reston, and local friends from high school.

A redheaded man with a thick neck and dark sunglasses stepped forward and captured Jenna's hand between both of his. He was short enough that she could almost look him in the eyes with her heels on. "Ms. Ryan, I'm Troy Griffin, CEO of Claymore."

Without thinking, she snatched her hand back, his rough palms chafing her skin like sandpaper. This man was responsible. Because of him and his company, Rob was dead.

*Oh, God.* Mortified by her rude, knee-jerk response, she opened her mouth to apologize. "I—"

"It's okay." He gave her a placating smile that emphasized the network of lines that framed his green eyes. "I just wanted to express my condolences. I'm deeply sorry for your loss."

She nodded, hardly able to make her head move. "Thank you."

Griffin shook hands with Mick next and then moved away. Could he feel the daggers she was shooting into his back with her gaze? Petty and irrational? Maybe. Did that change how she felt about the man? Not a bit. And it wasn't just about Rob. She couldn't fight the feeling that someone at Claymore was responsible for the invasion of her home.

As if sensing her struggle, Mick gave her shoulder a quick squeeze. She smiled at him, still unable to reconcile this man with the sloppy drunk from the night before.

Turning back to the receiving line, Jenna greeted Dan Molina, a PJ who'd joined Claymore with Mick and Rob. Behind him, Kurt Steele waited, his dark eyes pinched with sadness. His time with the PJs had ended when he lost both legs above the knee in a helicopter crash in the mountains of Afghanistan. The last time she saw him, he was still adjusting to his prosthetic limbs, but now he walked toward her without even a hitch in his gait. Some of the clients of his private security company were probably clueless about his injuries.

Dan and Kurt's handsome faces were drawn in sorrow as they gave Jenna hugs and volunteered their help anytime she needed it. After trading greetings with Mick, they stepped aside to talk to Tara. She looked stunning in an eggplant-colored dress that emphasized her tiny waist and brought out the deep highlights in her black hair. The two men lingered longer than necessary—as men often did with Tara—before wandering into the crowd.

Finally, the line dwindled, and people milled around in small groups or slowly made their way to their cars. Jenna was starting to fantasize about ditching her uncomfortable heels when a dark-haired man, huge and solid like a linebacker, came forward to shake her hand, completely enveloping it within his own. "Colin Di Ferio, ma'am. I'm sorry for your loss." He was handsome, but his big arms and brute strength were a little scary.

On her right, Mick stiffened. "Di Ferio."

Colin acknowledged him with a quick nod but said nothing.

"How did you know Rob?" Jenna asked.

"Claymore. We were on the same team for the last few months, and we went on a number of runs together."

"Thank you for coming," Jenna said.

"Wouldn't miss it," he said. "Rob was a stand-up guy." His dark eyes strayed to Tara and lingered there appreciatively.

Tara stuck out her hand. "Hi. Tara Fujimoto." The two kept talking as they moved away.

Jenna sighed, and Mick gripped her elbow, pulling her close. "Your friend might want to stay clear of that one."

She glanced back at them, watching as Tara reached out and touched Colin's arm. Both were smiling. It was probably too late. They made an odd pairing, but she recognized that look on Tara's face. Her friend always fell for the tall, protective type. "Why? Is he married or something?"

Mick gave a harsh laugh. "Hardly." His eyes hardened and he shook his head. "There's just something about him I don't trust. I can't say more than that."

It seemed there was a lot he couldn't say more about these days.

Tara returned alone and wrapped her arm around Jenna. "Sorry."

"What was that all about?"

"He asked for my number. He wants to take me out this weekend."

Jenna's eyebrows shot up. She didn't get it. Three minutes with a guy and Tara already had him hooked. "Did you give it to him?"

Tara's sheepish smile gave her away. "I hope you don't mind. I know this isn't the most appropriate place…"

"Why should I mind?" Jenna snapped. Never mind that they were standing next to her dead brother's grave. God forbid Tara go for one day without a man in her life.

"I'm here to support you, not find a date," Tara said, squeezing Jenna's shoulder. "I'm sorry. I wasn't looking…"

Jenna relented with a sigh. She didn't want to fight with her best friend, especially not today. "It's fine. Just be careful. Mick doesn't trust him."

"I will." Tara nodded. "Are you sure you're all right? What are you going to do about the break-in?"

Jenna had pulled her aside before the funeral to give her a quick recap of the morning's events. "We reported it to the police on our way here. Since no one was hurt"—not physically, anyway—"they said they could wait to examine the scene until I get home."

"Why don't you stay with me tonight?" Tara frowned. "You won't be able to sleep there tonight anyway."

Mick stepped in. "She's staying with me."

Jenna's head snapped around. "I am?" It was the first he'd said about it.

So much for never seeing him again after today.

Tara nodded solemnly, a gleam in her eye. "Good idea. He can keep you safe better than I can."

"And I don't want to bring you into this," Mick said, using the one argument that Jenna couldn't counter. She'd never willingly put her friend in danger.

"He's right," Jenna said reluctantly, giving Tara a quick hug. "Be careful with Colin this weekend. And just say no," she whispered into her friend's ear. After a string of one-night stands, Tara had made a new rule: no sex on the first date. Colin would be her first test.

"Yes, Mom." Tara scowled playfully, then turned serious. "Stay safe. I'll talk to you Sunday."

Mick watched her leave. "I guess you're not going to tell her to keep away from Colin," he said.

Jenna turned to face him. "She's a grown woman. I can't order her around, especially not based on your vague distrust of the guy."

"Yeah," Mick sighed. "I know." He squeezed her shoulders, kneading them with his strong hands. "How are you holding up?" he asked quietly, his bright blue eyes searching hers.

She shrugged free and turned away as tears threatened again. She might never be okay again, but she was done crying. "I'm fine." The light dimmed as a cloud blocked out the sun, and the breeze chilled her skin. She rubbed her arms, suddenly frozen to the core.

All around, fake flowers fluttered in their urns, bright

spots in the calm of the endless green lawn. So many lives reduced to brass plaques and plastic petals.

Mick wrapped his arms around her from behind, chasing the ice from her veins. He didn't speak. He just held her, and this time she didn't fight him. How easy it would be to let him take care of her, make all the hard decisions.

Too easy.

Not that he wanted the job. He was good when he was around, but he didn't ever stick around. Jenna had watched him go through a string of women over the last several years, and she had no desire to be another of his throwaway girls.

Somehow she'd find the strength to stand on her own.

Jenna pulled free from Mick's embrace again, leaving him cold and empty. She shuffled toward the deep hole in the ground where Rob's casket lay, as if reluctant to say goodbye to her brother. He could relate. Rob had been his best friend since basic training at Lackland Air Force Base in San Antonio.

Seeing right through Mick's carefree act, Rob had slowly begun chipping away at the walls Mick had built to protect himself. Because after watching his asshole dad charm everyone around him into believing he was some paragon of virtue, Mick had gotten into the habit of using his own brand of charm to keep people at a distance.

Rob had sealed their friendship by saving Mick's ass during an inspection. When he applied for PJ training a year later, Mick signed up right after him. They'd agreed that it was the perfect job, combining the adrenaline rush of jumping into a hot zone—sometimes fighting their way out—and saving lives. As a PJ, Mick had been too busy rescuing other people to worry about his own sorry existence. Nothing put life into perspective like war.

But now Rob was gone. They hadn't had a lot of heart-to-heart talks. Guys didn't do that shit, at least not guys like them. But somehow Rob had understood and accepted him for who he was. And that was a hell of a lot more than he'd ever gotten from his old man, who'd always taken the slightest excuse to whale on him.

He was close to Kurt and Dan, but Rob was the person who had known him best. Losing him was like being set adrift with no life raft. If not for Jenna, he might have let himself drown. Say, in a bottle of Guinness. Or Jack. But whether she wanted him around or not, she needed him. Which changed everything.

The thought made his heart pound.

He joined her at the gravesite, but didn't touch her or offer any more condolences. He'd known her long enough to understand that she hated appearing weak in front of anyone. In fact, that was half of her appeal. Imagining what she'd be like when she finally let go of her inhibitions never failed to excite him.

Not that he'd ever see it happen outside of his dreams.

But he would keep his promise to Rob to watch out for her. And he would do everything in his power to see that justice was served. It was the least he could do for the friend he'd failed to save.

At home after the funeral, Tara changed into sweats and flopped onto her overstuffed couch, pushing aside a stack of magazines with her feet to make room on the coffee table. She'd filled her townhome with all the frills and flowers and knickknacks she could fit, but it wasn't enough.

Her heart was still empty.

*Alone on a Friday night.* It would be the first one she'd spent solo in a long time, but she was proud of herself for turning down Phil from Marketing. Although, if she were honest, he probably shouldn't count since she wouldn't have gone out with him anyway. He thought much too highly of himself.

Now Colin Di Ferio was another matter. That was one handsome hunk of man. Too bad he hadn't asked her out for tonight. She so did not want to be alone, especially after the funeral. A distraction was definitely in order. Not one to be shy, she might have called Colin herself, but he already had plans for the evening.

Though she hadn't mentioned it to Jenna, she and Colin had already made firm plans for Saturday night. Tacky maybe, given where they'd met, but it wasn't like she'd actively been looking to hook up at Rob's service. The connection between her and Colin had been instant, though, and she wasn't going to ignore that, funeral or not.

It was amazing that she and Jenna were even friends, given how different they were. But they'd immediately clicked when they met during their new-hire orientation at QDS. Maybe it was because they balanced each other out. Jenna's quiet, methodical style reined in Tara's impulsive, outgoing nature. In turn, Tara pushed her friend to get out of her comfort zone.

Still, when she wanted to really let loose, there were other friends she called. She flipped through the contacts on her cell phone. It was only six. Maybe some of the girls from work were still available to go barhopping. If nothing else, she needed a drink. Thinking about Rob in that casket...well, she couldn't.

Truth be told, she'd always had a bit of a crush on him. Nothing serious, but his death had brought home her own mortality in a way she had no desire to think about. Not tonight, not ever.

The phone vibrated in her hand and she almost dropped

it out of surprise. "Shit." She fumbled and caught it, taking a deep breath before answering.

"Hey. It's Colin."

Her body heated. Had he read her mind? "Hey, yourself," she said in her calmest voice. He didn't need to know how excited she was to hear from him. Especially if he was calling to cancel. "What's up?"

"The guys I was going to hang out with tonight bailed. Any chance you're free?"

She wasn't sure whether she should be perturbed that he thought she wouldn't have Friday night plans, or ecstatic that he wanted to see her again so soon. Probably a bit of both, but she opted for the latter. "As it turns out, I am," she said. "What'd you have in mind?"

Jenna stared at her green front door, the one she'd painted to match the fake shutters that flanked every window on her home. Hers was the center unit of five attached homes with alternating brick and vinyl facades that made up a large section of multi-family buildings in her subdivision.

As much as she'd once loved this place and made it her own, she had no desire to go inside now.

The police had come after the funeral, declared her house safe, and left. But she'd never feel safe there again. Not after it had been so violated. Not after the thugs had torn apart everything, right down to the boxes in her garage.

Now she needed to take inventory for the cops and let them know if anything was missing. And she needed a list for her insurance company too.

"You don't have to do this today," Mick said, putting a hand on her shoulder. "It can wait until morning."

She opened the door. "I'd rather get it over with." She really needed him to remove his hand so she could think

again. Despite the purple shadows under his eyes, he looked
as handsome as ever in the dark slacks and button-down shirt
that didn't seem capable of containing all his energy. She got
the impression that if his silk tie came undone, he'd explode.

"Okay, let's get the groceries into your car first. We can
take them to my place." He moved away—both a relief and a
regret—and grabbed the bags they'd left in the foyer before
the funeral. "Pop the door and I'll load them up."

She unlocked the car with the key fob and closed the
front door to the house before following him down the stairs
and across the small patch of grass that served as a lawn. He
stopped a foot short of her Volvo—her own personal
armored vehicle—and held up his hand.

"What's wrong?" she asked, pushing by him to reach for
the door handle. Adrenaline flooded her system and she bit
back a scream. The seats had been slashed, their foam
peeking out like fat from under split skin, exposing the metal
skeleton beneath. She stumbled backwards and Mick caught
her. "They came back," she sobbed. "They came back."

Was this the reason they'd been followed earlier? So that
these animals would know when she was out of the house?
That part at least made sense. But what the hell did they
want? And why had they destroyed everything?

Mick tugged her toward his car. "We'll call the police
from my place."

She had no desire to stick around, so she followed
without a fight when he started to climb the grassy hill
toward his car. They were ten feet away when something
slammed into her back. Confused, she blinked and stared at
the blades of grass in front of her nose. When had she
fallen?

A roaring whoosh sounded to her right and she angled
her head for a better view. Her brick-faced colonial,

sandwiched between a unit with tan siding and another with white—the home she had once shared with her brother, the home that held everything in the world that was dear to her—roared with flames that danced skyward, blending with the sunset.

# CHAPTER FOUR

ADRENALINE RUSHED THROUGH MICK'S VEINS as he hauled Jenna over the small hill and covered her with his body, head down and hands over his neck. Gunfire popped around him and the sound of crackling flames filled the night. He groped for his M4 and his radio and then froze, squeezing his eyes shut.

Virginia. He was in Virginia, not Afghanistan. "Shit."

He raised his head quickly to take in the scene. Jenna's townhome was burning. The popping sounds were coming from inside. It wasn't gunfire, though, probably just gases being released as her things burned. Neighbors were running around, shouting and talking on their cell phones. There were no bloody bodies or burning Humvees. No insurgents with rifles. No IEDs buried in the road. He was in Virginia.

Jenna's house should not have exploded, but they hadn't been inside, thank God.

She moaned beneath him and he scrambled up so she could breathe, running his hands along her body to check for wounds. "Are you all right?"

"I will be when you quit molesting me," she said, her voice hoarse.

He breathed a little easier. She sounded okay. "If I were molesting you, honey, you'd know it." He removed his hands. "I didn't feel anything serious, but let me know if something starts to hurt." Pushing to his feet, he catalogued his own body, well aware that adrenaline could mask the pain of a serious injury. Other than a few scratches and bruises, he was in one piece. "Wait here while I make sure everyone else is safe."

Sirens pierced the night with their plaintive howl as he raced toward the blaze. His left knee protested, but the rest of his body performed without complaint. He'd dealt with worse. He approached the group of people huddled near the building. "Is everyone out?"

"Everyone except for the girl who lived in this unit," said an older woman. "I don't know if she was home, but her car's here," she added, her eyes shimmering in the flames.

"I'm fine, Mrs. O'Malley," Jenna said as she walked up from behind him. "We weren't inside."

The woman stepped forward and pulled Jenna into her arms. "The explosion rocked the house, and I had no idea what it was, but then I saw the fire. I was so scared for you…"

"I'm sorry," Jenna said, caught up in the woman's embrace. "I hope there's not too much damage to your place."

Unbelievable. Her house had just been annihilated and she was consoling her neighbor.

"What happened?" Mrs. O'Malley asked.

"I don't know." Jenna stared at the flames as if they might hold the answers. She had to be wondering if this was related to the break-in earlier. As he was.

"I'm just glad you're okay, dear. First your brother and now this… You must be reeling." Mrs. O'Malley let her go with a pat on the arm, shaking her head in sympathy.

"It hasn't been my best day," Jenna said, watching the flames lick at the roof, her back rigid as she hugged herself.

Mick reached out to steady her, afraid that she might collapse, but he needn't have worried. She was stronger than he gave her credit for, stronger than he could comprehend. He marveled that she could have a sense of humor about such a disaster, but it would go a long way toward helping her recover. He itched to wrap her up and carry her to safety, but she wouldn't let him. Of that he was certain.

Instead, he watched in horrified fascination as the vinyl siding on the neighbors' homes melted like wax at the corners, reminding him of a stroke victim's face—smiling on one side, sagging on the other.

Before long, the firefighters arrived, quickly blocking off a perimeter around the building and moving the crowd back so they could get to work with their hoses. EMTs checked the bystanders for injuries and cleaned the small cuts on Jenna's hands and face. They gave Mick an ice pack for his knee.

Shortly thereafter, the police interviewed them. The detective looked skeptical when Jenna insisted she had no idea who might have targeted her. Was she involved with some shady crime group? Did she have any enemies? Anyone who might want to hurt her?

Ordinary people did not have their homes ransacked and then blown up.

After the interrogation, Jenna watched silently as the fire crew worked, until nothing was left of her home but wet ash and smoke-blackened brick. A disaster cleanup crew arrived to board up the windows and cover the roof with a tarp.

"I'm not sure why they're bothering. There's nothing left."

She clenched her fists and pressed her lips tight, fighting for control.

Mick beat down the urge to hold her again. When he thought about how easily she could have been killed... He didn't want to care so much, hadn't known he was still *capable* of caring so much.

"Let's go. You must be exhausted."

She hugged herself as she stared at the remains of her home. The street was no longer filled with gawking spectators, the people in the neighborhood having returned to their regularly scheduled lives.

He gently pushed her along toward his car, which had been protected from damage by the low berm and a large truck that was parked next to it.

Back at his condo fifteen minutes later, he prodded her to take a shower, gave her a T-shirt and boxers to wear to bed, and dug up a travel toothbrush. Other than thanking him, she didn't speak to him at all. Nor did she cry. He knew the numb feeling all too well. In war, you either learned to distance yourself from the horror or you put a bullet in your head.

Hours after he'd tucked her beneath the covers on his futon, Mick woke with a start, his heart pounding after a dream he couldn't remember. Whatever it was about, it had left him gasping with feelings of pain and loss.

Too anxious to lie still, he crept into the living room to check on Jenna. In the dim light filtering through the window, she looked up at him, her eyes dry but wide with fear. Not of him though. She didn't shrink away when he slipped under the covers next to her.

Instead, she let him wrap around her like a cloak, and relaxed into his embrace with a small sigh. Within minutes, her breathing was deep and even, and the anxious creases in her face eased away.

She was beautiful, and he couldn't stop himself from pressing a kiss to her temple, though he managed to control his less dignified urges. Lying with her brought him a kind of peace he'd never experienced, one he needed as much as she did. One of his last thoughts before falling asleep was that he'd never just *slept* with a woman before.

He was surprised by how much he liked it.

"This one is my favorite," Colin said to Tara as they stood in front of the Korean War Memorial.

The statues glowed gray in the dark, oversized ghosts of a battalion—or regiment or whatever they called it—frozen in motion, stopped in their tracks, just like the men who'd died. It was a bit eerie, really.

Her first thought when he brought up the idea over dinner in DuPont Circle had been "ugh." Even for a former commando, visiting the monuments seemed a bit cliché. But she'd been wrong. It was powerful, moving, and somehow romantic. Most guys would have taken her to a movie or a loud bar. How were you supposed to get to know someone when you couldn't even hear your own thoughts?

They'd spent the last two hours strolling beside the reflecting pool under the canopy of trees, talking about everything and nothing. He was the oldest of four boys and had grown up in Illinois. He'd been in the Army and served with Troy Griffin before a knee injury forced him out of Airborne. Griffin had invited him to join Claymore from the very beginning, and he'd jumped at another chance to join the fight against the Taliban and insurgents.

"Our role is different as private security contractors. We're more of a protective detail, either for people, equipment, or buildings. And sometimes we train the local police forces. But every once in a while, we get to do our part to reduce the terrorist population," he'd told her.

His easy attitude toward killing others—even if they were the enemy—bothered her, but she supposed it was hard to stay objective when your life was in danger day in and day out. And then the tough guy had surprised her with his sensitive side, asking about her own upbringing in northern Virginia.

And speaking of sensitive, he must have noticed her goosebumps, because his hands slid along her arms as he tugged her back against his chest, instantly chasing away the chill. Her belly did a slow flip while her heart danced to a nervous beat. She hardly knew him, but the attraction was almost animal.

In an attempt to distract herself, she looked back at the memorial and said, "I think this is my favorite too. I've been down here dozens of times, but never at night. It's surprisingly beautiful."

"You're beautiful," he whispered in her ear, wrapping his warm arms around her.

A shiver chased across her skin. He was so big and strong and hard, and she thought briefly about Mick's concerns. But she'd seen nothing tonight to make her worry. Maybe she should be scared, but instead, she wanted to peel away his layers and learn more. Did he like dogs or cats? What kind of music did he listen to? What turned him on?

Well, actually, based on the evidence pressed tight to her lower back, she was pretty sure *she* did. It was either her or the ghost soldiers.

She rotated in his arms and ran her palms along the brick wall of his chest, feeling every ridge and ripple as she worked her way down his ribs. His hold tightened around her waist and he cradled her head in his giant hand. She had only a second to register the desire in his dark eyes before he captured her mouth.

His lips were soft but insistent, his tongue molten as he licked and teased his way inside. Her body buzzed with energy and heat pooled between her thighs as she and Colin waged intimate battle.

He won.

She wanted to climb him like a tree, wrap herself around him, and feel him deep inside. She was wanton and mad. God, what the hell was wrong with her?

He cupped her ass, and she forgot to care.

He broke the kiss with a low groan, his breath coming fast and heavy. "Stay with me tonight."

"It's nine a.m., Jay."

Jenna's eyes popped open to see Mick's face just inches away from hers. Close enough to kiss. And, oh God, how she wanted to know what he tasted like. Last night, she'd been too tired and numb to want anything but comfort, and he'd surprised her by sensing that. Now, though, wide awake in the light of day with his warm breath on her neck, something coiled in her belly at the sight of him.

He watched her, his pupils dilating until only a small ring of bright blue remained. "Breakfast is ready," he said.

And then, just like that, he stood, breaking the spell he'd cast. Why did he always have this effect on her? He was like fire. He mesmerized and danced and teased, but if she ever gave in and grabbed hold, she was sure she'd get burned.

Despite the goodness she could see in him, she knew deep in her soul that he'd break her heart if she let him. But the more time she spent with him, the less she cared. Which was stupid. She gave herself a mental shake. Lust was a fool's game, and she was better than that. When she finally gave her heart to a man, it would be for keeps, and he wouldn't be an unpredictable adrenaline junky like Mick.

Besides, she had more important things to think about, like who was gunning for her. The only important thing was to get her life back. She shot to her feet and grabbed her clothes from the coffee table where Mick had left them folded after they came out of the dryer.

Somehow it seemed fitting that all she had left in the world was wash-and-wear funeral clothes.

More aware of her surroundings this morning, she took in the decor of his home as she crossed the small living room. The condo had crown moldings, neutral colors, and plush beige carpeting, but that's where the designer touches ended. The only furnishings were the green futon she'd slept on, a scarred coffee table, two stools at the breakfast bar, and the huge flat-screen TV on the wall. No pictures, knickknacks, or plants. The word *sterile* popped to mind.

As she headed to the master bath through the bedroom, it became instantly clear that this was the only room where Mick worried about making an impression. A cherry sleigh bed took center stage, flanked by matching nightstands and neatly covered with a dark maroon bedspread. This room had probably welcomed more women than a gynecologist's office.

Pushing away the unwelcome thought, she ducked into the bathroom to get cleaned up.

Five minutes later, she sat at the granite breakfast bar, fork in hand. She had to admit that Mick made a mean omelet. Who knew he could cook? Somehow she'd slept through all of his banging around in the kitchen.

"That was delicious," she said. "Thanks."

He grinned and she ignored the extra thump of her heart. If only she could ignore him. That would have made life a lot easier. And she could use some easy for a change.

Her chest still hurt at the thought of everything she'd

lost, so she decided not to think about it, to focus on making lists instead. A master list of everything she needed got her started, followed by smaller sublists for things like potential apartment complexes, clothing basics to replace, and personal essentials she needed to pick up.

The only short list would be the one with ideas for who was after her and Mick.

She scooted back from the bar and cleared her dishes. "Do you have anything on your schedule for today?" Probably a hot date with some on-again off-again local girl, in which case, she didn't want to know. "I need to do some shopping, but I could rent a car. Now that my house is toast —" She stilled. "Oh, my God, I can't believe I said that."

Hysteria forced up little bubbles of laughter and she swiveled away from him, stricken that she could laugh about it. She didn't feel like laughing. What the hell was wrong with her? She covered her mouth with both hands, trying to hold back the unwanted sounds.

"It's okay, Jay. Happens all the time when our brain can't process something." He rested a warm hand on her shoulder. "When I was seventeen, my mom and I got rear-ended at a stoplight. I laughed until the paramedics came. I didn't want to, but I couldn't stop. She was pissed as hell, and I'm not sure she ever forgave me for it, even though the medic said it was pretty common."

She closed her eyes and focused on his smooth voice and reassuring touch. "Thank you," she said, dropping her hands as the manic giggles finally subsided.

"No worries. And my calendar is clear for the foreseeable future, so I'm all yours."

Until he left again. And he'd never be *all* hers. "When are you going back?" she asked.

"Eager to be rid of me already, huh?" When she didn't

return his smile, he cleared his throat. "I promised Rob I wouldn't go back, but I haven't figured out what I'm going to do next." Pain crossed his face for a fraction of a second, but he quickly masked it with a smug grin. "I'm sure I'll find something that's in my wheelhouse. Apparently, Dan knows a guy who's a flight medic. Or I might look into firefighter jobs."

Of course. He didn't talk much about his childhood, but she knew it had been rough. Was that why he always pushed his limits? Was he trying to prove something, or just running away? She held in a sigh. "Well, I should be able to find a furnished apartment in the next few days, and then I can get out of your hair," she said. Rebuilding her life would be a lot easier without him around as a distraction.

"Skip the apartment search for now. I want you here until we get this figured out. This place is already set up with security. Plus, I know the emergency exits, where my weapons are, and how someone would approach." The warrior came out as his spine stiffened and his jaw hardened. "I can protect you here."

He'd already lined up his strongest arguments without waiting for her to protest. Helplessness crept over her, heavy and thick as a wool blanket, her sense of control slipping out of her grasp. "And how long do I have to sleep on your lumpy futon before you declare that I'm safe to reenter the world?"

His gaze flicked to hers and he hesitated. Was he remembering how entangled they'd been earlier that morning? She couldn't stop thinking about his eyes just inches from hers, his mouth so close…

"We don't have to hole up in here, we just need to be careful. I can't be sure your home was the only target. I don't want to scare you, but please do this for me. I promised—"

She waved him off. "Yeah, I know. You promised Rob. You were busy making promises, weren't you?" She didn't wait for an answer. "But Rob never asked for my permission. Maybe I don't want you to feel obligated to me. I told you I'm not going to hold you to it. You're free to move on to your next death-defying job, and I can try to get my life back in order."

He shook his head. "You're stuck with me until I think you're safe. If you leave, I'll just follow you."

She huffed, not sure of what to say. The playboy had become a rock. For years, he had let her and everyone else underestimate him, never appearing to take anything too seriously. He was always the life of any party, telling dirty jokes and funny stories about his friends, making sure everyone in the room got his attention at some point during the night. Even Rob's shy, nerdy little sister.

But now she was seeing a new side of him. She'd seen evidence of his integrity before, but she'd never experienced its full effect. Maybe she finally understood why Rob had trusted Mick with his life. And hers.

Because he was there when it mattered.

"Is the futon really that bad?" Mick asked.

How could he not have noticed? She nodded.

"Then you take the bed tonight."

"What about you?" she asked.

He flashed his familiar playboy smile at her and lifted an eyebrow. "Is that an invitation?" She must have looked mortified because he laughed. "Kidding." He thumped the back of the makeshift bed. "Trust me. I've slept on worse."

After clearing her breakfast dishes and cleaning up Mick's kitchen, Jenna called Tara to fill her in on the latest disaster. She almost didn't leave a message, but she didn't want Tara to worry if she heard about the explosion on the news.

With that out of the way, she and Mick braved the mall. After working her way through four clothing shops, lunch, and the computer store, she was ready to quit. "I hate shopping."

Mick raised an eyebrow as he held up two large bags. "I thought women loved to shop."

"I lost my girl card ages ago. I think Tara took it by force and ripped it to shreds." She just couldn't muster enough interest in clothes or shoes to spend hours searching for the perfect item. Not that she didn't want to look good, but it took way too much time and money to get the flawless fashionista look Tara had perfected. More than she was willing to spend. "I'm more of a homebody than a homecoming queen."

"Quiet girls have their own appeal."

"Maybe." That wasn't her experience though. When she and Tara went out, Tara was the draw for the men who came to their table. Jenna was the consolation prize. And it went beyond looks. She didn't know how to flirt without feeling ridiculous.

She preferred to go slowly, getting to know a man as a friend first so she wouldn't be all hormonal and idiotic around him, trying too hard to impress. She wanted to be liked for the real her. Uptight, cautious, and bookish. Yeah, she was a hell of a catch.

"Is there anything else you need right now?" Mick asked.

"You mean besides a house, a car, and a life?" She hefted the bags weighing her down. "No. This will have to do."

Mick's mouth tightened into a grim line and he nodded. "All right. Home then." He slid his car keys from his front pocket and steered them toward the exit.

His eyes were alert, cataloging everyone who passed. No

one paying any attention could mistake him for a casual shopper. In spite of the bags he carried, she had the sense that he was ready for anything, hyper-vigilant and prepared to spring into action if needed.

Even though it chafed to let someone else take charge, which was the very reason she dreamed of working for herself someday, she couldn't help but appreciate the sense of security that Mick's presence provided.

"Can we stop and get my mail on the way back?" she asked.

They reached his car and he popped the trunk before looking at her. "Are you sure you're ready to see the place in daylight?"

"No." But the mail was a small connection to her old world. The one where everything was still normal. "I'll get a P.O. box later to make it easier, but I still want to pick up my mail today."

She spent the rest of the short drive watching the forest speed by. White dogwood flowers lit up the near-leafless stands of trees, seeming to float among the bare branches as if by magic. She had always loved the promise of spring. She could really use some of that promise right about now.

When they reached her building, she gaped for a minute at the burned-out shell where she used to live. She and Mick could have so easily been inside when it blew up. Too easily…

"Hey." Mick covered her hands, which she hadn't realized were shaking. "You're okay."

With a nod, she hopped out of the car, determined not to dwell on what could have happened. Like he said, she was okay. Still, she didn't look at the soot-blackened space again. She just blindly grabbed the thick stack of mail in her box, shoved it into her tote bag, then slid into the car and let Mick drive away.

They finished their errands—including a side trip to a jewelry store to pick up Mick's recently repaired watch—grabbed takeout, and made it back to the condo without any obvious tails. His building was in a great location within walking distance of shopping and restaurants. Perfect for a bachelor on the go. When he was in town.

The scent of ginger filled the small space as she opened the bag from the Chinese restaurant they'd hit on the way back. Her stomach rumbled in anticipation while she pushed aside her lists to make room at the breakfast bar, setting out place mats, bowls, and utensils before prying open her little white boxes.

She scooped rice into her bowl and dumped half of her cashew chicken on top. "Do you think they're done following us?" she asked before taking a bite.

Mick joined her at the counter, topping his rice with beef and broccoli. "Hard to say. They could've just been watching us to make sure they weren't interrupted at the house. But that doesn't explain the explosion. I don't know if it was triggered by the door and set on a delay, or if it was supposed to happen before we arrived. We can't assume you're safe."

"Could it be an accident? A gas leak or something?" She didn't really think so, but she clung to a sliver of hope.

A scowl marred his handsome face. "Could be, but it's too much of a coincidence for something like that to happen after the place was ransacked."

She nodded. "They had to be after something, don't you think?"

"Sure seems like it. But what?"

What indeed? "I didn't see anything strange in Rob's bag, but there was that missing memory card. I wish I knew what was on it."

Lost in vague thoughts about the culprits, she chowed

down, scraping the sides of the paper box to get every last bit of chicken into her bowl. It was like she had a hole in her stomach. Or maybe she was trying to fill the void in her heart with food.

What she really didn't understand was why someone would target her. The idea should have seemed preposterous, but it was hard to argue with an explosion...or the searches and the tails. And—

Nope. She wasn't going there. There was nothing she could do right now, and it would be better for her not to think about it. Especially with Mick around.

Being with him kept her off balance, and as if to demonstrate his skill in disconcerting her, when she was cleaning up after dinner he said, "Don't be mad, but I lied to you."

She frowned. How many lies were there?

He reached across the counter for the box the man at the jewelry shop had given him and handed it to her, his hands shaking. *Shaking.* Jenna's stomach took a dive, even as she chastised herself for being stupid.

"When we stopped at the jewelry store on the way home, it wasn't to pick up my watch. I actually ordered something for you a couple days ago."

Now she was the one who trembled as she pried open the box and lifted out a flat silver bracelet. Tears burned at the back of her eyes as she ran her fingers over the words engraved in the shiny surface. *IN MEMORY...ROBERT RYAN.*

"I thought you'd appreciate a memento of Rob, especially since you lost everything in the fire. But if you don't like it, I can exchange it for another style," Mick said, his words coming out in a rush.

"No, it's perfect." She looked up at him, her mind

whirling. Had she ever really known the real Mick Fury? "Thank you." The urge to launch herself into his arms nearly overwhelmed her, but before she embarrassed herself, he cleared his throat and broke eye contact.

Standing, he shoved one hand into his front pocket and gestured to her bag with the other. "So did you get anything good in the mail?"

His sudden change of topic pulled Jenna back to reality. She was still reeling from the planning and thoughtfulness that had gone into his gift, but when he mentioned the mail, she remembered an oversized envelope, and her curiosity trumped the mystery that was Mick. For the moment. She took the bundle of mail from her bag and spread the envelopes out on the counter, enjoying the new sensation of the cool metal of the bracelet on her wrist. Instantly the return address on the heavy-duty Tyvek envelope caught her eye, and she could have kicked herself for not checking sooner.

"There's something from Rob," she said, her voice oddly hushed. She was both eager and reluctant to see what was inside. Mick showed incredible restraint by moving into the living room to give her privacy.

She smoothed a hand over the thin material, working up the nerve to tear the thing open. Getting posthumous mail was creepy. When Rob had carefully sealed and addressed the envelope, he'd been planning to come home for good.

She ripped open the top and paused. A profound sadness pulled at her as she thought of her strong, handsome brother preparing this envelope the previous week. He'd been ready to quit Claymore and start a new life. Now that would never happen. With a deep breath, she shook off the melancholy and removed a sheet of paper and a small brown envelope that felt like it contained a spiral-bound notebook.

The letter was brief. A quick hello and a request to put the inner envelope on his desk. He reiterated his readiness to come home and signed off. That was it.

She stared at the manila envelope for a minute, not sure she should open it. It seemed like intruding, even though it really didn't matter anymore. Slowly, she peeled back the flap and removed an ordinary blue notebook of college-ruled paper.

When she glanced over her shoulder, she saw that Mick was watching an MMA fight on the big screen with the sound muted. He was still showing respect for her, for this final moment she had with Rob. She opened the cover. The first page was blank, but a small square had been stuck to the inside cover with 100-mph duct tape in olive drab. No self-respecting PJ would travel without the green duct tape, and her brother had apparently been no exception, out of the military or not. A smile tugged at the corners of her mouth as she gently peeled away the sticky strip.

She gasped at the sight of the memory card beneath. Could this be the key to the danger they were in? She opened her laptop, logged in, and inserted the card into the slot on the side, drumming her fingers as her computer scanned it for viruses.

While she waited, she flipped through the notebook, but the few pages Rob had filled with neat block letters contained only mundane entries about the heat, the sand, the food, and games of poker with the guys. Nothing about his missions or his plans for the future.

Setting the notebook aside for the moment, she opened the memory card files on her computer and scrolled through the photos. The first few—taken a month earlier according to the date stamp—showed Rob and Mick standing in front of a dusty supply truck, guns strapped to their thighs, sunglasses shielding their eyes from the bright sun.

Standard look-how-badass-we-are stuff. The kind of pictures that ended up on Facebook or circulating the Internet with derogatory subtitles.

Rob had looked good. Strong. Healthy. Alive. Breathing through the tightening in her throat, Jenna clicked on the next photo.

This image was different. Two men in profile leaned toward each other in conversation, their heads close, as if whispering. The image was grainy, as if the photographer had taken it from a distance. One man's head was wrapped, his shoulders draped with cloth, the other sported the standard Claymore uniform of a polo shirt and cargo pants. She didn't recognize either of them.

The next picture was clearer. It showed the same men from the previous image, along with another Claymore contractor, standing next to a crate of rifles. Following that was a photo of a crate filled with rectangular cellophane packages of yellowish-white powder. Drugs?

Unease skittered down the back of her neck. The remaining pictures were more of the same.

What were the photos for? Had the men been involved in breaking up a drug ring? The DEA used private security contractors in Afghanistan to help with drug raids, but she didn't think Claymore played any part in that. But then, Rob usually couldn't tell her what he was doing, so what did she know?

Nothing.

"Mick. Can you take a look at this?"

He was at her side before she even finished her request, as if he'd been waiting for her to call him over. "What is it?" He looked over her shoulder, then slid the notebook to her right and sat down next to her.

"Have you seen these pictures before?" She angled the computer so he could see the screen. "What do you think?"

In silence, he worked his way through the images, his jaw clenching tighter with each subsequent image. He sighed and looked up at her. "It looks like he was keeping track of illegal shipments in and out."

"Guns and drugs," she said, her heart picking up its pace as another thought occurred to her. "You don't think he was involved, do you?"

"*Hell* no," Mick said. "Rob wouldn't get mixed up in something like that."

Relief kicked in. She didn't want to believe her brother would turn to smuggling either, but it was good to know that Mick agreed with her. They were the two who had known him best.

He blew out a breath as he ran through the photos again. "Why didn't he tell me?" He massaged his forehead with his fingertips.

"I didn't know either."

"Yeah, but I was *there*." Anger laced through his deep voice. Or hurt. Probably both.

"Maybe he was trying to protect you."

He looked up and scowled. "Clearly I wasn't the one who needed it."

Jenna took a deep breath and pushed on, hoping to distract both of them. "Do you know the guys in the photos?"

"Yeah, Rizzo and Dolph." His tone of voice left no doubt about his dislike for the men.

"Are you sure Claymore wasn't helping the DEA or something?"

"The DEA is working with a different company. Besides, if my team was in on it, I would have been knee-deep in the raids. This is something else. An inside job." He tapped the notebook. "Anything in here?"

"Nothing helpful. It looks like he started a journal but didn't write in it much."

She thought about the official story about Rob's death. Afghanistan was a dangerous place, but she couldn't ignore the timing. Especially not in light of the attack on her home.

Taking a deep breath to steady her nerves, she studied Mick's handsome profile and worked up the guts to ask him a question she dreaded. "Do you think there's any possibility that Rob was murdered?"

His head shot up and he stared at her. His expression changed, as if something was clicking into place for him. "I never thought..." But then, like a light going out, his face went blank. "When you're killed in a war zone, they don't call it murder."

"That's not what I meant and you know it." She stood, her whole body trembling. "It's a simple question, Mick. Yes or no?"

He closed the notebook and covered it with his large hand. "I'm not sure." His voice was suddenly unsteady and he wouldn't meet her gaze.

"You were there," she said. "How can you not know?"

"A firefight is chaos." The muscle in his jaw jumped. "I was there, and Rob was shot. What else is there to say?"

"You know something else," she said, unable to believe that he would shut her out like this. "What if the guys who came to my house were looking for these pictures?"

He considered her argument for a few seconds, his face progressing from doubt to resolve. "It's pretty extreme to destroy a house just to cover up a small-time smuggling operation, isn't it?"

"Not if murder is involved," she said, frustration clear in

her voice. "You're being intentionally obtuse."

"Jay, the incident is still under investigation. I can't give out any details about what happened."

"Even if it might shed some light on what's going on now?"

He shook his head.

"Why else would someone be after me?" She'd assumed the State Department's investigation was a routine cover-your-ass kind of thing to make sure Mick's team hadn't used undue force, but what if there were more to it than that?

"I don't know." He slid off the stool and combed his fingers through his hair. "The investigators are working on it. Until they figure everything out, I'll keep you safe. That's what matters."

Jenna bit back a scream of frustration. Why was he lying to her?

One thing was becoming clear. If she wanted to find out what had happened to her brother and figure out who was responsible for upending her lackluster but stable life, she wasn't going to get help from Mick. She'd have to do the legwork on her own. She gave a loud sigh, kept her eyes on her hands, and nodded to herself as if reaching a difficult decision. Which she was, because from now on she would be at odds with the one person who was doing the most to help her.

"You're right. I'm seeing conspiracies everywhere." Sliding the notebook out from under his fingers, she held it close to her chest. Lying was not her strong suit, so she stuck to the truth. "It's just hard to let go."

His shoulders relaxed and he pulled her into his arms. "I know, but sometimes there's nothing else we can do."

But he was wrong. In her head, she was already making a list.

# CHAPTER FIVE

ON SATURDAY EVENING, TARA OPENED her front door and smiled at the glazed look on Colin's face. Apparently he liked the tight red dress that plunged low in front and even lower in back. Or at least the message it sent.

"Hi," he said, handing her a small bouquet of pink roses, already in a vase with water.

"You're so sweet." She placed the vase on the hall table before stepping out to join him, locking the door behind her. Flowers were a very good start.

Somehow, she'd managed to keep her panties on last night. It hadn't been easy. The man had a persuasive tongue, especially when he used it on that sensitive spot at the base of her neck. But she didn't want to keep making the same mistake over and over again, and in her experience, sex on the first date was always a bad idea.

Unfortunately, she had enough experience with it to have learned that lesson.

A little challenge would let him know she wasn't easy, giving him a reason to ask her out again. But one look at

Colin in his tailored pants and button-down shirt and she was a goner. If she didn't get into those khakis tonight, she might self-combust.

He descended two steps and turned back to face her at eye level. She drank in his woodsy scent and lost herself in the lust in his dark eyes. His hand snaked around the back of her head and gently pulled her to him as he pressed his mouth to hers.

He teased and licked and nipped until she was panting, too aroused to be concerned about the neighbors walking their dog on the sidewalk below or Mr. Farmer who was surely watching from his window next door.

"*You're* sweet," he said, his voice rough as he tangled his hands in her long hair. "And tonight, you're mine."

Sunday morning, Mick woke up early. The light shining around the edge of the blinds was still pale and gray. He had now slept two nights in a row on his futon. Actually, sleep might be too generous a term to describe the half-conscious state in which he'd spent the night. Jenna was right about the cheap mattress being lumpy, but that wasn't the problem.

The problem was the woman sleeping in his bed. Without him. And not just because he ached to join her there. He couldn't stop thinking about the photos. Or Jenna's questions. Mick couldn't answer them, but he couldn't bring himself to outright lie to her either.

She'd played like she was going to drop it, but he wasn't convinced. Even if he hadn't promised Rob not to tell her, he wouldn't want her to know the truth. And it was dangerous for her to know. He was sure that if he gave her even the tiniest thread of truth about that day, she would never let go until she unraveled the whole story.

Unable to lie down any longer, he got up and started the

coffee, then went online and started searching. There was someone he wanted to track down in light of yesterday's revelations. Given the new evidence Jenna had found, he was rethinking everything he'd seen on the day of Rob's death. He couldn't ignore the possibility that Rob had been murdered, which meant that he and Jenna were in big trouble.

An hour later, Jenna joined him, sipping coffee and nibbling on a bagel while she made phone calls to her insurance company and filled out a request for copies of Rob's death certificate from the Office of Vital Records. She needed certified copies to close down his accounts.

The bracelet Mick had given her encircled her wrist, a shiny reminder of a man they'd both loved. It was comforting to see her wear it. The tiny chip inside ensured he would be able to find her, even if she got mad enough to walk out on him. Or, God forbid, someone took her. His hands curled into fists. He'd die before he let that happen.

He took a deep breath and forced himself to relax. She'd be fine. They'd be fine. He turned his mind away from the danger they were in and focused on Jenna.

If not for the sad reason for it, he would have laughed at the image of her sitting at his breakfast bar surrounded by a neat stack of lists, a brand new laptop, and her cell phone. The woman could out-organize him any day. She had a list for notifications, one for potential furnished apartments, another for things she needed to buy—with columns for short-term and long-term—and a master to-do list to keep all of her other lists straight.

At the moment, she was busy transferring her notes into the MacBook she'd picked up at the mall. "I think that's all I can do until tomorrow," she said without looking up at him as she marked tiny checkboxes on the screen. "Is the dryer done?"

"Yep. I dumped the clothes on the bed."

"Thanks." She slid off the stool and rubbed the spot right over her heart with the heel of her palm. "I could really use a run."

He knew the feeling. Nothing unknotted his chest like a hard workout. "That sounds good. You change first."

She emerged from his bedroom a few minutes later, a simple act that stirred up all kinds of fantasies he couldn't afford. At least the loose-fitting shirt she'd bought covered up enough of her skin for him to focus on potential threats instead of her ass.

Ten minutes later they were on the trail that snaked past his building. Mick was used to running hard and long. Hell, he could never have made it through pararescue training otherwise. But, damn, Jenna's pace was killing him. She'd run cross-country at Virginia Tech, and apparently she could kick his butt.

She pulled farther ahead of him, and he had the feeling she was deliberately trying to avoid conversation. That would be okay if he could keep up without dying. After six miles of lung-busting torture, he called out in desperation, "Stop!"

She gave him a startled look and halted next to the asphalt trail. "What—"

He bent over and rested his hands on his knees, feeling like a fish out of water, starved for oxygen. "I just need a minute, okay?"

"You mean a big, bad PJ can't keep up with little old me?"

He ignored the barb. "Is this helping? Because I may collapse if you keep it up."

Her face darkened and she looked away.

"I'm sorry, Jay." *He* certainly wasn't helping. "I wish I could make this whole mess better. If there's something I can do…"

She stared him down, her lips compressed into a tight line. And somehow, she wasn't even breathing hard anymore, while he still felt like an asthmatic in need of an inhaler. "You can tell me what really happened out there."

Shit. How long had she been waiting for that opportunity?

"I want to know the truth," she said quietly, her eyes full of pain. "Everything."

He shook his head. "That's the one thing I can't give you."

Tara squinted at the bright sun that tumbled through a gap in her bedroom curtains. Without even turning to look, she could tell Colin was no longer in bed. If he had been, she would have been hard-pressed not to roll toward him the way the mattress sagged under his weight. In fact, at one point last night she'd been afraid the whole bed would come crashing down. She'd entertained thoughts of buying a firmer mattress if things worked out between the two of them.

It was a good memory, tempered by the fact that the house was now silent. He hadn't stuck around for the morning after. Tears threatened. She *knew* better. She knew that jumping into bed after two dates was too soon. She knew that once men got what they wanted, they left.

But she'd really liked him, and thought he felt the same way. That's what she got for believing men thought with anything but their dicks, that a little sweet talk and flowers meant he was after something more than an easy lay.

Her phone rang, and her foolish heart leapt with the hope that he might be calling to apologize or explain why he'd left so early. Okay, maybe not *early*. It was almost ten according to the bedside clock, but still. He could have kissed her goodbye or left a note on the pillow.

She ran into the kitchen, clutching the bedspread around her for warmth, and snatched up the receiver before it went to voice mail. "Hello?" She tried in vain not to sound breathless.

"Hey, it's Jenna. Did I call too early?"

Tara slumped into the counter, unwilling to admit to herself how devastated she was that it wasn't Colin. "No. I'm up."

Coffee called to her, so she took the bag out of the freezer and measured it into the coffeemaker. Startled by the sound of the front door opening, she jumped, spilling fresh grounds all over the granite and onto the floor.

"Is everything okay? Did you and Colin go out?" Jenna's voice filtered through her buzzing brain as if through water. Tara barely registered her friend's question because she was too busy smiling at the bear of a man who'd just walked in her front door with two paper coffee cups and a bag of bagels.

"Tara?" Jenna prompted.

She dropped the bedspread and watched Colin's eyes darken with lust. He set breakfast on the table and reached her in two strides, spinning her so she was bent over the counter, one large hand warming her bare breast. With a low groan, he nipped at the back of her neck and trailed his fingertips up the inside of her thigh.

It took every ounce of control Tara had not to whimper when he removed his hand to unzip his pants. Before she lost her senses altogether, she managed to squeak out, "I'll call you later. The date's not over yet."

Then Colin's heat pressed home and she dropped the phone.

"Huh." Jenna stared at her cell phone for a minute, not sure how she felt about Tara's revelation. She'd slept with Colin. And apparently he was still there. So much for her friend's intention to play it cautious with men from now on.

"What's up?" Mick asked, jolting her back to the present.

They hadn't spoken for the last two miles of their run, but somewhere along the way—without actually discussing it —they'd come to an uneasy truce.

"Tara's busy right now. She'll call me later." Jenna tucked the phone into her purse and wiped her forehead with the back of her hand. "I need a shower." She was sticky with salt and sweat from their run and probably didn't smell too pleasant either.

He studied her face, which heated a little more every second he held her gaze. "Is everything okay?"

Apparently for Tara and Colin it was. So far. "Yeah, fine. It sounds like she and Colin are getting along well."

Mick grunted and grabbed his water bottle.

"What was that for?" she asked.

"Nothing."

Now he had her worried. Could Colin be involved in this mess? Was her friend in danger? Maybe Mick was just jealous that Colin was getting some and he wasn't. After all, he'd been in the desert for almost six months, and now he was stuck watching over her, with no chance of hot sex with his slut of the week. Yeah, so she was a bit biased about the women Mick dated. Or maybe envious.

She squeezed her eyes shut and took a deep breath. It was past time to snap out of this pathetic crush she had on him. There was enough crap going on in her life.

After a hot shower and some lunch, Jenna pulled out her laptop and logged into work. Carl had already sent her three emails demanding to know when she was coming back to work and if she would have her project ready by the

Wednesday due date.

Never mind that she had lost her brother, her car, and her house. He hadn't even bothered to express his sympathy. *Asshole.* If she had her way, she'd never go back, but since she'd missed her interview with Travers & West, she had nowhere else to go. Besides, she wasn't sure she could handle any more changes. Working for a jerk was still less stressful than starting a new job. And work wasn't remotely challenging when compared to the stresses she'd been subjected to over the last few days. She was grateful to immerse herself in programming for a while.

At some point—it could have been thirty minutes or half a day, she had no idea—Mick tapped her on the shoulder. "Hey, you've been at it for hours. Are you hungry? I ordered a pizza, and it should be here any minute."

She stretched and nodded, surprised to see that it was dark outside. "That sounds great." Cheese, unlike french fries, she couldn't resist, and her stomach growled just thinking about it.

She shut down her computer and moved to the couch, leaving her things spread across the breakfast bar. Moments later, the doorbell rang. While Mick settled the bill with the delivery driver, Jenna tried to figure out the best way to get him to talk. She understood that he was under orders not to discuss the incident, but still…

Why was he so afraid to tell her what had happened? If Rob had been murdered, she wanted to make sure the killer didn't get away with it. Was that so wrong? And not knowing was driving her crazy. Not to mention that the information might be crucial to understanding why she was being targeted, why they both had been. She couldn't just let it go.

After Mick sat down, setting the pizza on the coffee table, she decided to try again. "I know you don't want to talk about what happened to Rob, but can you at least help me understand why?"

He glanced at her with a scowl on his face. "Besides that it might land me in jail?"

"I can keep a secret. And if there's any chance his death is related to what's been happening, how can you keep it from me?"

Mick lowered the piece of pizza he'd been preparing to bite into, setting it down on the open box with a sigh. "Jesus, you're like a broken record. Let's say he *was* murdered because he knew too much. We have no proof. The pictures are pretty damning evidence that Dolph and Rizzo were involved in smuggling, but they don't implicate either man in murder. Everything we have is circumstantial. It doesn't tie them to the threats on us, either. Hell, we can't even prove they know we have the photos. And if we show our hand, we might be putting ourselves in more danger. As for witnesses, I saw Rob die and I still can't tell you if it was murder or not."

He was right, but she couldn't let it go. "I want someone to pay for Rob's death, and I want to feel safe again. But I also want to understand what happened." Didn't he get that? "I realize you're trying to protect me, but I don't know if the reality could possibly be worse than what I'm imagining. I'd rather just know."

"Jay, stop. We can look into the smuggling, but I can't tell you anything about the day Rob was shot. I gave my story to the State Department team and it's done. I'm not supposed to talk about it." Jaw clenched tight, he stared at his hands. "If they want to release the details, they will."

She stood up, mad enough to stomp. "No, they won't. They'll sweep it under the rug like they've tried to do with everything else. I would take the pictures to them in a heartbeat if I thought it would do any good, but the government needs private contractors. They can't afford the bad press any more than Claymore can, and you know it."

He shook his head, his stern features reddening.

She was getting to him. She'd never seen him angry, and it was a bit scary, but she was determined to keep pushing. "Was it something Rob did? Was your team not supposed to be there? I don't care. I don't want to sue or talk to the press. It won't change my opinion of my brother." She hesitated as something occurred to her. "Or you."

Mick's fists clenched and looked away. She was getting close. And then another thought struck her. "Were you...did you have something to do with it?"

"For God's sake!" He jumped up, knocking the pizza box onto the floor with his knee. "How can you even think that?" Confusion crossed his face as he studied the mess on the carpet. "Shit."

He looked up at her, his blue eyes blazing with pain and frustration. In a low voice that was more frightening than if he'd yelled, he said, "Rob was like a brother to me. Closer. If I had been responsible for his death, I would have made damn sure that I died there too."

Then he crossed into his bedroom, slamming the door behind him.

She stood frozen for a full minute, her body trembling uncontrollably. Blinking back tears, she took a deep breath, finally unlocking her joints enough to pick up the slices of pizza that had flipped onto the floor. Grease from the cheese was already forming an oblong stain.

Should she leave or would that piss him off even more because of the damned *promise*? The promise that made her wonder if Rob had foreseen the danger, or if he was just being the same overly protective big brother he'd always been.

Either way, she was grateful for Mick's protection.

Maybe she shouldn't put so much pressure on him. She couldn't afford to lose him as an ally, but she still wanted answers. There had to be another way to find out what she wanted to know, because with or without his help, she was going to get the truth.

# CHAPTER SIX

MICK ROSE FROM HIS BED after forty minutes of reliving the day of Rob's death. *Enough*, he fumed, pacing his bedroom floor, vaguely aware of cars passing by on the parkway eight floors below. Goddammit, why couldn't Jenna just leave this alone?

He marched to the bathroom door and turned back again. Okay, he could understand her desire to know. In her shoes, he'd feel the same way. But there was too much at stake. Whoever had targeted him and Jenna—whether the brass at Claymore, or just some rogue team members—wasn't fooling around.

Why hadn't Rob told him what was going on? He'd noticed a change in his friend during their last few weeks in Afghanistan, but he'd figured it was because Rob had decided to go home. Why hadn't Mick asked more questions? Would it have changed anything?

God, he hated this whole mess. How he could be so amped up after having run eight miles that morning, he had no idea, but Jenna pushed all of his buttons.

Didn't she understand that the truth could put her in danger?

Somehow, he needed to distract her while he figured things out. Could he give her just enough of the truth for her to believe it was everything? He'd have to think about that. Maybe there was a way. In the meantime, he needed to mend things between them.

He opened the door, ready to apologize and placate. Instead, the words stuck in his throat. He processed the scene in one glance. Jenna was leaning over a shopping bag, dressed only in tan bra and bikini underwear. She probably considered the color sensible and boring.

But *goddamn*, sensible or not, the look was far from boring. She was flawless. Narrow waist, long runner's legs, and miles of creamy skin. He finally understood the meaning of *lithe*.

All of his anger, apologies, and promises twisted into one primal thought: *I want her.*

With more restraint than he knew he possessed, he turned his back on her and cleared his throat. Staring at the door didn't do a damn thing to erase the image of her from his mind.

"Mick!" she yelped from across the room.

"I didn't expect you to be changing out here. Sorry." *Liar.* He wasn't even a little bit sorry.

The sound of frantic rummaging reached his ears and he imagined her hastily covering up that gorgeous body with the oversized, striped pajamas she'd bought at the mall.

"Okay," she said. "Did you need something?"

He walked casually into the kitchen, avoiding her eye. "A drink. And I figured you might need to use the bathroom." He snuck a peek at her. Yep. Baggy jammies. *Pity.*

She eyed him cautiously, arms crossed over her chest,

probably wondering why he was being so nice. "Yeah. I was about to use my finger as a tooth brush," she said, but didn't move. "Look, I'm sorry a—"

"Don't apologize," he said. "I overreacted." Hope blossomed in her pretty eyes, and he had to quash it quick before she got the wrong idea. "And no, I still can't give you details, but I understand your need to know, I really do."

She raised one eyebrow and tilted her head. He felt like he was back at home trying to do the two-step around his mom's knowing stare. The one she'd pulled out whenever he did something wrong and tried to cover it up.

"Just know that Rob died with his honor intact, okay? I respected him more than anyone I've ever known, and nothing has changed that."

Her head dipped into the barest hint of a nod, and then she wordlessly grabbed her cosmetics bag and made a beeline for the bathroom. She stopped in the bedroom doorway, her hand gripping the jamb. "Thanks."

He held her gaze for several heartbeats, mentally cursing his team for getting into that firefight, the bastard who fired the fatal rounds into Rob's chest, Rob for his heroics, and himself for not finishing off Rob's killer when he had the chance.

And damn if he didn't want to sink to his knees and spill it all out to Jenna right then and there. Judging by the look in her eyes, that was what she wanted too, more than anything. Instead, he said, "How about tomorrow I give Dan a call? Maybe he knows something about the smuggling."

If they could figure out who was behind the illegal drug and weapons shipments, if he could find real proof, then maybe he could find a way to end this.

"That's a good idea. Is there anyone else you trust enough from your team to ask about it?"

"None who are still alive." Despite Dan's efforts, Olszewski hadn't made it either.

She blanched, then nodded and scurried into his bedroom.

No matter what, he couldn't tell her about that awful day. It was his cross to bear. The truth held too much power, and if it came out, she'd get hurt. She thought that knowing the truth would bring her closure. But it would only bring more pain.

It would be a long, hard fight to protect her from herself, but it was the only job he had, and he intended to do it or die trying.

On Monday morning, Jenna was back at the breakfast bar—it was either that or the futon—listening in while Mick talked to Dan. Based on his end of the conversation she was pretty sure Dan didn't know anything.

Mick signed off and met her gaze. "He had no idea that our guys were involved, or that Rob had been tracking them. I mean, we all knew drugs and weapons were moving in and out of Afghanistan illegally, but Dan didn't know Claymore was part of it."

Well, what now? If Claymore had any influence at the State Department, handing over the photos could put her and Mick in more danger. Same for the local police. If she gave them the images, they might be better equipped to solve the case on her house, but if local detectives started investigating the men on Rob's team, it would only confirm for Claymore that she had evidence. And who knew what they'd do then...

Besides, the cops had no jurisdiction over anything that had happened in Afghanistan, and she wanted the keep the evidence for use as leverage. Things had been quiet over the past couple of days, but she didn't think that would last forever.

Her affinity for following the rules plagued her, because surely withholding potential evidence was a crime of some kind, but she didn't think sharing it would be a good move right now. Mick didn't argue. In fact, he seemed relieved that she didn't want to turn over the photos, but when she asked him why, he wouldn't answer. "It's your choice," he said.

Some help he was.

Not sure what her next step should be, Jenna decided to check in with Tara at work. "Is the date over yet?" she asked, unable to keep the sarcasm out of her voice.

"I'm sorry. I didn't mean to cut you off like that yesterday." Tara giggled. "Colin was kind of, um…persistent."

Again, in the category of *don't need to know.* "I was just surprised that you let him spend the night on your first date." Kind of. Not really.

"Actually, I didn't. We ended up going out on Friday night. It was so romantic. We toured the monuments at night after having dinner at a great little kabob place in DuPont Circle. And you'd be so proud of me, Jenna. I turned him down the first night."

"Oh. Well, great. I hope it works out." *Be careful.*

"Me too." Tara's voice was rich with the excitement of new romance.

Wow, she was really falling for this guy. Jenna tried to dial back her cynicism, because she wanted her friend to be happy. She deserved to have a good man in her life for a change. Hopefully, Colin could be that guy, in spite of whatever misgivings Mick had. "It's great to hear you sounding so happy, Tara."

"Thanks. I can't give you a lot of details right now, though, because Wicked Wanda of the West is on a rampage today and she'll be back in a few minutes."

Jenna had to laugh at Tara's description of her new boss. The redhead was not well-liked in the HR department where she'd taken over for Tara's previous supervisor, a friendly old guy named Reggie who had retired after forty years at QDS. "You definitely don't want to mess with her. She might turn you into a toad."

"I don't doubt it." Tara sighed. "Any idea when you'll be back?"

"Soon, I hope. Mick wants me to wait a few more days."

"Are you doing okay at his place? Anything I should know about?" Tara asked, her voice heavy with innuendo.

Only in her dreams. *"Tara."* Jenna could only laugh at her friend's reliably dirty mind. "I'm fine. I feel safe here."

"Good. Any news on who destroyed your house?"

"No. The police are investigating."

"I hope they figure it out soon. I miss having you around."

"Believe it or not, I miss being there," Jenna said. "Hey, before you go, can you do me a favor the next time you talk to Colin?"

"Sure."

"Will you find out if he was with Rob's team the day he died? And if so, see if he'll tell you what happened."

"He's not big on talking about his time over there at all, but I can ask." Tara hesitated. "What's going on?"

How much to tell her? Jenna's instinct was to keep it close to the vest, but if she couldn't trust Tara, then there was no one left. "I'm not sure, but I don't think anyone's telling the whole story. And, I'm starting to wonder if maybe Rob was more than just a casualty of a war zone."

"Are you serious?"

Jenna considered mentioning Rob's photos, but something held her back. She'd trust Tara with her life, but she couldn't ignore Mick's instincts about Colin. And even if he wasn't involved, Colin might mention it to someone in Claymore who was.

Jenna sighed. "Yeah, I'm serious, but I'm probably delusional too. You know what? Just forget about it." She was starting to regret her decision to involve Tara. "I'm sorry."

"Don't be. I know things are hard right now. I'll poke around a little and call you later."

After thanking Tara, she thumbed off her phone and listened to the water from Mick's shower. She wasn't cut out for subterfuge. Sneaking around made her jittery. And she wasn't even doing anything wrong. She was just trying to see if she could get information from another source.

Still, she hated lying to him. It felt like a betrayal of one of the few allies she had left. But at least they weren't fighting. Now all she had to do was figure out how to keep from acting like a lovesick fool around him, and they'd be grand.

But then she'd always struggled with her feelings for him. Like that time when Rob threw a Christmas party during a month of leave from Claymore, and Mick cornered her beneath the mistletoe.

"I'm not supposed to kiss you." He leaned his forearm against the wall, looking down at her with sin in his eyes.

She licked her lips as her stomach flip-flopped and her heart beat wildly. She shouldn't want him. But those piercing blue eyes and that cocky grin did her in every time. She pressed herself against the wall, too aware of his body heat and clean, spicy scent. "Says who?" she asked with more bravado than she felt.

"Your brother."

As if she hadn't known. Though she was more than old enough to drink the beer in her hand, Rob still treated her like she was a naïve teenager. She took a quick swig from the brown bottle and suppressed a grimace at the bitter taste. "He's not in charge of me," she said, raising her chin in defiance. "I choose who I kiss."

Mick glanced at her mouth and heat flooded her limbs. Would it be so bad if she gave in? Just this once?

*Yes!*

Mick left behind a woman with a broken heart every time he left for Afghanistan. Her brother did too, for that matter, but apparently Rob wanted better for his little sister.

So did she.

Mick knew she was off limits, yet for some reason he loved to tease her. Maybe because he was certain she'd turn him down. Like a game.

What would he do if she actually said yes? Probably freak out and run the other way. Game over.

"Where are you going?" he asked as she scooted away from him, amusement sparkling in his knowing eyes.

"Far away from you, Romeo."

But even Afghanistan hadn't been far enough. He'd always been somewhere in the back of her mind.

And now she was stuck with him 24/7. He was a good man, an honorable man, but he was still a risk-addict and womanizer.

He was still not the man for her.

The object of her analysis emerged from his room a few minutes later and she pushed aside the dangerous memories.

They spent the rest of the morning running errands. She met with the insurance adjuster, who promised her the funds to rebuild the townhome and repair the neighbors' siding. Her policy also included money for a rental until she could move back home. Or sell. The thought of living there had lost its appeal. Maybe starting over would be a better idea.

Either way, she needed the money. Her mortgage was taxing enough, but paying for two places could put her in dire straits. Rob's savings would cure her financial problems, but probate of his will could take months. She needed to be conservative with the limited funds that were available to her right now.

Insurance sorted, she turned to other issues. Taking a circuitous route to ensure they weren't being followed, they opened a safety deposit box to store a flash drive backup of the pictures until she figured out what to do. The original media card was in her purse, and they had stashed several printouts in Mick's condo. The more copies the better, as far as she was concerned. They couldn't risk losing their only evidence.

In the afternoon she buckled down and spent time on her project for QDS. She broached the idea of going back to work, but Mick told her to wait.

"Why don't you give it a few more days? You can get some work done from here, can't you?"

Carl would never let her hear the end of it, but she caved.

Tara called during dinner, but Jenna had put her phone on silent. She didn't want to talk to her friend while Mick was around, particularly if she had any updates from Colin, but he had been sticking to her like a leech. She finally got a break later in the evening. He was on the phone, trying to track down someone named Smitty. She didn't ask why; he didn't say. Fine by her, since she had her own secrets. While he was preoccupied, she called Tara back.

"Sorry I missed you earlier," Jenna said.

"No problem. I don't have any real news for you anyway."

Jenna had known it was a long shot, but she still deflated a little. "That's okay," she said, trying to make sure her end of the conversation was as bland as tofu in case Mick was paying attention.

"I really tried," Tara said. "In fact, I was downright persuasive." The smile in her voice was a clue that Jenna didn't want to know more about her methods. "He was there when it happened, but he said he can't talk about it. Apparently, the whole incident is under investigation by the State Department for some reason." She paused. "Is that normal?"

"I think so, considering the outcome," Jenna said. "Standard procedure." Or not. She had no idea, but she didn't want Tara to start thinking about it too hard. No need for her to become any more involved.

"You're being rather careful with your words. I assume Mick is nearby."

"Yep. And how are you and Colin getting along?" she asked.

"Got it. And so far so good. I'm trying not to get my hopes up, but I really like this one, Jenna. He looks like a big grizzly, but he's more like a teddy bear. You know, without the fat for winter." She laughed.

Jeez. "Good luck, and thanks for trying. I should probably get back to work. Carl is breathing down my neck to get him this project by Wednesday."

"He's such an asshole. That man has no heart," Tara said, always her staunch supporter. "What are you going to do about getting your answers?" she asked.

Good question. "I have no idea." Jenna glanced at Mick. As if he'd felt her gaze on his back, he turned and caught her eye. Heat flooded her face and she ducked her head. Smooth.

On the other end of the line, Tara hesitated and took a deep breath. "Have you thought of seducing it out of him?"

Jenna must have reddened even more, because Mick raised an eyebrow at her.

She coughed. "Um, no. Not even once."

Thankfully, he became engrossed in his conversation again and turned away.

"Well, it kind of worked with Colin. And I probably could have tried harder, but I didn't want to risk pushing things too far. But what do you have to lose?"

Besides her pride? And her heart? "Well, gee, thanks."

"Do you have a better idea? Besides, I know you've lusted after him for years, even if you're careful not to say anything about it. That totally gives you away, you know. You might as well enjoy yourself whether or not it gets you any information."

Her? Seduce Mick? Ridiculous. Tara knew how awkward and hopeless Jenna was with men. Other women did this kind of thing. Women like Tara. But even if she had the nerve to do it, Mick wasn't stupid. He wasn't going to blurt out the truth over a blow job.

*Holy crap.* Her cheeks flamed. "I really need to get back to work. I'll talk to you soon, okay?"

"Yeah. Good luck, Jenna. Personally I hope you go for it."

Jenna laughed nervously and said goodbye. Tables and queries and charts were what she needed to focus on now. The deadline loomed.

But damn Tara and her nympho brain. All Jenna could think about now was how magnificent Mick would look towering over her in all his naked glory.


Watching Jenna from the corner of his eye, Mick had one ear on his phone conversation with his buddy Kurt, owner of Steele Security, and the other on her conversation with Tara. It sounded normal enough, but damn if she wasn't blushing repeatedly. What the hell did those girls talk about anyway?

Maybe Tara was dishing on her sexual escapades with that

asshole Colin. The guy got off on carrying big guns and was a little too trigger happy for Mick's taste. And since Mick wasn't sure what role Colin had played in the attack that ended in Rob's death, or whether he was involved in the smuggling, he might be a threat to Jenna.

"Mick?" Kurt said, breaking into his thoughts. "I'll get a guy on him and get back to you tomorrow, okay?"

"I appreciate it." Mick turned his back on Jenna. "Any other news?" Kurt had been discreetly looking into the destruction of Jenna's townhome.

"Nothing but the official line. The police don't believe in coincidences any more than I do, but whoever set it up did a good job. Any evidence of a crime was destroyed."

"Damn."

"Yeah." Kurt cleared his throat. "Hey, listen. If you're ready to stay in the States, you know you're welcome to join my team. I can always use guys with your skills for executive protection."

"Thanks. I'll think about it." But right now, Mick was focused on finding Smitty. Alan Smith. The only man in the world he'd ever *wanted* to kill. He'd thought that after he calmed down and got away from the heat and the dust of the desert, he'd be able to let it go.

Instead, the need to smear Smitty over the pavement was overwhelming. And if he were honest, it was unsettling. He had never taken a life in cold blood. Never even considered it. Now, he was almost mad with the idea, even as his rational mind dismissed it as a horrible fantasy.

Maybe he would have been able to let it go with time, but then Jenna had gotten him thinking about the specifics of Rob's death. At the very least, Smitty needed to answer some questions.

Mick's first instinct had been to take Rob's memory card

to the State Department. Maybe they would reopen the investigation now that the men were back home.

But he was torn. If the Feds started looking into the attack, the media would get hold of it. For the same reason, he'd been relieved when Jenna decided not to go to the police right away. He didn't trust either law enforcement agency to be beyond Claymore's reach, and if the media got wind of the story, whoever was behind the explosion in Jenna's house would know they had something concrete.

Hell, even if they sat on the evidence forever, they were still being followed. He hadn't wanted to scare Jenna—and he'd managed to lose their tail on the way to the bank—but the danger was far from over.

At this point, he only cared about two things: his promise to Rob and Jenna's safety. And, coward that he was, he cared about what she thought of him too.

If Mick could get some answers from Smitty, maybe he could find out the truth and remove the threat to Jenna. And then he could drown his visions of that horrible day in a pint of Guinness until her accusing eyes no longer sliced his heart in two.


That night Jenna curled up in Mick's bed, enveloped in the subtle scent of him that lingered on the pillow. How many women had been here before her, waiting with excitement for him to slip between the sheets and between their thighs? Jealousy knifed through her. She didn't want to know. Couldn't understand why she was so obsessed by it.

Tara had planted this horrible seed in her mind: the idea that she might get the two things she wanted most in one stroke. Except that her desire was the foolish lust of a schoolgirl. She could not find lasting love with a man like Mick. She wanted more than a few nights of animal sex followed by a *sayonara.*

Although, admittedly, her body was fully on board for the animal sex.

Anyway, Mick didn't seem like he wanted her to seduce him. He'd shown remarkable restraint over the last few days, which led her to believe that all of his flirting and teasing over the years had been nothing but a game. Tara was wrong in assuming that he was Jenna's for the taking.

There had to be another way to get the information she wanted, but as long as Mick was on her like duct tape, her ability to investigate was limited.

Too worked up to sleep, she flipped on the lamp and snagged a small notepad and pen from her purse. A list would calm her. She used them to get the ideas and questions out of her brain in an organized fashion. It made the impossible seem possible. Today, all of her attention was focused on how she could uncover the truth about Rob's death.

She had eaten, slept, and breathed that question until it was part of who she was. It had left her with an empty space inside that wouldn't go away until she knew the truth. Perhaps that was her flaw. She couldn't let things go. As a child, she'd nagged her mother for the truth about Santa Claus, even though she feared the answer. After her mom finally admitted that she and Jenna's dad were the ones responsible for all those presents under the tree, Jenna had cried for hours.

Her mom had warned her not to seek answers she couldn't handle, but that was one lesson she'd never learned. The need to know was part of her.

And deep down, she believed that the truth would make everything okay again. Whoever was after her would be foiled. Mick would move on. Life would go back to normal. Worse, because now she was more alone than ever, but normal. Predictable. *Safe.*

The blank page mocked her. After all, what were her options? Claymore wasn't talking. Mick wasn't talking. The State Department wouldn't tell her anything. The other men who were involved had no reason to tell her anything, nor could they be trusted. She wasn't an investigator. She didn't have a clue where to start, and she didn't have the money to hire someone who would.

Her only leverage was Rob's pictures, but she still felt she couldn't share them with the FBI or the police. If she did, the evidence might be buried. The government's track record so far was less than stellar. The only time they took the actions of contractors seriously was when the media got involved.

The media! Head-smack moment. Why hadn't she thought of it before?

A reporter had called her before Rob's funeral to get the details straight. If she could just think of his name… She snapped her fingers trying to remember. Something Longstreet. James. That was it.

After scrawling it on the paper, she turned off the lamp and lay back on the sheets.

First thing in the morning she was going to email that reporter.

# CHAPTER SEVEN

THE NEXT AFTERNOON, JENNA STARED at the email reply from James Longstreet. She had emailed him as soon as she woke up, asking if he had any additional information about her brother's death. He wrote in short bursts of thought separated by ellipses. She found herself mentally inserting "STOP" after each burst, like it was a telegraph transmission.

*Rumors of another Nisour Square…no confirmation…State Dept & DOJ not talking…what do you know?*

Nothing. She knew nothing. Her chest deflated like a popped balloon. And apparently he didn't know any more than she did.

Mick sat on the couch with his back turned, doing his own secret work on his computer. God, what a pair they were. Allies and enemies, all mixed up. The whole situation was exhausting. Even little things were starting to grate on her.

Like having to wear a bra until bedtime.

If he would just tell her what he knew, she wouldn't be sneaking around. She didn't want the media circus that might be sparked by her efforts, but Mick had left her no choice.

The other problem was that she couldn't focus on work. Fear, lies, and lust had twisted her shoulder muscles into knots, only adding to her stress about her deadline, being followed, and, oh yeah, her house blowing up.

Her eyes flicked across the email again. *Rumors of another Nisour Square.* She didn't recognize that reference, so she Googled it. Four Blackwater contractors had been charged with firing into a crowd of Iraqi civilians, killing seventeen.

Could Mick and Rob have been involved in something like that? Dread slid down her throat, bitter and slimy. *No.* They were honorable men. Mistakes happened in the heat of battle, but neither of them would hurt innocent people on purpose. And the skirmish had been small, involving only a few Afghan militants. At least according to the official version.

She reread Longstreet's email, her fingers lightly stroking the keys. Should she respond?

"What are you doing?" Mick asked from just behind her.

She jumped and switched the screen to the desktop before turning to glare at him. "Don't sneak up on me like that." Her heart raced beneath her palm.

He reached over and brought her email back up before she could stop him. "Damn it. Why are you talking to that scum? Do you have any idea what you could unleash if you get that guy sniffing around?"

Anger flooded her limbs with righteous energy. "How could I? You won't tell me anything."

His face turned crimson, his hands closing into fists at his sides. "What did you say to him?"

She'd never been afraid of Mick before, but when he reached for her, she ducked her head and hunched over to protect herself. It was pure instinct.

"Christ, Jay." He backed away, his eyes full of anger and pain. "You really think I would hurt you?"

"I don't know what to think anymore," she said softly, blinking back the damn tears that were always at the ready lately.

He stared at her, breathing like he'd just finished a race. "I've done a lot of things I'm not proud of, but I would never..." He ran his fingers through his hair and closed his eyes, lifting his head to the ceiling. "I wish you could just trust me that you should leave this alone."

"Don't you realize that every time you say something like that it only makes me want to know more? That's like telling Pandora not to open the box."

"But if I told you the box could explode if you opened it, would it make a difference?" He rubbed his face and leaned against the couch. "I'm not trying to patronize you. I'm trying to protect you."

"Well, by forcing me to look elsewhere for information, you're getting exactly what you're trying to avoid." Her argument was perfectly logical. There was no defense against it.

"I don't know how to make it more plain," he said, fatigue threading through his voice. "If you pursue this, you'll not only put both of us in danger, but that reporter too."

"Then just tell me the truth and I'll stop." It really was that simple. Why was he being so stubborn? It was too late for her to go back to believing the official account.

"No."

"Why not, Mick? I don't understand."

He sprang up from the back of the couch. "Because I don't want you to know what happened. Is that clear enough?" He dropped his voice and held her gaze, speaking slowly and deliberately. "I don't want you to know."

* * *

Mick watched Jenna back away. The hurt and confusion on her face cut through him like a hot blade. The worst part was that she'd read him correctly. He *had* wanted to hit something. Not her, but something.

"Mick?" she asked in a near whisper.

He cut her off with a shake of his head. "Don't." His head buzzed with anger and frustration that he didn't know how to contain. He needed to leave before he did something monumentally stupid. Like scare her witless. Or spill his guts.

Palms pressed to his temples, he closed his eyes. He could really go for a beer. Or twelve. He felt his car keys dig into his thigh from his front pants pocket, demanding his attention. He knew a long stretch of deserted road where he could rev up the Camaro's engine. His nervous system practically sat up and begged him to do it.

But he couldn't really leave Jenna alone, because even what she didn't know had the power to hurt her. They'd already seen that. There'd been no direct threat since the destruction of her house, but he knew she wasn't safe. They were still being followed, and she was intent on continuing to dig. Sooner or later someone would find out.

How the hell was he supposed to deal with this? He'd never expected to be in close quarters with her for this long. Under normal circumstances, he could have easily avoided her and her questions, but not when she was living in his home, sleeping in his bed.

He opened his eyes and met her gaze. She took a tentative step toward him, and then another. His feet felt like they were mired in cement as she crossed the plush carpet in bare feet, bringing with her that sweet scent that turned him inside out.

She stopped mere inches from him and put her hands on his biceps. Her fingers were cool as she stroked his arms down to his wrists before starting back at the top again. "I'm sorry," she said. "I don't want to fight."

He shivered under her touch, both energized and soothed. The red haze of anger ebbed, but more dangerous feelings started to take over. In a perfect world, she would never stop touching him. In this world she had to—right goddamn now. As she reached up to start again, he grabbed her wrists, careful not to hurt her. She let out a surprised gasp that drew his attention to her pink lips, so moist and soft. "Hey," he said, releasing his grip slowly. "I'm not made of stone."

Her eyes widened and she shifted away, hugging herself. "You just looked so... I don't know, but I needed to do something to help you calm down." Picking at a thread on her T-shirt, she said, "I'm not trying to hurt you."

For a long moment, he just looked her in the eyes. "Rob is dead," he finally said. "He's not coming back. Nothing can change that."

She cringed at his blunt words. "I can't turn off my desire to learn the truth," she said, with an edge of frustration to her voice. "But I'll try to stop asking you about it."

That wasn't quite the reassurance he was looking for, but it was something. "Thank you." And then against his better judgment, he hugged her. "I don't want to lose your friendship, Jay. You're too important to me." He skimmed a palm along her silky curls and kissed her forehead, wishing he had the right to do more.

He released her before he could change his mind.

Jenna was shaking when Mick let her go. He'd been so tender. *I'm not made of stone.* Maybe he wasn't immune to her limited charms, after all. Maybe he really did think she was beautiful. Or maybe he was just a sex-starved man who'd take any woman he could get.

Except that he'd pushed her away. So clearly she was easy enough to resist.

Still, would he give in if she pushed a little harder?

Tara was right: Jenna had nothing to lose. Mick had already stolen her foolish heart, and she probably only had another week or two with him. He'd have to find work eventually. He couldn't play bodyguard forever. Once he left, her chances of finding out what happened to Rob would drop dramatically. With that in mind, she had a sudden idea of how to start. Only one type of clothing could give her the strength and confidence to pull off something like this.

"Would a run help?" she asked. In workout clothes, she wasn't just a woman, she was a kick-butt runner. For some reason, that changed everything. It made her feel powerful. Silly, maybe, but true.

His brow furrowed. "Help what?"

"You're wound up tighter than a spring." She glanced at the front of his jeans. Her face went hot, but she soldiered through. "You keep reaching for your keys, and I'm guessing you want to go do something stupid."

He whipped his hand from his front pocket, but didn't deny it.

"Running will dull the urge. You know it will. We can drive over to the trail across the freeway for a change of scenery. If you let me set the pace, you'll be too exhausted to think of anything but sleeping in your bed by the time we get back."

"Honey, I can always think of something to do in a bed besides sleep." He smiled and his shoulders relaxed a degree.

"I'll bet," she said, surprised by how relieved she was to have the old playboy Mick back. He was so much less intense, so much easier to handle than warrior Mick.

"You change first," he said.

*Game on.*

The butterflies in her stomach took flight, but she would not back down now. There was too much at stake. She chose her outfit from one of the shopping bags she was using to hold her new clothes and closeted herself in Mick's bathroom.

Once dressed, she examined herself in the full-length mirror on the back of the door. *Oh, no way.* She couldn't go through with it. The woman in the jog bra and spandex shorts wasn't her. She was showing way too much skin.

Except, that was kind of the point, right?

Sure, *Jenna* would never dress like this. She was all about practicality and comfort and modesty. So she needed to think like someone else. She needed to think like Tara. What would Tara do? *WWTD?* Jenna giggled and then took a deep breath. Okay, she could be serious about this. She could become her sexy alter ego, Jay. A woman Mick couldn't resist.

At least not in close quarters after months without sex. No one said she had to play fair.

She covered her indecency with sweats—no need to give away her plan too early—and with one last fortifying breath, she opened the door and stepped into the living room.

"Mick's on to us," Beavis said as soon as Troy Griffin—a.k.a. Ghost—answered his phone. "I stayed out of sight, but he managed to lose me for a couple of hours. It was definitely on purpose. Riz called in when they got back to the condo."

Griffin stood next to the office window in his Georgetown condominium and idly watched a powerboat cruise down the Potomac. Late afternoon sunlight sparkled on the water, blinding in its intensity. "You're going to install a tracker to prevent this from happening again, right?" He fought to keep the exasperation out of his voice.

"Yes, sir. Working on it now."

The smuggling operations were lucrative, but he was already regretting his involvement. If the Feds got wind of what Claymore had been up to, it could lead right back to him. And all because the idiots working the operation had let Rob Ryan find out. It didn't exactly help that they'd made such a mess of their efforts to clean up the loose ends after his death. A fucking explosion. Real subtle. If Griffin's guys took out Mick and Jenna now, the police would look much more carefully at the cause of death. Jesus Christ, he should have just taken care of this himself from the beginning.

He'd have to take an indirect approach to keeping tabs on Jenna and Mick and wait until an opportunity presented itself. There was too much at stake for Claymore to come under more scrutiny now, before the multi-billion dollar contracts with the Department of Defense were finalized. His influence within the government and law enforcement only extended so far.

Besides, Mick had all kinds of reasons to keep his mouth shut, and so far he was behaving. According to Griffin's sources, Jenna was asking questions about Rob's death—even going so far as to contact a reporter. He balled his fists at the thought of the *other* thorn in his side. For some reason Longstreet had it in for Claymore.

The fact that Jenna had gone to an outside source meant that Mick wasn't talking, and maybe didn't even know the truth about Rob. On the other hand, something had made her suspicious. The attacks on her house would have done the trick, but his gut told him either she or Mick had received something from her brother, something that Beavis and Riz had missed when they combed through her house.

The pictures, a letter…something. Or maybe he'd just

told her of his suspicions. She couldn't do anything without proof, but she was still a liability. She and Mick both were.

"Sir?" Beavis asked, pulling him out of his thoughts.

Red-hot rage flowed through Griffin's veins. Beavis and his team of dunces were risking everything he'd worked so hard for. And now, when he stood on the brink of securing the most lucrative contract of his life, this band of dumbasses could bring it all tumbling down around him.

A plan sparked in his mind like flint against stone—a way to clean up this entire mess and deflect the suspicion away from him. He smiled. "Call me back when you have something to report."

Without waiting for the man's response, he cradled the phone.

If his new plan worked, all of his problems would disappear in just a few more days.

Mick stood at the trailhead under a canopy of trees that were fuzzy green with new leaf buds, stretching lightly as he waited for Jenna to get out of her sweats. She began peeling off her pants, and his pulse picked up. He'd known her for more than a decade, and he still couldn't control his response to her.

Her long, toned legs emerged, and when she pulled off her sweatshirt, she stood in front of him wearing nothing but a black jog bra and matching shorts that hugged her hips and thighs. Creamy skin glistened everywhere he looked.

Was that a tattoo peeking out from beneath her waistband?

His mouth went dry and all the blood in his brain rushed south as he thought about uncovering the design. Not in a million lifetimes would he have expected her to have ink.

"Okay," she said with a smile. "You ready to run?"

He nodded and blinked. God, what was she trying to do to him? *Get a grip, Fury. This is Rob's little sister.* The thought should have doused his desire like an ice bath, but it wasn't enough to counter the vision before him. She walked onto the trail and he followed, trying in vain to keep his eyes off her butt. Her shorts clung to every curve, and there was no panty line in sight. He stifled a groan. Running had been a bad idea. They should have gone for coffee. Or ice cream. Or, hell, anything.

They ran in silence for the first mile, which was good because he could barely talk at her speed anyway. At least running beside her meant she wasn't in his line of sight. The fine line of guilt was all that was keeping him in check. That and the promise he'd made.

"You could have borrowed one of my running shirts," he huffed out.

She hesitated and he glanced at her. Something flickered across her face before she said, "No, thanks. I have another one, but I was too warm last time." She bit her lip and looked away.

He'd seen her do that before, when she was trying to pull something over on her brother. But why on earth would she lie about a shirt?

Turning to face him, running backwards, she gave him a grin. "Want to race?"

Hell no. He was having enough trouble keeping up with her as it was.

She took off without waiting for his answer. He put on a quick burst of speed and caught her around the waist, tugging her onto the grass under the shade of a large oak. She squealed in protest and slapped his hand away. "Hey!" Her peaked nipples pressed against the thin fabric of her bra, and he closed his eyes to block the sight.

"You're too fast," he rasped.

"Yep, that's us," she said, already breathing easy. "The fast and the fury-ous."

He shook his head as he rested bent over to catch his breath, hands propped on his knees. "Very funny."

"You know me, a laugh a minute." She put her arms over her head and stretched backward, revealing a bit more of her tattoo as she wiggled her hips.

Was it a flower? His fingers itched to find out. "Aren't you cold?"

"Nope." She straightened up and looked him in the eye. "Running always makes me hot."

Mick had never seen her like this before. Sure, he'd sensed that their attraction was mutual, but she'd never come on to him. In fact, he'd always counted on the fact that she never would. "What are you doing, Jay?" He stepped close and gazed down at her.

For a split second her eyes widened, but then she schooled her features and licked her lips. She laughed nervously and looked at the ground. "Trying to get your attention." The breeze tugged at her ponytail, and loose strands of blond hair stuck to her glistening face.

"You've always had my attention." Not that he'd ever wanted her to realize it.

She glanced up at him and her look was a mixture of hope and confusion. It totally undid him. Giving in to years of suppressed longing, he cupped the nape of her neck and pressed his mouth to hers. Desire mixed with anger as he swept his tongue past her shocked lips and plundered her sweetness.

Damn her for tempting him like this. Couldn't she see that she was playing with fire? She might think she wanted him—or at least a walk on the wild side with a bad boy to make her forget her troubles—but he knew better. She wanted love and flowers and forever. She wanted someone who was nothing like him. And if he gave in to his lust now, he'd be shattered when she finally realized she could do better than a risk-junky like him.

But before he could back away, her arms snaked around his waist and she pressed her palms to his back, bringing him closer as she responded to his kiss. He groaned and grabbed her butt, grinding his erection against her pelvis, kneading the soft flesh beneath his fingers.

The world around him disappeared as he molded to her warm body, finally indulging in a craving that had haunted him for years. She was even sweeter than he'd imagined. Why had he waited so long to find out? He ran his fingers along the waistband at the back of her shorts, dipping beneath the stretchy fabric to touch the softness beneath.

*Heaven.*

Her body melted against his, sleek and smooth and willing... God, had he ever wanted a woman this much?

Except—*fuck*—what was he doing?

She moaned into his kiss and he pushed her away, instantly regretting the loss of her hot lips and warm skin. "Damn it." He clasped his hands over his head so he wouldn't reach for her again. "You weren't supposed to like that."

"What?" She wiped her mouth with her fingertips and then dropped her arms to her sides. "You kissed me."

"That wasn't a kiss, that was an assault. I expected you to run away screaming."

The hurt on her face twisted his gut, but he stood firm and unsmiling, ignoring the way the waning sunlight set her pale hair on fire and bathed her sweat-beaded skin in gold.

"Why?" she asked softly.

"Because you're Rob's sister," he said, unable to keep the

anger out of his voice. Didn't she get it? Hell, he couldn't handle this right now. It was enough of a struggle to curb his interest when she was ignoring him. If she took an active interest, he was toast.

She put her hands on her hips and glared at him. "So what? Rob loved both of us. I don't think he'd object. Or is this part of that stupid promise you made to protect me?"

"Your brother made it very clear that you were off limits to me," he said, pissed at his friend for putting him in this position.

"He had no right," she said. "Stop treating me like a little girl, Mick. I'm a grown woman."

No shit. That was the problem. "You're playing with fire here, honey. You *know* me. You know I never stick around for long. And then what? Friendships don't survive that kind of thing, Jay."

She stared at the ground in front of him, lips pressed tight, arms folded across her chest. "Maybe I don't want to be friends."

God help him. He needed to nip this in the bud. The girl was as stubborn as Rob when she got an idea in her head. He took a deep breath and steeled himself, angry that it had come to this. "If you're that hot to get laid, I know a guy who's a sucker for uptight blondes. I can give him your number."

Her head jerked as if he'd smacked her. He could have sworn her eyes filled with tears, but she took off running before he could tell for sure.

# CHAPTER EIGHT

JENNA'S FEET FLEW OVER THE asphalt under the broken shade of the oak and poplar trees lining the path. She pumped her arms and ran flat out. Mick had to be following her, but it didn't matter. He wouldn't be able to catch her if she didn't want him to.

God, when she'd decided her only option was to seduce him, she'd almost jumped for joy. She finally had a reason to do what she'd been dreaming about for years. But this heavy feeling of rejection in her chest was why she rarely flirted, let alone expressed overt signs of interest.

The worst part was that he'd been turned on—there was no mistaking that—and he'd still pushed her away. How would she even look him in the eye again?

"Jerk." Mick seemed to be a sucker for anyone with breasts. Except for her. She might not be the hottest thing on two legs, but she knew she wasn't hideous. So why'd he single her out for exclusion from the Make-It-with-Mick club?

She reached the end of the trail and sank to her knees on the grass in front of his car, fighting a wave of nausea.

"Are you okay?" a deep voice asked.

Jenna recoiled and looked up at a tall man in bicycle gear and a red helmet. Suddenly aware that there were other people in the small parking lot, she nodded and rose to her feet. "I'm fine. I just ran too hard. Thanks." She tried for a reassuring smile as she brushed dirt and bits of grass off her knees.

"Okay," he said, looking her up and down before hopping on his bike.

Moving behind a bench, she started to stretch before her muscles cooled down. It would help pass the time as she waited for Mick. He couldn't be too far behind.

"Jenna?"

When she turned around, a man in track pants and a gray polyester running shirt that barely fit his wide shoulders and huge biceps stood in front of her. Startled, she realized it was Colin. "Oh, hi." She crossed her arms over her chest. What had she been thinking going out in public half dressed? "What are you doing here?"

"Going for a run before Tara comes over for dinner."

Was it a coincidence that he was here, or had he been following them? And where the hell was Mick? He wasn't *that* slow. Goosebumps spread across her skin as her body cooled. Or maybe it was Colin's presence. Despite all the glowing things Tara had said about him, he scared her a little. "You live nearby?" she asked.

He nodded and pointed toward a string of buildings down the street. "I have an apartment where I crash when I'm home," he said.

Okay, so maybe it was just a coincidence.

"Speaking of which, Tara told me about your house," he said. "That's tough."

Understatement of the year. "Not my best week, for

sure."

He nodded and frowned in sympathy. "Do the police have any suspects?"

Was he curious, or could he be fishing for information? She held back a tired sigh. This sucked. Not knowing who to trust, constantly thinking the worst of everyone. And if someone *was* following her, she'd left her protector in the dust. *Way to go, Jenna.* When had she become a hothead, acting without thinking? Now was not the time to toss logic out the window.

"No suspects yet. It's starting to look like the explosion was an accident, unrelated to the break-in." Not that she believed it. These special forces types could blow up anything. Surely they knew how to engineer an "accident."

"Yeah, fire makes it tough." His eyes flicked to her chest and then back up to her face. "Do you need a ride or something? You look like you're freezing."

She pulled her arms tighter around herself, shook her head, and glanced back toward the trail. *Come on.* "Mick's right behind me. Maybe he had to stop and tie his shoe."

Colin snorted. "More likely he ran into a cute girl."

Her body flushed with angry heat at the idea. She could vividly picture Mick chatting up a cute little redhead in spandex.

"Tara said you guys are just friends," Colin continued. "That's probably smart on your part. He's not exactly a one-woman kind of guy," he said, not telling her anything she didn't already know.

"And you are?" she asked, surprising herself as much as him.

"I am now." He smiled and glanced at his watch. "Are you going to be okay? I need to get moving or I'll be late."

She looked back and saw Mick cresting the low hill,

headed her way. Was he limping? "There's Mick now. Thanks. Enjoy your run."

Colin gave her a little two-fingered salute and started jogging. He and Mick exchanged nods, but didn't speak. As soon as Colin passed him, Mick's head whipped around to watch him go.

Jenna ran over to Mick, her anger temporarily forgotten when she caught sight of his bloody knee. "Are you okay?"

He nodded. "Fine. What the hell is *he* doing here?" he asked, jerking his thumb behind him.

"Running."

"Right now, when we're here? Doesn't that seem a bit too convenient?" Mick asked as he flopped onto the bench and examined his leg, brushing away tiny stones and dirt with his fingers.

"Maybe, but he lives nearby. This trail is closer to his place than yours." She knelt in front of him for a closer look at his injury. "What happened? If I'd known you were hurt, I would have come back for you."

He used his key fob to unlock the Camaro's doors and stood up. "A bicyclist collided with me." His voice was hard. "Big, tall guy. I thought it was an accident, but after seeing Colin here, I'm not so sure. I think maybe it was a diversion so he could talk to you."

Her stomach jumped. Could it be the same guy who'd talked to her before Colin's arrival? "Red helmet? I think I might have talked to him too."

"*Christ*, Jay." His words vibrated with anger. Or fear. Or maybe a bit of both. "Either one of them could have taken off with you and I wouldn't have been there to stop it. I don't care how mad you are, don't run away like that ever again."

She started shaking. "I'm in control of what I do, not you." A minute ago she'd been relieved to see him, but the hurt and anger roared back, his domineering manner fanning the flames.

"How am I supposed to protect you if you won't let me?" he asked, his frustration evident.

"I'd be more inclined to listen if you didn't kiss me one minute and hurl insults the next."

He ran a hand through his sandy blond hair and pinned her with a look that made her knees weak. "What's your game? This isn't like you." He waved a hand at her clothes. Or lack thereof.

"Did it ever occur to you that sometimes I get tired of being like me?" She'd been trying to build up the confidence to break out of her tightly controlled bubble for years. Inside, she was colorful and passionate, but she couldn't quite bring herself to put it on display. Could a person learn to be more spontaneous, more playful, less rigid? Or was she stuck?

One thing was for sure. Every time her world came crashing down, she crawled back into her shell to take comfort, and spontaneity left the building.

"I'm not a cure for your control issues," he said. "You need therapy for that."

"Well thank you so much, Dr. Freud." *She* had control issues? "Can we go now?" She was tired of showing the world her belly button, because the one man she wanted to notice it was busy looking anywhere but at her.


After a silent drive home from their run, Mick showered and threw together spaghetti and a jar of sauce while Jenna got cleaned up. When she joined him, damp hair curling around her in a cloud of pale silk, tension filled the air like bitter smoke.

His normal wit failed him, so he opted to keep his mouth shut. Better to maintain the distance between them than to say something stupid.

She ate with her head down, not making eye contact. "Thanks," was all she said before loading the dishwasher and claiming a spot at the breakfast bar with her laptop.

He cleared his bowl and punched Kurt's number into his cell phone while he stared at Jenna's back. What the hell was he going to do with her?

"Smitty is still in town," Kurt said after they exchanged greetings. "He's been looking for work, but Claymore has blackballed him."

That was a risky move on Claymore's part. If Smitty grew desperate, he could start talking. "Any idea where I might be able to find him?"

"I know you said you just want to find out if he knows who's after you and Jenna, but I'm sensing something more in your voice, man."

Mick struggled with how much to say. Kurt had known him for too long not to read his moods. But he couldn't be the one to tell Kurt about Rob's pictures or the truth of how he'd died. He hated lying to his friend, but he didn't have a choice.

He took a slow breath and focused on getting his temper under control. "I just want to talk to him."

Kurt was silent for a minute before he let out a sigh. "Be careful with this guy. He can't get a job, his wife just left him, and his friends have abandoned him. He spends every night getting drunk. He's got nothing to lose."

"Thanks, Mom, but I'm not paying you to dispense advice," Mick said. "Besides, I'm not going to lay a finger on him." He had questions for Smitty, and he needed to look the man in the eyes as he gave him the answers. That was all. He wrote down the information. "Thanks, man. I'll be good."

"I'm pretty sure I'm going to regret this," Kurt said

before he hung up.

Mick chuckled and glanced over at Jenna, who jabbed at the keys on her computer as if she was stabbing the machine with each letter she typed. Her project was due tomorrow, and her boss had already called twice today to check on her progress. Each time she hung up, her face was splotchy and pinched. She'd explained to Mick in elaborate terms how much she hated the guy.

"The project due date isn't even real," she'd said. "He just made it up to give me a deadline. The customer—the shipping department—won't be ready for it until they get their new computers in two more weeks. I have no idea how Carl got this far. Maybe people kept promoting him to get him out of their departments."

Watching her now, tense enough to crack, he couldn't resist saying something. "Maybe you should quit if your boss is such a prick." He leaned against the wall a few feet away from her, keeping his distance in a vain effort not to smell her shampoo or accidentally brush up against her soft skin.

"I was trying, remember?" she answered without stopping her work. "I had an interview lined up the day you called me with the news." She quit typing and looked at him, the pain of that memory still fresh in her eyes. "I'm sure they've already filled the position by now. I probably didn't have much chance of getting it anyway. Finding a job in this town is all about who you know, and that's just not my thing."

He'd forgotten about the interview. "I thought you wanted to work for yourself."

She grimaced and shook her head. "I love the *idea* of it, but the reality? I don't know." Her fingers flew over the keys for a few more seconds, and then she slapped the counter and sat back. "There, now it's done and submitted. A day early. Maybe the jerk will finally get off my back."

"Until next time. Seriously, what's the worst that can happen if you go out on your own?" he asked.

Her cell phone rang again before she could respond. She listened quietly, jaw tight, hand trembling as the loud-mouthed bastard on the other end of the line railed at her. For a minute Mick thought she might break down and cry, but then color stained her cheeks, her lips compressed into a flat line, and her eyes sparked.

*Atta girl.* He nodded at her and leaned forward to speak to her in a low voice. "Life's too short, Jay."

Her eyes locked with his for a second before she nodded back. Then, clearing her throat, she said, "Carl? I quit."

Jenna stared at the phone after ending the call with Carl, her whole body shaking. God, had she really just quit her job?

She dropped the phone into her lap and stared at Mick.

He reached across the granite, gripping her shoulders as he met her gaze. "You did the right thing. No one should have to put up with that kind of treatment, especially not when you work so hard. That guy didn't appreciate you and he didn't deserve you."

"I'm not so sure this was a good idea." Resting her elbows on the counter, she put her head in her hands and tried to take normal breaths around the tightness filling her chest. Her job had been the last tether to her old life. This had to be the dumbest thing she'd done in a long time. How could she have made such a big decision on impulse?

And yet…a small part of her was doing a little dance. The little part inside of her that had always pushed to be free began to assert itself. She finally had an excuse to make the changes she'd yearned for. She could do whatever she wanted with her life, and she wavered between hyperventilating and cheering.

Mick stepped back and watched her carefully. Other than touching her shoulder just now, he'd been giving her a three-foot berth since they returned from their run.

"Well, I guess that settles it," she said, looking up. "I don't have to go back to work tomorrow."

"I'm sorry, Jay." He looked genuinely distressed for her. "I know you wanted to have something else lined up before you left QDS."

"Yeah, but maybe this is a good thing." Looking at it any other way would only bring her to tears. "Now I truly have nothing to lose. I could go anywhere, do anything." She'd never imagined having no strings, no attachments to a particular place.

"Where would you go?" he asked.

"Good question. I've never considered it." No, that wasn't entirely true. "Well, except that I'd love to live near the ocean." Some of her happiest moments had been at the beach with her family, back when things were good.

"You should do it," he said. "When this is over, you could start your own consulting business and move to the beach. You can work from anywhere now."

*When this is over.* When would that be? What was *this*? How would she even know when it was over?

"Trying to get rid of me already, huh?" If she moved away, he wouldn't feel obligated to watch over her anymore. He'd probably welcome the reprieve.

"No, it's not that," he said, apparently missing the teasing note in her voice. He ran a hand through his hair, giving it a sexy disheveled look. "I want you to be happy. Nobody should have to go through everything you've survived this last week. Hell, these last few years." His look of concern deepened. "It's time for something good to happen to you."

Yes, it was. "And when do you get to be happy?" she

asked, shutting her laptop and pushing it aside.

He gave her a wry smile. "Who says I'm not?"

*Liar.* "Okay, fine then. I think we should celebrate all of this unexpected happiness." She was suddenly feeling reckless. Reckless and numb.

His eyes narrowed and he put his hands on his hips, stretching his ratty Air Force T-shirt tight across his chest. Her belly did a little flip and she swallowed hard. Now that they were speaking again, she finally realized something that should have been obvious to her all along. His harsh words on the trail had been his attempt to push her away. It was that damn promise to Rob again.

She wasn't going to give up. Now that she'd given herself permission to give in to her desire, she was impatient with longing. But she'd have to be more careful this time. She'd have to lure him in before he knew what was happening.

As if she knew how to do that.

"What did you have in mind?" he asked. "We could go out for ice cream."

She laughed. How old did she think he was? "I was thinking beer."

He frowned. "That's not a good idea. For either one of us."

"For years you and Rob have been telling me to loosen up, lighten up, let go a little, and when I finally want to, you tell me it's not a good idea?" She stood up, a sudden surge of energy shooting through her body. "How about this? I'm going out. Either join me or don't. I may not have Tara's glam, but I'm sure I can find someone who's willing to drink with me."

Besides, she needed to lose a few inhibitions if she wanted the confidence to come on to Mick again.

He sighed and shook his head. "Fine. Someone has to

make sure you don't do anything stupid."

"Hah. But who's going to watch out for you?"

"Good question," he muttered under his breath.

"What?"

"Get changed. I know the perfect place."

For the first time in her life, Jenna was going to let go. She was either really excited or scared out of her mind. Maybe both.

# CHAPTER NINE

TARA SMOOTHED HER HAIR IN Colin's bathroom mirror and walked through his bachelor bedroom with its plain oak furniture and bare walls, moving past the disheveled bed where they'd just had incredible sex. Her hunger had been forgotten the minute he opened the door and pulled her in for a kiss. Five days and his touch still turned her to putty.

But now she was ravenous and almost shaky with hunger. Lunch had been a long time ago. She reached for the handle of the door leading to the living room, but stopped when she heard his voice.

"No suspects."

He paused, and she could hear cupboard doors squeaking open and being slammed shut.

"I can't really talk right now…yeah, keep it up and let me know."

Pots clanged and the kitchen faucet started running.

"Roger that. We'll talk tomorrow."

She forced herself to wait at the door for another thirty seconds so he wouldn't know she'd listened to part of his conversation. But why did she feel like she had to hide? She hadn't overhead anything incriminating. He worked in security, and he probably wasn't supposed to talk about his work with her, but it wasn't her fault if she heard something she shouldn't. Besides, wasn't he supposed to be on R&R right now?

She thought of Mick's warning and frowned, but Colin had given her no reason to doubt him. He was probably just talking shop with a friend. And, truth be told, she didn't *want* to doubt him. He was tender and thoughtful when she needed it. Rough and wild when she wanted it. The first guy in years who'd stayed interested for more than one or two nights. She was probably just getting paranoid because she really liked him.

Shaking off her thoughts, she walked into the living room that adjoined the kitchen. "It smells great out here. What are you making?"

"Nothing fancy. Spaghetti and meatballs. My grandmother's recipe." He reached her in two steps and took her hands, twirling her toward the stereo where he punched a button. Slow, sexy jazz filled the tiny room. "Dance with me while the sauce simmers," he said, leaning in to plant a hot kiss on her mouth.

God, she loved this big man who cooked and danced and kissed like a dream.

*Oh, no.* Her heart skipped a beat and her steps faltered. It was too soon, but she still couldn't deny the truth.

She was definitely falling for him.


Mick scanned the large room crammed with billiard tables, video games, and low-slung club chairs gathered around short tables. The sharp crack of someone breaking the rack on a nearby pool table reverberated in the dark green room.

Smoke hung in the air, filtering the dim light, as music with a heavy bass pulsed over the din of conversation.

Nobody in the crowd looked familiar.

According to Kurt, this was Smitty's favorite hangout, but it was early yet, only eight. Bringing Jenna to this place was probably not his best idea ever. Still, she wanted to go out, and he wanted to talk to Smitty. This way they could both get what they wanted.

"I thought you couldn't smoke in public places in Virginia anymore," she said, waving her hand in front of her nose. She wore a green v-neck top over blue jeans that showcased her cute little ass. Her white-blond curls hung loose, almost to her shoulders, glowing brightly in the dimly lit room.

"The law doesn't apply to the bar area if they keep it separately ventilated from the restaurant," he said. He'd frequented them enough to know.

"Oh," she said, wrinkling her nose in distaste. She looked around, her eyes landing on an air hockey table before she turned to him. "Can we play?"

"Sure, let's get our drinks first." He ordered two beers and met her at the table, choosing the side that faced the front entrance. Digging into his pocket, he pulled out the quarters he'd gotten from the bartender and handed them to her.

"Thanks." She got everything set up and placed the puck on the table, leaning forward to push it to him.

The move provided him with a quick glimpse of her bra, and he faltered, almost missing the puck as it glided in his direction. They went back and forth, the flat disk pinging off the bumpers with a high-pitched *tink* until he finally sunk a shot into her goal. He downed half his beer and did a quick check for any new patrons.

Jenna took a couple of swigs from her bottle, unable to hide her brief grimace in response to the bitter flavor. She swallowed, then set her drink down, giving him a dazzling smile. What was it about her? One smile could reduce him to a teenager in heat.

She was beyond distracting, and Mick missed some easy shots. And he wasn't the only one who was noticing her charms. A couple of guys sitting in a nearby lounge area were enjoying the view, especially when she reached across the table. She won the game, celebrating with a little squeal of delight, and one of the men whistled. "Nice job, Blondie!"

Red crept up her neck and into her cheeks, but she grinned and faced the group, finishing her beer off with a quick gulp. "Thanks. Who wants to play me next?"

A dark-haired man with muscles to spare rose and walked toward them, his eyes never leaving her face. "I'll play." He nodded toward Mick without breaking eye contact. "If it's all right with your boyfriend."

Jenna glanced from Mick to the interloper. "Oh, no, he's not my boyfriend," she said with a giggle. "I'm not his type."

The man looked at him with disbelief. Mick forced himself to nod, even as something ugly worked its way through his blood. He couldn't afford to act out or lose his cool. The guy was right to think he was crazy. This beautiful woman had offered herself up on a platter for him today... and he'd turned her down.

Not only that, he'd insulted her. Oh yeah, and he was lying to her.

"I'm Brad." The man reached out and shook Jenna's hand.

She smiled. "Jenna. You ready?"

No way was Mick going to stand there watching them like an idiot. Not that he'd let her out of his sight. She could still be in danger. He approached Jenna. "Want another beer?"

"It's on me," Brad said, handing Mick a ten like he was

some kind of waiter.

"Thanks," Jenna said. She turned away, dismissing him altogether.

Well, Brad had swooped in quickly. And Jenna had come out of her shell a little more than Mick would have liked. What had happened to the shy girl who didn't even have the confidence to flirt? He preferred her. He could handle her. As he stood at the bar waiting for his drinks, he checked out every person in the large, plus-sign-shaped room. The bartender brought him the bottles, and as he stepped away to make change, a familiar face walked in the front door.

*Smitty.* Mick tensed. This was why he'd come, but now that he had the man in his sights, he was having trouble controlling his rage. He turned away and strode back toward Jenna and her new buddy, setting her beer and Brad's money on the corner of the game table.

"Thanks," she said, her eyes on the puck as it ricocheted around the table and finally into her goal. "Oh, crap."

He took the opportunity to whisper into her ear. "I see someone I need to talk to. Will you be okay here with your new friend for a few minutes?"

Her eyes met his, and he could've sworn he saw disappointment there. What did she want from him? If this whole little show with Brad was her attempt to make him jealous, it was working, but he wasn't going to be manipulated. If she wanted to blow off some steam, fine. She should enjoy her newfound confidence and leave him out of it.

She nodded and grasped the white disk from its return slot, placing it on the table.

"Don't go anywhere that I can't see you. I'll be back in a few minutes."

"Have fun," she said in a flat tone and then smacked the

puck across the table.

Shit. This was why he didn't want long-term involvement with her or any woman. Emotions were messy and they complicated everything. Give him a no-strings-attached fuck any day over a relationship.

Relaxing his muscles as much as possible, he strolled toward Smitty, who was watching a group of people play pool.

The man's face was red and he was leaning against a support column. "Nice shot." He raised his glass as one player sank a striped ball in the corner pocket. The men ignored him, but he didn't seem to notice. He swayed on his feet a bit before taking a sip and bumping back into the post. Had he started drinking before he arrived?

Mick walked right up next to him, undetected. Bruises were still faintly visible on Smitty's ugly face, and Mick had the small satisfaction of knowing he'd put them there.

"Long time no see, Smitty," Mick said.

The man jumped and the remainder of his drink sloshed onto the cement floor. "What are you doing here?" he asked, eyes wide.

"You and I have some unfinished business."

Smitty backed away, glancing around for help that wasn't there. He'd come in alone. "You can't touch me in here, man. They'll call the cops."

"I have no intention of touching you." Although he could easily imagine shoving his fist through that oversized target of a nose. His hands clenched with intent, but he shook them out. *Relax.*

Mick shoved his hands in his pockets. "I just want to talk."

Jenna tried to ignore Mick and enjoy the attention of her new friend, Brad. When was the last time she'd felt this sexy and interesting? And why couldn't she be happier about it?

She finished off her beer, the second in less than an hour, and her brain was buzzing. The hockey puck slid past her again, sinking into the goal with a metallic thunk.

"My game," Brad said, coming around the table. "You want another drink?"

"Not right now, thanks." Unable to help herself, she glanced over at Mick and the man he had backed into a corner. Mick's jaw was hard, his shoulders tense, and he looked ready to spring. When he'd told her he needed to talk to someone, she'd expected a woman. She was relieved that it wasn't.

"He's really not your boyfriend?" Brad asked. "Because the way you guys look at each other…"

Not for lack of trying. She sighed and gave Brad her full attention. "No. He's just a friend. An overprotective one, for sure, but nothing else."

"Well, he's crazy. You're the prettiest woman here."

"Thanks." She wasn't sure that was much of a compliment, but she'd take it. Men didn't often go out of their way to call her pretty.

Brad wandered over to an empty love seat and set his beer on a low table. Jenna followed. In the corner, Mick was staring down the man with the big nose, his handsome profile harsh in the dark room. Could this be the infamous Smitty that he'd been looking for? Had he only agreed to bring her here to confront this guy?

She slumped back against the leather cushion. "So, Brad, what do you do?" *Please, anything but security or military.*

"I'm a physical therapist. How about you?"

Perfect. A nice, normal job. No high-risk assignments, guns, or long deployments. "As of today, I'm an unemployed programmer. I'm here to celebrate my freedom."

He gave her a confused look, apparently not sure if she was serious. "Well, congratulations, I guess."

"Thanks." She stood up. "You know what? I think maybe I will get another drink. I'll be right back." When she reached the bar she ordered another beer. Her last—otherwise she was likely to pass out.

"Hey," Brad whispered into her ear from behind. "I'll get that." He leaned forward to throw down some bills and sandwiched her gently against the bar.

That's when it became clear. Brad might be nice and normal and attractive, but he didn't interest her. Not really. If Mick had pulled that move, sparks would have shot across her skin and her legs would have gone weak. If it had been Mick, she would have turned to face him, threaded her arms around his neck, and pulled him down for a kiss...

A crash followed by a shout drew her attention to the other side of the room. Mick was sprawled across a pool table, Big Nose towering over him with his fist drawn back. Mick was holding the guy off with one arm, yelling something she couldn't make out. What the hell was going on?

Jenna squirmed away from Brad, heading toward the gathering crowd. She wriggled through the onlookers just in time to see Mick push to his feet and land a blow on the other man's nose. Blood spurted everywhere, and the man roared before throwing a kick to Mick's stomach.

Mick stumbled back and doubled over with one arm across his middle before coming in for another charge. "I should have killed you when I had the chance, asshole." He pummeled Big Nose's face.

Momentarily stunned, Jenna stood rooted to the floor, unable to believe the ferocity on Mick's face and the violence of his fists. Without a conscious thought, she stepped forward and put a hand on his shoulder. "Mick, stop!"

Startled, he used his elbow to shake her off. "Get back!" He connected with her solar plexus, knocking the wind out of her, and she stumbled into a pair of strong arms. Brad. Mick glanced her way and his jaw went slack, but she couldn't breathe, much less process his response.

Brad helped her into a chair, concern furrowing his brow. "Are you okay?"

She shook her head. Her chest hurt, and panic began to set in as she struggled to make her lungs work. Oh, God, why wouldn't they work? She was dying, and Mick had killed her. It was like drowning without water, and she clutched her shirt collar, desperate for oxygen. Tears ran down her cheeks as the seconds ticked by, whole lifetimes measured out by the smallest hand of a clock.

"Relax, Jenna. It's okay. If you panic it will only get worse." Brad squeezed her shoulders gently. "Sit up and take a slow breath."

Oh, how she wanted to, but she couldn't. She shook her head. How could he be so calm when she was dying?

"Jenna, look at me."

Their gazes locked and she focused on the deep brown of his eyes. Why couldn't she love *this* man? This handsome, friendly physical therapist who thought she was pretty and bought her beer. Who handled crises with calm strength instead of causing them? Whose gently kneading hands and softly spoken words were helping her relax in spite of herself.

And all of a sudden, she could breathe again. She gulped in huge lungfuls of air, afraid it would stop coming.

"Oh my God, Jenna." Mick slid into place beside her, kneeling next to her chair. "I'm so sorry. I didn't mean to hit you. I was just trying to keep you from getting hurt." His gaze roamed over her. "Are you all right?" He reached up to wipe the tears from her cheeks, but she jerked her head away from his bloody hands. Staring at his palms as if they belonged to someone else, he stood and wiped them on his shirt, backing away. "Jesus, I'm sorry. I—"

"Why don't you leave her alone?" Brad suggested, cutting him off.

For a minute, Mick looked like he might take on Brad, too, but instead he nodded and stepped away, keeping an eye on Big Nose, who was leaning heavily against the wall holding his face while the crowd looked on in disbelief.

A small commotion near the front of the pool hall drew everyone's attention.

"Shit." Mick slumped into a chair and closed his eyes as four policemen entered the bar.

An hour later, Mick opened the door to his condo and waved Jenna through. She still wasn't talking to him. He didn't blame her. Not only had he ruined her night, he'd freaking elbowed her in the chest. The look on her face after he'd connected— the shock, the hurt, the pain—had broken through his angry haze and wrung his heart out. And it had probably saved him from killing Smitty.

Mostly, he was glad about that. Mostly.

Damn the man for getting physical. All Mick had wanted was answers. Okay, maybe that's not *all* he'd wanted, but questioning the asshole was all he'd intended to do, no matter how satisfying breaking his nose had been. To his surprise, Smitty had declined to press charges, though it wouldn't have been a clear-cut case anyway. After all, Smitty had started the fight. Since no damage had been done to the bar, the cops had released them both after taking the report.

Jenna set down her purse and marched into the kitchen,

where she poured herself a glass of water and leaned against the counter, staring into her drink. Somehow, he needed her to trust him again. Or, barring that, he at least needed her to feel safe with him.

He'd start by cleaning up. He dashed to the bathroom and emerged five minutes later, bloodstain-free. Jenna was still standing in the kitchen.

Approaching cautiously, Mick cleared his throat and leaned against the fridge. "I'm sorry, Jay. Really." What else could he say? His feelings were stronger than that, but he had no way to express them, no way to make her understand.

"You said that already." Without looking at him, she doused the sink sponge and began wiping down the counters, picking up the can opener, the toaster, and the knife block in succession to clean under them.

He moved in behind her and grabbed her hands. "Stop."

"Fine." She yanked free of him and moved to the living room, leaving behind the fresh scent of her shampoo mingled with a hint of cigarette smoke.

"I'm sorry about Brad. I know you wanted to have fun tonight and I ruined it." Although, he wasn't really sorry about Brad. He'd wanted to punch him almost as much as he'd been gunning for Smitty.

She turned and gave him an incredulous expression and let out a bitter laugh. "You think this is about Brad?" She shook her head slowly. "You think I'm so desperate that I'd go home with someone I just met in a bar?" Pink splotches colored her cheeks and she straightened to her full height as she said, "That may be your style, but it's not mine."

*Ouch.* He had no response to that. Apparently, he had no response for anything tonight.

"Beyond that," she continued, her voice rising, "has it not occurred to you that I might be a little upset that you got into a fistfight?"

His throat tightened. "I didn't intend for that to happen. I just wanted to ask him a few questions."

She hesitated, and he could almost see the gears working as she cocked her head and stared at him thoughtfully. "Is he the real reason we went to that bar in the first place?"

She'd figured him out. Maybe even before the police had mentioned that the man's name was Alan Smith. "I wanted you to have a good time, but I thought I could use the opportunity to talk to Smitty too. I wasn't planning to—"

"Murder him?" she asked.

Well, yeah, that. He couldn't look her in the eyes anymore. She read him too well.

An exasperated sigh hissed through her teeth. "What's going on? What's so important about this guy, Mick?"

He glanced up. *Mistake.* The pleading in her eyes nearly undid him, but he held his ground. She didn't know what she was asking. "That's between me and him."

"Does this have something to do with the pictures? Are you investigating this yourself?" She put her hands on her hips and stared him down. "Were you ever planning to tell me?"

"It's not about you, Jay. It's about me." She didn't get it—he didn't want her to—but he was walking a fine line here. "There's nothing to tell."

"There has to be something. You were ready to *kill* him."

The scary thing is that he might have. He'd wanted to, after Smitty slammed him into that table. Who was kidding? He *still* wanted to.

What did that say about him?

There was real fear in Jenna's eyes when she looked at him, and he hated himself for that. He'd never wanted to hurt her or have her see him like that. Taking her to Smitty's hangout had been a bad idea. One of his worst. Right up there with wanting to yank her to the floor and rip her clothes off.

But his need to keep watch over her at all times was trapping them both. He couldn't keep her safe if he was off hunting down Smitty, and his sense of duty wouldn't let him pawn her off on someone else while he did. That, and he didn't want to leave her.

Maybe he owed her something. A small nugget to satisfy her curiosity. He expelled a long breath. "You're right. I wanted to ask him about the smuggling, but I couldn't be direct about it because I didn't want him to know you had evidence." Mick ran a hand through his hair. "The little asshole wouldn't tell me anything. He just came at me."

Her face softened a little and she crossed her arms, shifting her weight to one foot. "Did it occur to you that maybe he was goading you into hitting him? If you go to jail, you're off his back and no one's the wiser."

Yeah, the thought had crossed his mind. Later. When he was thinking rationally again. But that made Smitty a first class idiot, because he could have gotten himself killed.

"He was drunk and not thinking clearly. If he'd been sober, he wouldn't have provoked me. Smitty's no genius, but he knows how much I hate him."

"And why do you hate him so much?"

In spite of himself, Mick chuckled. "You're a good interrogator. Ever thought of being a cop?"

She put her hands on her slim hips. "I must not be that good. I can never get the truth out of you."

He rocked back in surprise. That sounded like a challenge. And maybe an opportunity to regain her trust. "Ask me a question about anything besides Rob's death or this thing with Smitty, and I promise to answer it honestly."

Her eyebrows rose in surprise. "Anything?"

He nodded.

"How many questions?"

What was fair without opening himself up too much? "Three." He moved to the futon and sat down, propping his feet on the coffee table. "Take your time."

She watched him carefully, chewing her lip. "Have you ever killed anyone?"

"Jeez. Don't pull any punches, okay, babe?" He closed his eyes for a second. As much as he wished he couldn't, he remembered every fatal encounter. "Yes."

His answer couldn't have been unexpected, but she still gasped and backed into the wall. Okay, maybe this wasn't such a good idea after all.

"Why?"

"You want that to be question two?"

She scowled at him. "No. You can't just answer the follow-up out of the goodness of your heart?"

"Who says I have any goodness in my heart?"

"You should have been a politician." She sat on one of the bar stools and gripped her water glass, taking a quick sip before she continued. "Okay, question two. Why did you make a point of talking to me every time Rob called?"

Dropping his feet to the floor, he swiveled around so he could see her. A sexy blush stained her cheeks again, and with sudden clarity, he knew the real answer. An honest reply would give away too much, but if he lied, he'd undo any ground he was making up here.

He took a deep breath and held her gaze. "I missed you."

# CHAPTER TEN

JENNA HADN'T EXPECTED MICK'S RESPONSE. His answer did strange things to her nervous system. She wasn't just a substitute sister to him; he'd missed her. Not just home, *her*. Flutters rose in her belly and spread down to her toes.

Good thing she was sitting down, because his direct gaze was suddenly full of heat. She was useless when he looked at her like that.

This was the direction she needed to take things, though, because in spite of how much he'd frightened her tonight, she still wanted him. She wanted him to get used to sharing his secrets with her. And she wanted him to think about her as a woman, not as Rob's little sister.

She cleared her throat and rubbed her palms on her thighs in preparation for question three. Did she have the guts to ask? She channeled her inner Tara. *You can do it.* With a fortifying breath, she hopped down from the stool and walked over to him, standing by his feet.

His eyes followed her every move. "Uh-oh," he said with a grin. "You look way too serious."

"Number three." *You can do it.* Shoving her shaky hands into her back pockets, she forced herself to look at him when she spoke. "Do you want me?"

He launched to his feet, gripping her shoulders with warm hands. "You have to ask?"

"After today, yes." His rejection had killed her confidence.

He tilted her chin up and leaned in, answering in a low voice, "If you knew how much I want you right now, you'd run away."

"You tried that last time," she said, lust swirling through her body at his nearness and the memory of their kiss beside the trail. She'd run from his rejection, not his passion.

His hand slid along her neck and up into her hair, cradling her head in his large palm. She closed her eyes and savored his touch as his fingers caressed her scalp. He pulled her against his chest, wrapping his other arm around her waist. She ran her hands along his back, feeling the strong cables of muscle through his soft shirt.

He was all heat and strength and spice, and her body flared to life as they connected from shoulder to toe.

"I want you like I've never wanted anything or anyone," he whispered in her ear. "It's always been that way with you."

His words had the power to melt her, and when she looked up at him, she was surprised to see the raw honesty and yearning on his face. "Could have fooled me," she said, thinking of all the years she'd pined for him, believing that he couldn't possibly be interested in her, convincing herself that she didn't want a man like him.

"I was trying to. You were off limits, remember?" He stepped back, running his hands down her body until they rested at her waist, holding her at arm's length. "You still are. God, what am I doing?"

Her body leaned into him, begging silently for his return.

"You were about to kiss me." Her inner Tara rejoiced at her boldness.

Mick shook his head. "I can't, Jay. I—" His face reddened and his hands tightened on her waist, but he just stared at her.

"I know. You promised." Maybe it was the last of her beer buzz, or maybe it was the final desperate act of a woman who'd lost everything, but at this moment, she wanted nothing more than for him to kiss her. So she set confident, brazen Jay free. "Why did you promise? Did you owe Rob?"

"He was my best friend. You're his sister," he said, as if that explained everything. He shot her an exasperated look laced with longing and frustration.

"Why do you call me Jay? Does it make it easier for you to think of me as someone else?"

He opened his mouth, but then shook his head without answering.

She plowed on and gave him a flirty smile, running her fingertip along his collar. "Well, maybe you'd like to tell me what really happened—"

"Stop," he murmured against her mouth, invading her personal space suddenly and without warning. He pressed his lips softly to hers, tugging at her lower lip. "Just stop."

His warm hands stroked up and down her spine, bringing their bodies closer together with each pass. Her nipples peaked with the first brush of his chest. She wanted to rub against him like a cat.

Standing on her toes, Jenna reached for another taste. He met her halfway and slowly stole her breath with feather-soft kisses along her jaw and down her neck, sending tiny jolts of electricity across her skin. He returned to her mouth, licking and nibbling his way inside. She moaned when their tongues met, smooth and rough and eager. His hand slid down to her buttocks and urged her closer, rocking her against his growing erection. Oh, yeah, she was a goner.

With a low groan, he snatched her legs up by the thighs and wrapped them around his waist before staggering back to the futon. His heat and hardness pressed against her core and she writhed in his lap, drunk with desire. Her jeans needed to go now, but she didn't want to stop to take them off.

"You're so beautiful, so sexy." He spoke in between kisses as he lightly dragged his fingers down her chest.

The way he made her feel, she could almost believe him. And, God, if he would just…she arched her back, pressing her breasts against his hands. He chuckled and obliged her unspoken request by covering them completely with his palms as he stroked her nipples with his thumbs. A little buzz started along her nerves and traveled from low in her belly out to her fingers and toes. Oh, yes. That was precisely what she wanted.

Until he whipped her shirt up and over her head, slipped a finger beneath the satin of her bra, and touched her bare skin. "Mmm, yeah." *That* was what she wanted. Exactly that.

And then he unhooked her bra, skimming it down her arms. Leaning forward, he took a nipple into his mouth.

"Mmm…Mick." She bit her lip at the exquisite pleasure, her hips jutting eagerly against his, her breath coming in shallow gasps. *This* was what she'd been waiting for.

Until he withdrew.

No, *please*. She grabbed his biceps. "Don't stop."

"Never."

He captured her other breast in his mouth and licked until she thought she'd explode. She was a powder keg on fire, her fuse getting shorter by the second. Who needed control? Control was definitely overrated. Writhing in his lap as sensations hit her from everywhere at once, she completely gave in to him.

He owned her.

She wanted to own him too.

Running her hands down his sides, she found the hem of his shirt and pulled it up. He broke contact for just long enough to fling it across the room and then he lunged for her again, muscles rippling from his broad shoulders down to his abs.

His stomach jumped under her tentative touch, and he alternated his attention between her breasts, caressing them with his hands, his tongue. If not for the intense need to touch him, to feel his skin beneath her fingers, she would have been content to collapse as pleasure washed through her.

Sensations were building between her thighs, each wave tied to the pull of his mouth as if by a string. Suddenly she needed more. She wanted him inside her with a fierceness she'd never experienced. She kissed his forehead and skimmed her fingers along the waist of his jeans, dipping inside and beneath the elastic of his boxers.

"Jenna," he whispered hoarsely. "You make me crazy." He launched to his feet, still holding her, supporting her by her thighs, and kissed her hungrily as he swayed toward the bedroom.

For one brief moment, her body tightened. What the hell she was doing? This was Mick, reckless playboy, arrogant womanizer.

But this was her plan. She was finally going to get what she wanted.

He laid her on the bed and unbuttoned his jeans, his hungry gaze heating her skin to boiling. Who cared about the truth when the sexiest man alive wanted her? *Her.* Mousy, computer geek Jenna. Her throat went dry as he stripped bare and kneeled over her on the bed, the bad-boy tribal tattoo on his biceps dancing.

The reality was better than any fantasy she'd come up with while lying alone in his bed these last few nights.

He reached for the zipper on her pants. "Your turn," he said.

Worries long forgotten, she lifted her hips in invitation.

Mick laid his hand on Jenna's tight, flat stomach and traced the edge of her tattoo. This was crazy. This hot, sexy woman who melted when he caressed her was Jenna. *Jenna,* for God's sake—Rob's no-touch, hands-off little sister. But for the first time he didn't care. And he couldn't have stopped touching her if his life depended on it. In fact, he wanted to touch her everywhere.

When he didn't immediately undo her pants, she reached for the button herself.

"Uh-uh," he said, playfully slapping her hand away. "I want to do it."

"So what are you waiting for?" she asked, rising up on her elbows to nibble his lips.

Her pink nipples were tight with desire and he flicked his thumb across one while cupping her breast in his palm. She gasped and closed her eyes.

"I'm not done playing," he said as he delved into her sweet mouth. How could he resist? She was at once wanton and demure, seductive and staid. He'd been dreaming of watching her shed her inhibitions for years. Now here she was in his bed, half-naked and begging for him.

No man alive could have turned her down.

Time lost all meaning as he slowly peeled away her jeans. The delicate tattoo slowly revealed itself as a flowering branch that followed the curve of her pelvis in the hollow of her stomach. "What is it?" he asked, gently rubbing her inked skin with his thumb and slipping her white cotton panties down to see the complete design.

"A cherry blossom branch."

Her hips moved in a slow, sensuous rhythm beneath him, and he pressed his thigh between her knees to part her legs.

"What does it mean?" he asked, his mouth replacing his hand to kiss each delicate flower and tiny leaf.

Her belly tightened with each press of his lips, and her fingers dug into his shoulders. "It's supposed to represent…" She moaned as his fingers stroked the silky smooth skin of her inner thigh. "It represents the beauty of life, but also how short it is. I wanted to get it done after my parents died. I finally got the nerve after Jimmy succumbed to his injuries."

He kissed her, pouring his regret for her loss, his admiration for the woman that she was into every stroke of his tongue and nip of his teeth. He wanted more than anything to make her forget the sadness of the last week— hell, the last several years—of her life.

Eager to learn every inch of milky-white skin, he trailed his hand along the side of her breast, into the hollow beneath her ribs, around the flare of her hips, and down to her knee. There were so many lovely parts of her. He didn't have enough hands to touch them all at once.

He lay on his side, propped on one elbow and pressed his body against the length of her, swinging a leg over her thigh to pin her down. For tonight at least, she was his.

She reached up to him, and he kissed her lips once more before moving to her breasts. As he caressed them, he brought one hand up to the apex of her long, shapely legs, and pressed a finger into her. She was so warm and moist, and she clenched around him, moving her hips to take him deeper.

"You're so hot, baby. I have to taste you."

She whimpered and his cock twitched in response, begging to replace his fingers. *Easy.* He wasn't ready for the end yet. He kissed his way down from her breast, following the line of her tattoo.

"Beautiful," he said, gently spreading her delicate folds to reveal the prize.

He flicked his tongue lightly across her sensitive nub and she bucked and cried out. A smile crossed his face. He had done this to her in his dreams, but the reality was infinitely better. At this moment, he was the luckiest man on earth.

Going in for another taste, he gripped her hips with his hands and held her in place as she strained against him, every muscle taut. "Don't fight it," he murmured. "Just let go."

His fingers joined the party, and suddenly her whole body went rigid. She panted and moaned and squeezed her eyes shut, gripping the bedspread like it was a lifeline. "That's it," he whispered, nearing the edge himself. "Come for me, Jenna."

Her breath hitched and she arched up, a sexy cry escaping her lips as he stroked her with his tongue. He tasted her release as it shuddered through her and she went limp in his arms.

He wanted to cry at the sight of this gorgeous angel who had so completely given herself over to him, this woman who glowed as if lit from within.

Mick had thought there was no greater rush than risking death, but he'd been wrong. Bringing this amazing woman to climax could easily become an addiction. In fact, he already wanted to do it again.

Jenna floated, every nerve ending buzzing as she lay limply across Mick's bed. She'd expected to explode after he worked his magic a second time, but she was still there, heart pounding as he rose above her with a gleam in his eye.

"You're like a drug," he said, stopping to nuzzle her breasts before planting a kiss on her mouth.

She could taste herself on his lips, but instead of being weird, it was erotic. God, what had he done to her? He'd turned her into a shameless hussy. She tensed up and pressed her legs together, suddenly embarrassed at how she'd let him strip her bare.

He slid his knee between her thighs and caressed her hip. "Don't get shy on me now, baby," he whispered in her ear as his fingers trailed back to her heat and dipped inside. "I want to be right here," he said.

Her body reacted instantly to his presence and she pushed against him, giving in to the pleasure. She wanted him inside her too. More than anything.

"That's it," he murmured as she relaxed.

He magically produced a condom from somewhere—the bedside table?—and rolled it on, pinning her to the bed with his blazing blue eyes. She would *not* think about how expertly he sheathed himself. She would *not* wonder how many women had had this intimate view of the Adonis who moved over her with such confidence and grace.

Lowering himself to his elbows, he peppered her face with kisses and gently spread her legs, pressing his erection against her eager flesh. He hesitated. "Jenna?"

Not Jay, *Jenna*. She loved hearing her name on his lips. She met his questioning gaze with a quick thrust of her hips, taking the sweet invasion with a gasp of pleasure. He was so large and hot and the pressure was unbearably exquisite. "Yes," she whispered. Something coiled within her, a restless ache that only he could ease. *More*. She widened her legs, inviting him deeper.

"God, Jenna." He closed his eyes and groaned. His head

fell to her shoulder and he gripped her hips, his breath coming in short bursts as he set a hurried pace, pumping hard, meeting her stroke for stroke as they both raced toward the edge. "Come with me," he rasped, nipping at her shoulder and squeezing her buttocks.

She couldn't. She wasn't ready, but...oh, wait. She gripped his shoulders, digging her nails into his back, pressing him closer, deeper. And then the tight cord inside her snapped, sending sparks of electricity through her veins as lights burst in her vision.

Mick cried out and locked up, eyes shut tight as he dove off the precipice and joined her in the pool of rapture. She floated there with him, adrift in the aftermath of their lovemaking. It should have been one of her happiest moments, an oasis in an otherwise disastrous week. But a thought popped through her bubble of joy and she couldn't shake it.

*What have I done?*

# CHAPTER ELEVEN

TARA AWOKE ALONE IN THE dark. Her back was cold where Colin had been wrapped around her. According to his alarm clock it was after midnight. She slipped one of his large shirts over her head and padded out to the living room. He rarely slept, she'd learned, but perhaps she could coax him back to bed. It had worked before.

In the dim light that filtered through the blinds from the street lamps, the townhome sat empty and cold. Where was he?

"What's going on?" She could hear his muffled voice through the opening of the sliding glass door to the balcony, where he stood partially hidden by vertical blinds that had been pulled back.

She started toward the door, thinking she could slip outside and hold him while he talked. But her steps faltered as she approached the door. Who would he be talking to this late? Would he be mad if she overheard his conversation? But what if something had happened to someone in his family and he needed her support?

Or maybe he was just trying to be considerate and let her sleep.

She didn't want to start out their relationship by sneaking around listening to his phone calls. He'd share when he was ready. Trust went both ways, after all. With that decided, she turned to tiptoe into the kitchen. She'd flip on the light switch to let him know that she was awake. But his next words stopped her in her tracks.

"Mick's not talking, and Jenna hasn't learned anything new. If she were planning to turn in any kind of evidence, she would have done it by now. He's probably keeping her in check for his own reasons."

Tara started to shake. He was keeping tabs on Jenna and Mick? She stood rooted in place, unable to walk away.

"He did what?" Colin asked, his voice rising. "Sorry." He spoke more softly. "What did the police say?"

He was silent for a minute and she strained closer to hear. She could see the heel of his right foot peeking out from behind the blinds, so at least he was facing away from her. Keeping tabs on his position, she waited anxiously for him to speak again.

"Okay, I can do that."

His feet turned suddenly, and when she looked up at him, he was peering at her through the screen door. Their eyes met and he frowned. "Tara, what— Shit. I have a problem. I'll call you back."

He yanked open the slider, his face a mask of anger. *He* was mad?

She didn't back away when he entered the living room. Instead she put her hands on her hips and faced him down. "What the hell is going on?"

His anger morphed into a look of regret. "It's not what you think."

"So you're not spying on Mick and Jenna?" She hesitated as another thought occurred to her. "And using me for information?"

He gave a self-deprecating laugh. "Okay, well, it's kind of what you think." With one finger, he lifted her chin and caught her eye. "But I was not using you for information. Using what I learned from you, yes. Using you? Never."

Semantics—and totally irrelevant besides. Why did she suck so much at choosing men? Maybe she should join a convent. "You were lying to me."

She stalked into the bedroom and slid into her jeans before grabbing her overnight bag and purse. He followed and stood in the doorway, filling it with his large frame.

"Tara, wait."

She tried to push past him, but he didn't budge.

A trickle of fear slid down her spine. "Colin, let me go."

She dropped her bags and pummeled him with her fists, but he was too big, too strong. He caught her knee before it connected with his groin and pressed her up against the wall. For the first time since she'd met him, his size scared her. He could snap her like a twig without even trying.

The large hands that had caressed her so tenderly just hours before gripped her tightly, holding her immobile. "Stop fighting, honey. Just listen."

She quit struggling, but not because she stopped being scared. She would save her energy in case he let his guard down. He had her trapped right now and she would only wear herself out if she kept fighting him.

"That's better," he whispered into her ear. "I'm not going to hurt you."

Turning her face away, she squeezed her eyes shut to hold back tears. "Forgive me if I'm no longer inclined to believe you," she said into his shoulder.

He released her and backed away, positioning himself between her and the exit. "Sit on the bed."

"Or what?" Would he kill her? Beat her? Take by force what she had so freely given him over the last five days? She shivered.

"Damn it, Tara, just sit."

Giving him a wide berth, she sat on the edge of the firm mattress.

He crouched in front of her, rubbed his face with his hands, and let out a weary sigh. "Look, I can't always tell you about my job. That's par for the course. And it's especially true in this case, since you know Mick and Jenna."

"Why are you watching them?"

"I can't tell you that," he said, his face full of regret that she didn't buy for one minute.

A scarier thought occurred to her. "Did you blow up Jenna's house?"

"According to the police that was an accident."

*Oh my God.* "That doesn't answer my question." She stood up and tried to move past him.

"Where are you going?" He held her elbow firmly.

"Home." She let him see the fear that was surely on her face and the tears welling in her eyes. "I just want to go home."

He pushed a tendril of hair behind her ear and gave her a sad look. "I can't let you do that."


The next morning, Mick tucked Jenna close against him and kissed her hair, inhaling deeply. He couldn't stop touching her, even though guilt had settled over him like a fog. What would Rob think if he were alive? *He'd want to kick my ass.*

But Jenna was right. She was a grown woman who could make her own choices. She knew Mick, knew what he was

like. Hell, maybe women weren't always looking for Prince
Charming to sweep them away and live happily ever after.
Hadn't she said she was tired of being the good girl?

The spark between them had been there for years. Why
was it wrong for them to finally give in to it?

For the first time in ages, he had spent the whole night
with a woman after sex. Actually slept with her. Like he had
that first night, except now she was nestled naked in his arms,
all soft and warm.

His biggest concern was that he might never want to
leave the bed. She was the only woman who'd ever had him
thinking it might not be so bad to stick around. The idea
scared him to death, but something needed to change in his
piece-of-shit life. Maybe Jenna was the key.

He couldn't believe he was thinking about starting a
relationship—a real relationship, for Christ's sake—with this
woman. He wasn't sure he dared. God knew he didn't deserve
her. Still, he had to try. He wanted to keep her close, but he
couldn't do that with this secret thick like a wall between
them.

Mick looked down at her, and the urge to wake her and
spill everything he knew overwhelmed him. Maybe if he told
her part of it, she'd quit arguing with him. Or would she hate
him for waiting so long? But she already knew he was keeping
things from her, and she was still here, in his bed. Naked and
beautiful.

Jesus, he wanted her again. Couldn't imagine ever *not*
wanting her.

But how could he expect more if he was still holding
back? She didn't need to know everything, just the key parts.
As he warmed to the idea, his shoulders relaxed, the tension
he'd been carrying around for days slowly draining away.

There was risk in telling her. Risk that she would hate him

for what he had to say. Risk that she would pull away. But he
lived for risk, didn't he? Thrived on it.

He was starting to think that she would be in danger
whether she knew the truth or not. Someone had decided she
and Mick were a problem. Jenna ought to know why. Or at
least the important elements of it. Then they could figure out
how to move forward together.

In the early morning glow she looked like an angel, her
pale hair spread over his arm, those alluring freckles
contrasting against her nose and cheeks like a negative of
stars in the night sky. His chest squeezed in fear as he felt the
perfect moment slipping from his grasp.

Afraid to break the spell, he held her until she awoke an
hour later. When she finally opened her eyes, he kissed her
neck and smoothed his palm along her arm. "Good morning.
Did you sleep well?"

"Mm hmm." She turned to face him, tucking her arms
against her chest and pulling the sheet up to her neck.

He kissed her softly. She returned the kiss, but pulled
away quickly and stared at his chest. What was that all about?

"Mick."

Was there a note of regret in her voice? *Please, no.* Before
he could lose his nerve, he took a deep breath. "There's
something I need to tell you." He ached to smooth her hair
away from her face, tilt up her chin, and lose himself in her
soft lips, but he needed to get this over with. Keeping his
hand firmly planted on her hip so he wouldn't scare her off,
he waited until she looked at him. "I think you're right. You
deserve to know what happened to Rob."

Her eyes widened in surprise, and something he didn't
understand flashed across her face. If he didn't know better
he would have called it guilt. Maybe she felt bad about
badgering him for so long. Maybe it was unease or fear of the

unknown. Maybe after all of their fighting, she was actually afraid of what he had to say.

"Are you sure you're ready for it?"

"Yes," she whispered, clutching the sheet tighter to her body.

He didn't want to break contact with her, but he couldn't talk about something this serious while lying down. He rolled onto his back and sat up, covering his lap with the sheet and resting his forearms on his bent knees. She followed suit, wrapping the comforter over her shoulders.

"I still can't give you details about the firefight, okay? That part isn't relevant to what's going on anyway." He glanced at her to catch her nod of understanding before continuing. She'd probably agree to anything to keep him talking. "There was a point when we needed everyone to stop shooting.

"Rob and I were going up and down the line shouting at them to stop. I had to jump up on Colin's truck to get his attention. Rob did the same thing with Smitty." Adrenaline made him jittery, as if he were back in that hellhole, the deafening sound of gunfire exploding around him.

Understanding began to dawn on Jenna's face even before he finished his story, but he pushed forward, his throat tight. "Smitty turned his fifty-cal and shot Rob in the chest." He held her shocked gaze, helpless to stop the tears that trailed down her cheeks.

"I couldn't save him. I tried, but…" He couldn't finish that thought. She didn't need to know how bad it had been. "I swear to God it never occurred to me that it might be anything but an accident until this whole smuggling thing came to light."

"Now I understand why you were so mad at Smitty last night," she whispered. "I almost wish I hadn't tried to stop you from hurting him."

She covered her mouth then, her shoulders shaking as she sobbed. Cursing himself for bringing her more pain—even though she'd asked for it—he pulled her back against his chest, wrapping the bedspread around her so she wouldn't feel like he was taking advantage of her nakedness. She burrowed into his arms.

He held her tightly and buried his face in her hair, pretending he wasn't taking as much comfort as he was giving. "I'm so sorry, honey. I would have given anything to bring him back to you." He would have given up this time with her, even his own sorry life.

She hugged him close while she cried, but then tugged out of his arms. "Thank you for telling me," she said.

"Hey," he said softly. "Are you going to be all right?" Stupid question, but he didn't know what else to say. He didn't want her to leave the bed. He wanted to rock her beneath him until they both forgot—even if only briefly—about murder and death and the threats that lurked beyond these walls.

Instead, she nodded and scrambled from the bed without making eye contact. "I need a shower."

He considered following her, but when the door locked with a loud *click*, he rolled back onto his pillow. How could he blame her? She'd just discovered that her brother had been shot by one of his own teammates, possibly intentionally murdered, and Mick still had sex on the brain.

Twenty minutes later, Jenna came out in jeans and a crew-neck shirt, all covered up. Her damp hair curled around her scrubbed face, giving her a young, innocent look. "Your turn," she said, heading for the door to the living room without looking at him.

"Hey." He leaped from the bed, not even bothering to

throw on his boxers, and snagged her hand. "Are we okay?"

She met his gaze briefly before looking away, a slight frown drawing her lips down.

"Are you having second thoughts?" *No, no, no, no.* He'd denied himself for too damn long to give her up after one night. "If this is about Rob—"

"It's not."

If not Rob, then what? Did she think he was using her for sex? "Baby, you're beautiful and sexy, and last night was amazing. You're not a one-night stand to me, Jenna. You have to know that." He leaned in to kiss her, to reassure both of them, but she stepped back.

*Oh, shit.*

"Why don't you get cleaned up?" she said. "I'll make breakfast."

He watched in shock as she shut the door behind her. What the hell was going on?

He took the fastest shower on record and dressed with Superman speed, the smell of something frying drawing a rumble from his stomach.

Jenna was laying out ham and egg sandwiches when he walked out of the bedroom. "Do you want coffee?" she asked.

"Not until we talk," he said, blocking her way out of the horseshoe-shaped kitchen.

She tried to squeeze past him, but he caught her waist in his hands. She instantly went limp, eyes down, hands at her sides. Not quite the response he'd expected from the wild woman who'd shared his bed last night.

"Jenna, you're scaring me here. I just had one of the best nights of my life and I could have sworn you enjoyed yourself too." At least his words got a blush out of her. That was a good start. "Why are you running away now?"

"I'm sorry." She stared at her feet. "I...I enjoyed last night too. I don't regret it, but I think we should sleep in separate beds again."

Her words hit him like a shot to the chest. Was this how it felt to be used? "Can you at least tell me why you're having this sudden change of heart?"

Hugging her arms around herself, she chewed on her lower lip for a few seconds and then looked up him. "If we hadn't slept together, would you have still told me about Smitty?"

He jerked back, mind reeling. Would he have? "I don't know. Last night changed things." He met her gaze. "At least for me."

"Is that what you were holding out for? I've been hounding you for days, and all it took was a roll in the sack?" She gave a derisive snort. "If I'd known it was going to be that easy, I wouldn't have waited so long."

"It wasn't like that." His heart skipped painfully. How could he make her see? "I wasn't planning on telling you, but when we...took things to the next level, holding back didn't feel right." He shifted toward her, tantalized by her familiar scent, aching to touch her.

"But you're still not telling me everything. There has to be more to the story or you wouldn't have felt so strongly about keeping it from me."

Good God, seriously? He stifled a sigh. "For your safety and mine, there will always be things I can't tell you. I can't talk about some of the places Rob and I went as PJs, and I can't give you more details than I already have about the day he died. That's just the way it is."

She cast her eyes down. "I'm not sure I can live with that."

Adrenaline rushed through him. He wanted to shake her.

Why the hell had she jumped into bed with him then? *Before* he'd told her about Smitty? If he didn't know her better he would have thought she'd set the whole thing up to get the truth out of him.

He stilled as he processed that thought. Could it be? What had she said? *If I'd known it was going to be that easy, I wouldn't have waited so long.* Had she played him?

But, no, this was Jenna. She might have grown tired enough of her straight-arrow reputation to seduce him, but she'd never be so underhanded. More likely she'd just realized what he'd known all along: He wasn't good enough for her. He could never be the sane, stable kind of man she deserved.

And so he'd never again watch her come apart in his arms while he filled her to the hilt. He'd finally had a taste of the one woman who could convince him to stick around, and she didn't want him.

Karma really was a bitch.

Pressing back the tears that threatened to spill down her cheeks, Jenna watched Mick stalk into his room. Her plan had worked too well—particularly since she'd decided she couldn't go through with it. Their lovemaking had been too special to tarnish like that.

Too bad she was lying to *him* now. About her feelings, her motives for sleeping with him, and her reasons for not sleeping with him again. What she hadn't planned on was how hurt he'd be. If she didn't know better, she might believe that he actually wanted more than sex from her.

More likely he was just hoping for a few more days of it. Mick was nothing if not a smooth talker.

He cared. She knew that. And he'd been such a generous lover. Even more so than she'd expected. But she would never be dumb enough to get her hopes up for more than that, and she couldn't fall into bed with him again. Not after she'd taken advantage of him.

Her fists clenched as she replayed the confrontation in the bar. If she'd known last night that Smitty was responsible for Rob's death, she might have attacked him herself. How had Mick managed to hold himself back?

Was Smitty involved in the smuggling ring, or had it been nothing more than an accident, what they called *friendly fire*? The words ricocheted through her brain like bullets. Friendly. Fire. Her breath stalled, and her heart squeezed. Could there be a dumber name for it? As if shots from your own side were something you'd welcome. Like a hug.

A few rounds to the chest were the least friendly thing she could imagine.

If Smitty had killed Rob on purpose, how would they ever prove it? Mick hadn't told her everything about that day; he'd admitted that much. He'd also said that the rest of the story wasn't relevant, but how could she be sure?

If only she knew what he was so worried about.

*Argh*. This whole ordeal was driving her mad. She dialed Tara at work to see if she could meet for lunch. Talking things out with her friend always made her feel better. Mick would just have to get over tracking her everywhere she went. He could wait in the car or something.

"Tara Fujimoto's desk," an unfamiliar woman's voice answered.

"Uh, I'm calling for Tara. Is she there?"

"No, this is Wanda. Tara called in sick today."

Ah, Wicked Wanda of the West. "Oh. It must be serious," Jenna said. It wasn't like Tara to ditch work, and she almost never took sick days, even when she was really ill.

"Undoubtedly," the woman said with obvious scorn. "If you want to leave a message, I'll take it, otherwise I have work to do."

"Uh, no thanks."

Jenna ended the call with a sense of unease. Tara was the most dependable person she knew when it came to work. She may have fallen head over heels for Colin, but Jenna still couldn't imagine her friend missing work for anything but an emergency. And if it *was* an emergency, it was surprising that she hadn't called. She tried Tara's home and cell phones, but both went to voicemail. Had she passed out, was she too weak to get to the phone? If she had a stomach bug, it could quickly turn dangerous if she became dehydrated.

Mick's concern over Colin's character came back to her and her gut clenched. What if Tara wasn't sick at all?

"Call me back as soon as you can," Jenna told the machine. "I'm worried about you."

She knocked on Mick's bedroom door. She was wary about facing him, but what choice did she have?

"What?" came the muffled response.

"Mick, I think something's wrong. I…" She took a deep breath. "I need your help."

He opened the door and her belly did a little flip.

"What is it?"

After last night, just looking at him had the power to take her breath away. He was sexy as sin in a black Dos Equis T-shirt, jeans, and bare feet. God, why did life have to be so complicated? She wanted to go back to bed with him, where she'd felt safe, desirable, and cherished.

She was shocked to notice that his eyes were red, as if he'd been rubbing them. Could he really be that upset? Maybe he was thinking about Rob and feeling guilty for sleeping with her. That was much easier to believe than that *she* might be the cause for his distress.

"Do you have a way to reach Colin?"

His head jerked back. "Di Ferio?"

She nodded. "Tara called in sick today, but I can't reach her by phone. It's not like her to skip work, even when she's feeling awful." She held his gaze, silently pleading with him to take her seriously. "So, either she's gravely ill or something else is going on. Either way, I need to make sure she's okay."

He stared at her for a beat before nodding. "I'll call him." Then he shut the door in her face.

# CHAPTER TWELVE

MICK CLOSED THE BEDROOM DOOR and resisted the urge to beat his head against it. He knew he was acting like a petulant, heartbroken teenager, but it didn't matter. He hadn't felt this way since Kimberly Fenton had broken up with him before going to college.

He'd enlisted the next day.

But he couldn't run away this time. He'd promised to protect Jenna, and he wasn't going to turn his back on her just because he'd made a mistake. No matter how much she had wanted him at the time, he should have recognized how vulnerable she was.

Or maybe she'd come to him precisely because one night was all she'd wanted. He'd never given her any reason to expect he'd give her more. She knew what he was usually like.

The worst part was he still wanted her. So much it hurt. Every time he looked at her pretty, freckled face, he wanted to kiss her until she melted in his arms the way she had last night.

With a disgusted sigh, he dug up his phone and called

Colin. All he got was his voicemail. "Hey, man. Give me a call. Jenna can't reach Tara and she's worried."

He couldn't bring himself to say more than that. He was worried too. Colin was still on his list of people who might have been involved with the smuggling.

Reluctantly, he sought out Jenna and found her on the sofa surfing the Internet on her laptop. The keys clicked in an uneven rhythm as her fingers flew across the keyboard.

He cleared his throat and she looked up with a hopeful expression. "Did you reach him?"

"No."

Worry etched her face as she stared at the computer screen. "I know something's wrong." Setting down the MacBook, she hopped up from the couch. "We need to check her house. What if she fainted and fell down the stairs or…"

He could almost see her brain processing all of the bad things that could happen to a woman living alone, and she didn't need to go through that. "Okay," he said, interrupting her thoughts before she took them too far. "Let's go."

"Thank you," she said on a relieved breath, glancing at him quickly before switching her focus to something behind his head. "I'm sure you're not very happy to be stuck with me right now, but I appreciate your help."

"No worries, Jay," he said, falling easily back into playboy mode. "We're big kids. I think we can both handle it." He crossed his arms over his chest and leaned against the wall. "Now that we've gotten the sex thing out of our way, we can get back to figuring out what we should do next."

Her face reddened and she turned away, clasping her arms around her waist. It took every ounce of his willpower not to go to her, but that would get him nothing except more heartbreak.

He needed his head on straight so he could sort this out

and get the hell out of Dodge.

Riding shotgun in the Camaro fifteen minutes later, Jenna didn't know what to think about him. She'd always thought she could read Mick, but now she had to wonder. His feelings seemed to be all over the map when it came to her. Their relationship had been strained before their night of passion, but now it was stretched tight, like an overburdened rubber band. But she didn't have time to dwell on it, because Tara was her primary concern right now.

Mick parked along the curb in front of Tara's place and scanned the area before letting Jenna out of the car. They mounted the steps together, with him keeping her close to his side, all business. When they received no response to the bell or loud knocking, Jenna tried Tara's home phone again.

They could hear it ringing through the door, but no one answered.

Mick leaned over and peered through the front window before shaking his head. "I can't see anything. Let's go around back."

"I have a key," she said.

"Okay, good. We'll use it if we need to, but let's check in back first."

They marched around the building through the tall, wet grass—Tara's was an end unit, which made for a quick trip—and Mick pulled a gun from the back of his jeans, holding it in front of him as he examined the sliding door to the basement.

"What's that for?"

"Just being careful," he said, trotting up the deck staircase to the main back door. "Stay there for a second." He crouched low and looked in each window before returning to her side.

"Did you see something?" she asked, her concern growing by the minute.

"No." He tucked his gun away. "Let's use your key."

They circled to the front and let themselves in, entering through the living room. The green walls, ruffled floral upholstery, and lace curtains were a complete contrast to Jenna's own style. And the place was a bit of a mess. Old issues of *Cosmo* and *People* littered the coffee table, and piles of laundry on the sofa threatened to fall in an avalanche at any minute. Everywhere she looked, another surface begged to be cleaned.

"Tara?" Jenna called.

No answer. If Tara was truly sick, wouldn't she want to be home where she'd be comfortable?

Mick prowled the cluttered space like a panther trapped in an English garden, keeping his arms in close as if he were worried that the smallest disturbance of air would send one of the many ceramic kittens crashing to the ground.

Turning from the living room, he glanced at her. "Stay behind me."

"Okay." Jenna fell in line, every sense straining for a sign of Tara.

"This place must be driving you nuts. Is it always this messy?" Mick asked as they finished searching the main floor.

"Yes."

"What's upstairs?"

"Two bedrooms and a bath. Tara used to have a roommate, but now she makes enough money to have the place to herself." She followed Mick as he took the steps two at a time and cut left at the landing.

They searched through the spare room and bathroom, even checking closets, large cupboards, and the shower stall. In the master bedroom, pieces of colorful lingerie were piled on a chaise lounge in the corner. Judging from the unmade covers and misplaced pillows, two people had recently slept in the bed.

They looked in the closet and master bath before moving downstairs to the basement and garage. No Tara. No car.

"Nothing," Mick said.

Where could she be? Something had to be wrong. Fear knotted Jenna's stomach and she slumped against the wall.

"Hey," Mick said, wiping away her tears, which she hadn't even realized were there. "We'll find her."

She broke down then, crying not just out of fear for her friend, but for how badly she'd botched things with Mick, the stress of wondering whether someone was out there watching her every move, and the loss of her life as she knew it. In spite of the bad start to their morning, he moved closer and held her, his touch soothing.

His slow, deep breaths and steady heartbeat helped ease her anxiety, and the tears finally stopped after a couple minutes.

Embarrassed, she pushed his chest lightly, ignoring how warm and strong he was, and slid out of his arms. "I'm sorry. I just can't help wondering if she's in trouble. What if Colin hurt her? Or what if—"

"Stop, Jay. Let's get out of here and we'll make some calls."

She took a deep breath and forced herself to calm down, to ignore how much it hurt that he'd gone back to calling her Jay. "Okay." He was right. She needed to stay focused on what they could do, not get caught up in the endless game of what-ifs.

"How about we check out Colin's place too? If she's sick, he might be taking care of her."

She couldn't imagine Tara wanting anyone to see her

when she was sick, but then she'd never been this serious with a guy in the three years Jenna had known her. "Good idea. Thanks."

They detoured to Colin's apartment, but no one answered the door and the blinds were drawn.

Back in Mick's car, they both pulled out their phones. While Jenna was on hold with the hospital, Mick called the police to see if Tara had been in an accident or, hell, even arrested. They couldn't assume anything at this point.

Half an hour later they'd turned up nothing.

"Where could she be?" Jenna asked, barely keeping her panic at bay.

"Have you considered the possibility that she might have run off to Vegas with Colin?"

"No way," she said. "Tara's spontaneous, but when it comes to work, she's solid. And she would definitely call me before doing something like that." Wouldn't she?

Mick's look echoed her last thought. "Sometimes people do unexpected things." He raised an eyebrow at her.

Her face heated under his accusing gaze. He had a point. She'd totally broadsided him last night, but still. In her gut, she was certain that Tara was in danger. "Can you please call Colin again, just in case?"

"I did. Right after I finished with the cops. He's still not answering."

The cool breeze buffeted her face as she stared through the open car window at Tara's front door. Slowly, an unwelcome thought wormed its way into her brain.

"Do you think her disappearance has anything to do with everything else that's going on? Especially since Colin's not answering his phone either?" She turned to look at Mick, her brain firing on all cylinders now. "What if he was just using Tara to keep tabs on me, and she found out?"

"I don't know," he said, starting the engine and pulling out of the parking lot. "But it has occurred to me that Colin might be involved in this whole mess. It wouldn't surprise me at all, actually."

Jenna rubbed a hand over her acid-filled stomach and stared out the car window. *Where are you, Tara?*

Mick hit the freeway, heading out of town, away from D.C., away from his condo.

"Where are we going?" Jenna asked, her voice tight.

"I just want to see if anyone's following us."

He didn't spot a tail as eased into the middle lane of the freeway, got up to speed, and set his cruise control to five miles over the limit. The accelerator was too much temptation, and Jenna wasn't likely to appreciate any reckless driving. After all, the guy who was responsible for the accident that had destroyed her family had been joyriding in his new car, redlining the speedometer before he lost control and plowed into the Ryans' vehicle.

Rob had just left the Air Force when it happened. The medical care for Jimmy had racked up astronomical bills that ate through their parents' life insurance money like a fire burning through dry grass. Rob had stuffed all of his feelings about his loss deep inside, joined up with Claymore to pay the bills, and never looked back. He hadn't become angry or vengeful, he had just done what needed to be done. Mick could relate to that.

And now Rob himself was dead, and the way things were going, Mick wouldn't be surprised if his friend decided to haunt him for all of his failures with Jenna. He shook off the thought and focused on driving like a grandma as he exited the freeway, turned onto the overpass, and took the on-ramp heading back toward town.

As they got closer to his condo, traffic picked up and he had to slow for merging cars. He tapped his brake, but nothing happened.

"What the hell?"

He pressed the brake pedal again, but it went all the way to the floor without resistance. The Camaro didn't even hiccup as it raced toward the brake lights ahead of them.

"Shit. Hold on. The brakes are out." Which shouldn't have happened, because his car was new. Someone must have tampered with them. *Goddammit.*

Jenna inhaled sharply as her head swiveled in his direction. "They're out?" He could feel her gaze on him, but he kept his eyes on the road. "Oh my God," she whispered.

There was no time to reassure her. The car thunked into fourth gear as he downshifted, and the engine howled in protest, his RPM needle pegging in the red zone. He flipped on his hazards and honked as he crossed the fast lanes, heading for the outside shoulder. His heart raced as they careened along the gravelly asphalt.

Mick pressed and released the brake repeatedly. Still no pressure. *Shit.* "I need some way to slow us down without spinning out," he said, thinking out loud. Could she tell his hands were shaking? Or that part of him was savoring the exhilarating rush of danger? Because, oh yeah, he was totally fucked in the head.

He held the button on the emergency brake and slowly pulled it back. The car got squirrelly, so he stopped. He downshifted again, wincing at the beating his transmission was taking, its high-pitched whine sounding like a dying animal.

"Hold tight. I'm going into the grass."

"Can't you shut off the engine?" Jenna asked, her voice tight with fear.

"If I do I won't have full steering control."

"What can I do?"

"Just trust me."

Out of the corner of his eye, he saw her nod. "I do."

If he'd been a praying man, he would have recited a psalm or something, but instead he spoke to Rob. "Come on, man. I could use some help here," he muttered.

All around them, cars were slamming on their brakes—lucky bastards—and honking as Mick and Jenna flew by, kicking up debris. Gripping the wheel tightly with both hands, he eased his left wheels off the shoulder and onto the sloped grass, fighting as the car tried to veer sharply off the road.

Jenna screamed as they bounced along, then covered her mouth with her free hand.

His muscles strained to keep the car on a shallow trajectory so that they wouldn't flip. He maneuvered all the way onto the grass, using his knee to help keep the wheel straight as they were jostled by the uneven ground. He pulled the handbrake again and downshifted. Forty miles an hour. *Still too fast.*

A stand of trees loomed like a brick wall in front of them —much too close. Mick's mouth went dry. If he yanked the brake to a full stop, he risked flipping the car. But they weren't slowing quickly enough…

At this rate, they were going to crash head-on.

His ears buzzed and time slowed. In a steady move, he pulled the emergency brake all the way back. The car slowed, but then one of the wheels caught, and the vehicle skidded sideways.

Jenna screamed and reached for him as the forest loomed in her side window. The fear on her face cut through his soul.

"No!" he yelled. *Not Jenna.* With all his strength, he jerked the wheel. The car spun one hundred and eighty degrees.

Mick braced for impact as the driver's side of his shiny Camaro slammed into an oak.

# CHAPTER THIRTEEN

JENNA SAT IN THE CAR, momentarily stunned by the impact and their sudden lack of motion. Coming out of her mental fog, she unlatched her seatbelt with shaky fingers.

"Mick?"

Sirens wailed in the distance.

He moaned and pressed his forehead with his fingers, pulling away from the deflated side airbag. Their eyes met and he pulled her onto his lap, fumbling to get her over the center console. "Thank God you're okay." He held her tight against his chest.

She wanted to cry with relief. "Are you hurt anywhere?"

"Nothing serious. My head's still spinning, and I'm sure we'll both be sore tomorrow, but I think I'm fine." He brushed her hair back from her face and smoothed it. "What about you?"

How was she? Nothing specifically hurt except her head where it had bumped the window when he spun the car. "Thanks to you, I'm good." She stroked his cheek. He'd risked his life to save her.

He cupped her face in his palms and kissed her—a hot, feverish attack that left her breathless and wanting. "Don't you know I'd do anything for you?"

She looked at him, and she could tell the exact second when he remembered how she'd pushed him away that morning. The light went out of his gorgeous blue eyes and he released her with a sigh, letting his head fall back onto the seat.

Ignoring the ache in her chest, she scooted carefully over the gear shift knob and handbrake, and pushed her door open. Two men and a woman were approaching from where they'd parked their cars at the top of the hill.

"Is anyone hurt?" the first man asked, out of breath from his descent. The suit he wore barely stretched over his wide belly.

"Not seriously," she told him. "We're just a little banged up."

The other man, a thirty-something with long hair and a goatee, dressed in jeans and work boots, leaned into the car and spoke to Mick in a low voice.

A pretty brunette with a ponytail took Jenna's arm and led her to a flat spot to sit down. Jenna thanked her and turned down her offer of water. "I'm all right. Really."

Mick climbed over the seats and out of the passenger door of his demolished car. He shook Goatee's hand and nodded before joining Jenna on the grass, careful not to touch her again.

Sadness engulfed her. She wanted to be free to love him. When he spun the car, her very last thought before the impact had been "not him too." Why was this so damn complicated?

She shut down her train of thought as a fire truck and police cruiser stopped on the shoulder above them. The next hour passed in a frenzy of activity. They were checked for signs of injury by the EMTs, and then police officers interviewed them both, taking statements from the witnesses who had stopped.

Now, unable to tear her eyes away, Jenna stared at the crumpled driver's side of the Camaro. From the exterior damage it looked like Mick should be dead. She couldn't even bear the thought, so she focused instead on the tow truck as the operator hooked the car up to the massive chain.

When the tow truck lifted the car, Mick asked to look under the chassis, and he rolled onto his back and scooted beneath it. After a minute, he called out to the police officer, who went under with him. They conferred for several minutes, pointing and taking photos. Then the cop pulled something small off the underside of the Camaro and they looked at it for a moment before the officer stuck it in a bag.

They slid out, wiping dirt off their clothes. The cop took some notes, handed a slip of paper to Mick, and walked away.

Finally, his face grim, Mick waved Jenna over.

"What did he take off your car?" she asked as she joined him next to the truck.

"A GPS tracker." He shook his head, clenching his jaw. "I can't believe I missed it."

"You looked for one?" When had that occurred to him?

"I checked the obvious places, but it was well hidden. I would have needed a mirror." He ran a hand through his hair and sighed. "They've been keeping tabs on us, and the brakes were tampered with. This definitely isn't over."

In her heart, she'd known it. But she'd hoped... Adrenaline flooded her system and she began to tremble with fear and rage.

"All of this for a few images? We need to stop these guys."

"This is a dangerous game," he said. "We don't want them to up the ante."

"How can it get more dangerous than this?" She gestured to the damaged Camaro. "We can keep hiding, but maybe the next time they target us they won't miss."

Mick studied her for a minute and then sighed, running a hand through his hair before holding it out to her. "You're right. But first we need a rental car."

"Something built like a tank," she said, twining her fingers with his.

He nodded as he tugged her toward the tow truck and helped her up onto the bench seat beside him.

Just another crappy day in her new life.

"He's become a liability," Griffin said, working hard to keep his voice calm. "In fact, if you do it right, we can get rid of both of them *and* cover our asses."

"Understood, sir. What's my deadline?"

"Yesterday," he snapped. *Calm down, dammit.* He closed his eyes and took a deep breath. This whole clusterfuck should never have dragged on for so long. Too many mistakes had been made, and now it was time to clean up and move forward. "You understand how much is at stake?"

"Yes, sir. I'll get it done."

"When it's over, you'll need to disappear for a while. How about joining the team in Venezuela?"

"Sounds good, sir. I like the tropics."

Griffin signed off and then slouched back into his favorite armchair with a bourbon on ice. One more day and it would all be over.

When they arrived back at his condo after renting a car, Mick was exhausted and achy. His body complained loud and clear about the abuse it had suffered in the crash—sore muscles, bruises, and all. He downed some Advil and offered the bottle to Jenna.

She took two pills and got a glass of water. "I still need to track down Tara," she said after swallowing. "Will you call Colin again while I try her home and cell numbers?"

"Sure." Jesus, what a screwed-up day. Who knew that living with Jenna could be so exciting? Of course, this wasn't exactly the type of excitement he craved.

He dialed Colin, watching Jenna as she made her calls. A bruise darkened the right side of her forehead, and the anger he'd felt when he saw the cut brake lines rushed through him again.

"Di Ferio here."

Mick's head snapped up in surprise. He honestly hadn't expected Colin to answer. "Hey, it's Mick Fury. Did you get my messages?"

"No, sorry, I just turned my phone back on. Forgot I had it off this morning. Didn't want any interruptions, if you know what I mean."

Mick rolled his eyes. "Yeah, I get it. I'm calling about Tara. Jenna's been trying to reach her, but she didn't show up for work today. She's not answering her phone either. We checked her house, but she wasn't there."

Jenna watched him expectantly.

"She's with me," Colin said, an apologetic thread in his voice. "Didn't mean to make you guys worry. We're at the beach."

Mick nodded and gave Jenna a thumbs up. "Can Jenna talk to her for a minute? She's been really worried."

"Sure thing," Colin promised. "I'll have Tara call her when she gets out of the shower."

Mick ended the conversation. That was probably the

friendliest exchange he and Colin had ever had. Hopefully it would ease Jenna's worry. "They went to the beach."

She frowned.

"Why don't you look happier? Colin said Tara's fine."

"And you trust him?"

Good point. "Okay. Let's wait and see if she calls."

"I still can't believe she'd be this irresponsible. You don't know her like I do." She bit her lower lip. "I hope he's not one of those controlling types. I knew a girl in that kind of relationship, and it grew steadily worse until he started beating her and locking her in the house."

How could he respond to that? Despite his feelings about Colin, he'd been ready to take him at face value for some reason.

Jenna fidgeted and looked around the kitchen, probably itching for something to clean. She appeared ready to collapse under the strain of the day. He couldn't hold her, but he could still take care of her.

"Why don't you sit down," he said. "I'll make us some lunch."

She slumped against the counter and her gaze settled on him. "Why are you being so nice to me?"

*What?*

She must have read the confusion on his face, because she said, "After this morning…"

He crossed his arms. Now she wanted to talk about it? "I'm not thrilled with how things turned out, but I don't need to be an asshole about it."

"You should be. I deserve it." She hugged herself and stared at the floor for several moments before speaking. "I wasn't completely honest with you this morning."

He watched her carefully, his stomach burning with a sudden inkling that he knew what she was going to say. He desperately hoped he was wrong.

"I—" She cleared her throat. "I tried to seduce you because I thought you might tell me the truth if I did." Her gaze met his and then skittered away.

The words were like a blow from a sledgehammer straight to his stomach. He stepped back. *Son of a bitch.* She'd slept with him for information. Had she enjoyed it? Hell yes, he'd made sure of that. What a sucker. He put his hands on his waist and tried to catch his breath. Jesus, did he even know her at all?

Mick shoved his phone in his pocket and stared at the ceiling as he tried to rein in his stormy thoughts. "Well, congratulations. It worked." He couldn't keep the bitterness out of his voice.

"I'm sorry. After...after our night together I changed my mind. I didn't want to find out like that, but I couldn't bring myself to stop you when you started talking."

He didn't even know whether to believe her. He'd thought her incapable of such deceit. Clearly he didn't know her as well as he thought he did. That little speech she'd given him this morning about not being with someone who'd lie to her? What a load of crap. It had probably all been part of her strategy.

"What was your plan?" His fists clenched. "Did you think that by withholding sex, you'd get me to spill the rest of the details to get you back into bed?"

Her eyes widened and she moved away from him, heading deeper into the kitchen. He followed.

He wasn't ready for how much her betrayal hurt, but he shoved the pain aside, like he'd done so many times before, and leaned in close. "I thought you might be playing me this morning when you ran into the bathroom. 'But no,' I said to myself. 'This is Jenna. She would never be so dishonest. Truth is everything to her.'"

She winced and ducked her head, refusing to look at him. "It wasn't like that."

He pinned her with a hard glare.

Her throat worked as she swallowed heavily. "Not entirely." She met his gaze and gave him an imploring look. "Last night was special to me and I hated that I had an ulterior motive." She gripped his shoulders. "I wanted to be with you. I always have."

He wanted so badly to believe her, but he wasn't going to play the fool again. A sound of disgust rumbled through his chest. Every lie was like a cut from a knife. Any more and he'd be in shreds. How could he have been so stupid?

He straightened, dislodging her hands, and made his decision. "You know what? I'm done." He couldn't forget his promise to keep her safe, but he didn't need to be the one doing it, did he? "I'm going to call Kurt to come babysit until we figure out a safe location for you." He pointed to her shopping bags. "Start packing your shit."

At the entrance to his bedroom, he looked back, fingers holding the doorjamb in a death grip. Goddamn her for her lies. For making him think a woman like her could ever want more from a guy like him. Jenna had always been the one pure thing in his life, someone who represented everything good and right in the world. Everything he could never be.

"Mick, wait." She ran to him, her cheeks splotchy and red, stopping two feet short of him. "I'm sorry. I never wanted to hurt you." She lowered her eyes and twined her hands in front of her. "I was desperate."

He stilled, his heart bleeding in his chest as her beautiful face dissolved into tears.

"Well, babe, you might have been desperate, but I'm sure as hell not." He slammed the door in her face and dialed

Kurt.

# CHAPTER FOURTEEN

JENNA STARED IN SHOCK AT the door. Mick was going to leave her.

But then what had she expected? She'd betrayed him in the worst way possible. She wouldn't undo their night together for anything, but if she could go back and change her motives, make her intentions completely pure, she'd do it in a nanosecond. Not that she didn't still want the full truth from Mick. She did. But using his emotions like that... Her stomach twisted with nausea.

She hadn't intended to tell him, but the lie had been eating at her all day. His kindness had done her in.

Leaning against the wall, she wiped her damp face. Time to regroup. Regrets wouldn't help her now.

How long would it take for Kurt to arrive? Chewing on a fingernail, she circled the room and finally slumped onto the futon. She wasn't cut out for this espionage crap. She was sick of cowering, waiting to find out what her enemies were going to do next. Clearly, after today, they were no longer merely following her and Mick. They wanted to destroy them.

If Tara would just call, she'd be able to rest a little easier. Stress gnawed at her insides, and it didn't help that her head still hurt from the accident.

While she was waiting, she filled the department-store bags she'd saved from her shopping spree—had it really only been a few days ago?—packing her new clothes neatly inside. The makeshift suitcases wouldn't last long, but they'd get her through the day.

Twenty minutes later, Mick stomped out of his room holding a green duffle bag, not even looking her way as he opened the front door. Kurt stood in the hall, phone in hand. He was tall like Mick, but with a stockier build—definitely solid—thick dark hair just long enough to lie over, and the darkest brown eyes she'd ever seen. Like black coffee. He was handsome in a mafia gangster sort of way, and she was glad she already knew him or she'd be seriously intimidated.

"Thanks for showing up on such short notice," Mick said, shaking his friend's hand as he backed up to let him in.

"No problem." Kurt's eyes practically danced with unspoken questions when he met Jenna's gaze.

Mick stepped through the doorway, rattling his car keys in his palm. "I need to clear my head. I'll let you know when I have a plan."

"Actually"—Kurt snagged his upper arm before he could leave—"we have a problem."

Irritation flashed across Mick's handsome face, but he moved inside and shut the door, dropping his bag. "What is it?"

"Smitty's dead. I figure you have about thirty minutes before the police come knocking."

Jenna gasped and her limbs went cold. Mick hadn't hit him *that* hard. Had he?

Mick stilled. "How?"

"Shot in the head."

She sagged in her seat, nearly dizzy with relief. If the man had been shot, Mick couldn't have killed him.

"Word on the street is that you got into it with him last night." Kurt's voice was sharp as a blade. He crossed his arms. "I knew I shouldn't have told you where to find him."

"You fucking think I killed him?" Mick reddened and stalked past his friend into the kitchen, grabbed a beer from the fridge, and popped the top with a bottle opener he kept in a drawer next to the sink. "I was here all night." He gestured toward her. "Ask Jenna," he said, his voice laced with anger.

Her cheeks heated under Kurt's speculative gaze, and she could only nod in response.

"Are you sure he didn't sneak out while you were sleeping?" he asked. "Or did you not sleep at all?"

Oh, God. Where was a hole to crawl into when you needed one?

"Hey," Mick stepped forward, his free hand balled into a fist. "That's uncalled for."

Kurt stared him down. "You don't think the cops are going to ask the same thing?" His voice rose. "I don't care what you did last night, but if your alibi isn't rock solid, you're screwed."

Mick scowled, but gave a resigned nod, still not looking her way.

In response to a raised eyebrow from Kurt, she swallowed and said, "I slept, but I would have noticed if he'd left the bed." Wouldn't she? Her face warmed again.

"But you can't be one hundred percent sure, can you?"

She wanted to tell him he was wrong. She wanted to be able to say without a doubt that Mick had been next to her all night. She wanted to reassure him—and herself—that Mick was innocent.

But she couldn't. Her shoulders slumped. "No."

*Could* Mick have killed Alan Smith? Yes. After seeing the rage on his face last night, she believed he could have. He could have killed Smitty in the heat of the moment at the bar. But he wasn't capable of doing it in a cold, calculated way. He couldn't have made love to her like that and then crawled out of bed to commit murder.

Could he have?

Mick forced himself to look at Jenna and then wished he hadn't. He could tell she was wondering if he'd done it. "It wasn't me, Jenna. I was with you all night."

"I wish I knew for sure," she said, her voice small, her eyes on the floor. "I want to be able to say you were, but I slept for hours."

Unbelievable. "What man in his right mind would willingly leave his bed when you're naked in it?"

Kurt made a strangled sound and Jenna flushed for about the thirtieth time in the last five minutes. Her gaze moved to Mick's hands. Was she remembering how he'd run them along her smooth skin or picturing him beating the pulp out of Smitty at the bar?

"Uh, I'll just go in the bedroom and return some calls," Kurt said, practically running for the door.

Mick hardly noticed. He couldn't take his eyes off Jenna. She really thought he might have done it. *Goddammit.* His chest ached with the realization that she trusted him so little. And apparently she had no idea how gorgeous she was, how addictive, how irresistible. Because he hadn't been kidding about never wanting to leave her alone in bed.

But he had no time to stroke her ego. Nor did he want to. She'd slept with him because she wanted to know the truth about Rob's death. He'd do well to remember that. "It won't be long before the police show up." They could be pulling up outside even now. "Someone's setting me up. Obviously I wasn't the only one who wanted Smitty dead, and the timing —after our fight last night—is a little too convenient."

She nodded.

He really needed her to believe in him, because if someone had gone to all of this trouble to frame him, she was still in danger too. "Maybe the brakes on my car were supposed to fail sooner, and when they didn't, the people who are after us got desperate." He paced behind the counter while she watched warily from her perch on the arm of the futon. "Or maybe they needed to take out Smitty, and since I have a motive, they figured it would get me out of the way. It's perfect if you think about it."

"In that case, I have just as much of a motive as you do," she said. "But you told him in front of all those people that you should have killed him when you had the chance."

"Did I?" he sputtered, dropping his bottle to the counter with a loud *thunk*. Beer bubbled over onto the granite and spread into a foamy puddle. He snagged a dish towel off the oven handle to mop up the mess. Had he really said that? Probably. It was how he'd felt. Hell, he still did. But that was so not helping his case.

His head felt like it was about to explode. If he let the police arrest him, there was no telling what kind of evidence had been planted at the scene. If the big guys at Claymore were behind it, Mick was well and truly fucked. "I can't go to jail," he said. "I have to figure out who's behind all of this and put an end to it. Otherwise, neither of us will ever be safe."

"I thought you were done looking out for me." The way she hugged her middle undermined the bravado she was trying to project.

He'd thought so too, but he couldn't turn his back on his promise to Rob. And as pissed as he was at Jenna—for using him, for believing he could have killed Smitty—he'd never forgive himself if something happened to her. Plus the sad, desperate sucker in him wanted her around. Which made what he had to do even harder.

"I'd like nothing more than to cut you loose, but I owe it to your brother to protect you, whether you deserve it or not."

Spots of red bloomed on her neck and cheeks. She crossed her arms and glared at him. "So what do we do now?"

"We split up."

*Split up?* Jenna narrowed her eyes. Hadn't the plan changed? "But you just said you owed it to Rob to protect me."

She knew she was being inconsistent. She had been telling him for days that he was absolved of his promise to Rob. But now the situation was more perilous than ever. They needed to stick together. And despite his unwillingness to cooperate, he was still her best chance for learning the rest of the story about Rob's death. She was almost certain that everything she'd gone through since then was linked to that awful day.

"The best way to keep you safe is to get you away from me. The police are going to be coming after me, not you. I can't get you involved."

She gave an incredulous laugh. "Are you serious? I'm already involved. In case you've forgotten, the whole reason I'm hiding out is because someone is following my every move."

"Which is why I called Kurt. I'd trust him with my life. He'll keep you safe."

"I'm sure he's fine, but I don't want to be stuck with a guy

I hardly know." Jenna kept her voice low. There was no reason to offend the man in the next room, especially if he was going to be her new bodyguard. "Maybe it will help to have me around. The police won't be looking for a couple."

Mick toyed with his beer bottle before dumping the dregs into the sink. "They will be if you suddenly turn up missing."

"They can call me anytime they'd like."

"Not if you come with me. I'm leaving my cell behind so that it can't be used to locate me. And I'm going to hit the bank and pull out a wad of cash so that they can't track my credit cards. I'm going off the grid, Jay. If you came with me, you'd have to do the same, and then Tara wouldn't be able to reach you."

Her stomach twisted into a knot. He'd found her weakness.

"I can't take you along," he said again, moving to the front door and hefting his bag. "By tonight or tomorrow at the latest, my picture will probably be all over the news. If you come with me, yours will be too."

He was right. It made no sense for her to go with him. If she did, she'd become a fugitive from the police too. But there had to be a way for them to stick together, didn't there? She couldn't just let him walk away with all of this unresolved tension between them. She opened her mouth to argue again, but Mick cut her off.

"Kurt and his guys can protect you better than I can now, and if I take you with me, you'll only slow me down." His jaw hardened and he looked her straight in the eye. "I'm going alone. End of discussion."

And that's when it hit her. She wanted to be with him because despite his flaws he was an honorable man she could trust.

More importantly, she wanted to be with him because she

loved him.

Before she lost her nerve, she walked up to him, stretched up onto her tiptoes and kissed him, pressing him into the wall next to the door. His bag fell to the floor with a thud and his arms cinched her waist, crushing her to him. He was warm and hard and he returned her kiss with total abandon.

All thoughts fled her brain as he consumed and caressed her, stoking fires deep within. She could have stayed like that for days, but without warning, he pushed her away, depriving her of his warmth and his roaming hands.

He studied her with a fierce gaze, his chest heaving as if he'd been running. "What was that for?"

Tears burned behind her eyelids. He thought she was trying to play him again. "Just goodbye."

Jaw tight, he picked up his bag and peered through the peephole before opening the door a crack to scan the corridor. Looking over his shoulder at her, he said, "I'll call Kurt with my plan in a few minutes. Do whatever he tells you, Jenna. He's here to keep you safe."

She nodded in defeat.

He held her gaze, and for one shiny moment she thought he might kiss her. But then, for the second time that day, he shut a door in her face.

Jenna rested her forehead against the cool, metal door and closed her eyes. Now what?

"Did Mick leave?" Kurt asked from behind her, his voice full of disbelief.

She took a fortifying breath and turned. "He said he'd call you in a few minutes with a plan."

He scowled, but then nodded after a moment. "Fine. I'll line up somewhere to take you."

She frowned. The last thing she wanted was to be stuck in a hotel room with a bunch of brooding bodyguards.

The jingle from her cell phone made her jump. She didn't recognize the number, but she answered it anyway, thinking it might be Colin's phone.

"Jenna? It's me."

"Tara, thank God! Are you okay? I've been so worried about you." Jenna sagged against the wall as her throat tightened. She hadn't realized how much Tara's disappearance had been weighing on her. Her body trembled and she fought back tears. Her best friend was all she had left, especially since Mick was headed God knows where, and losing her might be more than she could handle.

"I'm fine," Tara said brightly. "Colin asked me to go to the beach with him, so I told Wanda I wasn't feeling well. I feel bad lying, but I've been such a good employee. I think I deserve a little break, don't you?"

Jenna's heart skipped a beat. "Uh, yeah, sure." Something wasn't right. Her friend's voice was even more cheerful than usual, almost manic. "Wanda wasn't pissed, though? I mean, come on, this is the lady that chews you out if you're two minutes late even *after* you call in about being stuck in traffic. She didn't sound happy when I talked to her."

"Oh, no," Tara said. "She's such a pushover. We can pretty much get away with anything in that department."

Okay, Tara was definitely trying to send her a message. She was in trouble. "Oh, well, good. So, this trip sounds exciting. Where are you guys going?"

"We're in Virginia Beach, right near that place you and I stayed last year for my birthday. I'm excited. In fact, I need to get going because I promised Colin we'd hit the water before it gets too late."

They'd never been to Virginia Beach together. And the only place they'd ever gone to for Tara's birthday was The Ranch House Grill in Leesburg. Her favorite restaurant.

"Got it," Jenna said. "Call me later if you can."

"I will. Thanks."

Reluctantly, Jenna let her friend go, the leaden weight firmly back on her shoulders. Looking up, she met Kurt's dark-eyed gaze.

"Everything okay?" he asked.

"I don't think so."

After shutting the door on Jenna, Mick sprinted along the corridor, quickly picked the lock on the fifth door down, and slid inside. No one would think to look for him so close to home. He stood in the living room of his neighbor's condo for a full minute, his brain still fuzzy from Jenna's kiss. His dick, however, was wide awake. *Goddamn.* He didn't know what her game was, and he had no time to figure it out. Had she wanted to prove he couldn't resist her? Or maybe she'd just been hoping to guilt him into staying.

Either way, she didn't seem so immune to him herself.

"Tori?" He checked the unit, thankful that neither Tori nor her husband Damon had come home for lunch. Moving into the kitchen, he picked up the handset of the telephone hanging on the wall.

Kurt answered after several rings and Mick laid out his plan.

"Tara just called, but Jenna is positive she's being held against her will," Kurt said.

"Shit."

"Yeah." Kurt paused. "She's pretty upset."

And Mick wasn't there for her. "I understand, but she needs to worry about herself right now. Get her the hell out of my condo before the cops show, and make sure you don't lose her." Mick paused for a moment and then added, "Please."

Kurt gave a low chuckle. "Roger that."

They discussed the plan, and then Mick ended the call, shoving aside concerns he couldn't afford to entertain. He walked through the condo to the master bedroom, hoping Damon wouldn't mind if he borrowed a few things. The room had blue walls, a king-sized bed piled high with decorative pillows, and lots of tropical plants in bright pots. Quite a switch from his own bedroom, which was filled with furniture he'd inherited from his grandmother.

He entered the walk-in closet and rummaged around until he found what he needed. Damon was a large guy, but soft around the middle. He'd been a football player in college, but he'd let himself go in the years since graduation.

Mick picked out a sweatshirt and baseball cap, and found a spare pair of reading glasses on the dresser. Next, he went through the bathroom cabinets. Tori changed her hair color every few weeks, and he would bet good money that she had a stash of dye somewhere.

*Bingo.* Under the bathroom sink, mixed in with the clutter of toilet paper, random bottles of whatever women collected, and a basket of first aid supplies, several boxes of Clairol were stacked in a row. He chose black to hide his own sandy color and went to work.

A loud knock down the hall made his nerves jump. It was followed quickly by a shout, "Police! Open up!"

He hoped like hell that Jenna and Kurt were long gone. If not, the cops would never believe they hadn't helped Mick escape. A loud crash echoed along the corridor. So, that answered one question. Kurt would have opened the door if he and Jenna were still in the condo. One less thing to worry about.

Once the police cleared the place and realized he was gone, they'd start canvassing the neighbors, most of whom would still be at work. By the time they combed through the building after work hours, he'd be long gone. The key was to make sure they had no reason to kick in Tori and Damon's door.

He quickly rinsed out his hair and used some mascara on his eyebrows—which would look odd if he didn't darken them too—and got dressed in the borrowed clothes. He snagged one of Tori's throw pillows and slipped it under his T-shirt, which he tucked into his jeans. Then he threw on the Redskins sweatshirt and topped it with the well-worn Yankees ball cap. He added the glasses and stepped in front of the mirror.

His pants were too trim, making him appear top-heavy, and his cheekbones were too hollow. Careful to stay silent while the police started knocking on neighboring units, he found a pair of Damon's jeans.

Replacing his pants with the larger pair, he added a belt to keep them and the pillow from falling down, and tucked his own jeans behind the padding so he could change back into them later. Next step, his face. In the middle drawer of the bathroom vanity, he found cotton balls. He stuffed three into each cheek, working them back so they wouldn't be seen if he spoke to anyone.

Checking his reflection once again, he marveled at the changes. The glasses completely altered the look of his eyes, and combined with his new doughboy figure and jet-black hair, he was confident he wouldn't be recognized.

He flinched at the knock on the door, but forced himself to stay calm. They couldn't enter without probable cause. He just had to keep his cool until they left the floor. No doubt someone would be watching the building, but he'd be able to walk right past them.

Based on the muffled conversations he could hear from

the hallway, the police were continuing their door-to-door search, questioning the few people who were home.

To pass the time, he went over his plan for the rest of the day. First, he needed cash. For the amount he needed, he'd have to go into the bank, which meant dismantling enough of his disguise to convince the teller it was really him. It also meant she'd have seen his new hair color, which was why he'd pocketed a bottle of red dye too.

After the bank, he would go off the radar for good. The cops or the bad guys or both could be watching Jenna, but Kurt's crew would keep her safe, so at least he didn't need to worry about her.

Not that he could stop. He slouched into an easy chair and let his mind wander back to their last kiss. He'd wanted to devour her on the spot. Walking out that door had been one of the hardest things he'd ever done.

Several minutes after the corridor went quiet, Mick rose from the chair and checked the hallway. Clear. He opened the door and strolled into the corridor as if he belonged there.

Since he was in full costume now, he took the elevator instead of the stairs down to street level, and strolled through the lobby, keeping his stride loose and his shoulders tipped forward. He fought the urge to run as he left the building and turned toward the commercial strip across the street.

He was two yards from the door when a young policeman stepped in his path, hand on his gun holster, and told him to stop.

# CHAPTER FIFTEEN

As soon as Kurt ended the call with Mick, Jenna grabbed her bags and followed the security specialist out the door. She had questions, but getting out before the cops showed up was more important.

Now they were on the freeway in his black truck, trees zooming by the windows. "I know you can't give me the details, but does he have a good plan?" she asked.

Kurt glanced at her before changing lanes. "Under the circumstances, I think it's the best he can do."

Mick had to trust Kurt a lot to keep him in the loop like that. "You're not worried about lying to the police and helping a fugitive? Won't it hurt your business?"

Instead of giving her a direct answer, he gestured to his legs and said, "Mick pulled me from a downed bird, patched me up, and picked off any unfriendlies until help arrived. I owe him my life." Kurt's gaze traveled between the road in front of them and his rear and side view mirrors in a constant, watchful arc, but he didn't look at her again. She stayed silent, sensing there was more to the story.

"He was the best shot on the team. He never hesitated to use his weapon when absolutely necessary, but he only fired when it was needed. I don't believe he could kill this guy in cold blood."

Jenna absorbed Kurt's words. "I feel the same way," she said. "In the heat of the moment, maybe, but not with premeditation. Don't you think the police will suspect Mick was framed after what happened to my house and then his car?"

"Hard to say. They might think he killed the perpetrator."

She sighed. *What a mess.* Not sure what else to say, she fixed her attention on the passing scenery.

Five minutes later, they parked behind the Steele Security building, which was an old two-story brick colonial that had been converted to commercial use like so many others in the area. "One of my guys will meet us here when everything's ready."

He entered the back and led her through a galley kitchen into the living room turned reception area. The room boasted an unmanned gray metal desk, a black leather love seat flanked by end tables, and not much else.

"This is nice," Jenna said. It was fine, but it could use a decorator's touch.

Kurt gave her a knowing glance. "Not really, but it's a start." He waved her toward a short hallway. "There's a bathroom here"—he pointed to a half bath tucked beneath the stairs—"and my office." The scuffed wooden floors creaked as he moved behind a desk that matched the military-issue one in the front room. He gestured for her to take a seat in one of two worn wood dining chairs across from him.

"How many employees do you have?" she asked.

He wiggled the mouse next to his desktop computer and then typed a few keystrokes on the keyboard. "So far, it's just me, Todd, and Jason, but I'm working on getting Dan and Mick to join me." He clicked the mouse and watched the screen as he talked. "And I need a business manager."

"So things are going well?"

He finally turned his dark eyes her way. "Not bad. I could probably get more if I had enough guys to fulfill the contracts. It's a bit of a catch-22."

She nodded absently and looked around the spartan office while he checked email or looked at porn or whatever he was doing. There were no pictures in here to break up the monotonous tan walls. Really there wasn't much of anything. She set her purse down and withheld a sigh. How long were they going to sit here? What was Mick doing? Was he okay? Would she ever see him again? And what about Tara?

"Is there anything we can do to help my friend?" she asked. "I'm pretty sure she's in Leesburg. Can't we track Colin's phone or something?" She fiddled with the bracelet Mick had given her. The feeling of uselessness made her restless in her own skin.

"Why don't you call the police department and tell them about her phone call? Even if Di Ferio turns his phone off, they can at least put out a BOLO—a Be On The Lookout alert."

Happy to have something productive to do, she stepped into the hall to make the call. She relayed everything she could remember about her conversation with Tara, giving the detective the number of the phone her friend had used to call her. The woman sounded skeptical, but she promised to put out an alert on the couple. It wasn't enough, but it was all Jenna could do at the moment.

When she returned to Kurt's office, he roused and offered her a soda, bringing back a can of Pepsi and a few magazines. She feigned interest in *Men's Health* while he got back to work.

Finally, after another agonizing hour crept by, a rangy man with military-short red hair entered the office. "It's all set boss," he said with a slight twang she couldn't identify. Texas? Alabama?

Kurt stood and introduced her to Todd, who turned his bright blue eyes her way. "Ma'am, you can't keep your phone, but if you give it to me, I can have all the calls transferred to this one. It's clean." He produced a no-frills flip phone.

Why hadn't Mick thought of that? Of course, he'd been under a time crunch.

Or maybe he just hadn't wanted her to come with him.

Pushing that thought aside, she nodded and switched phones. "Where are we going?"

"I have a small house lined up," Todd said. "It's fully furnished and between renters, so the owner has agreed to let us use it for a few days."

A few days. One way or another, she needed for all of this to be settled...and soon. She couldn't live her life in limbo forever. As soon as she got to the safe house, she had to come up with a plan to end this sequestration and get her life back.

After locking up the building, they returned to Kurt's car and followed Todd's gray Charger out of the parking lot.

"Here's how it's going to work," Kurt massaged the back of his neck with one hand as he spoke. "I'll have Todd and Jason outside, but they'll be inconspicuous enough for the neighbors not to notice. There'll be another guy inside. Everyone's in place, so the house is already secure."

"Is it really necessary to have someone on the inside too?" She didn't want to feel like a prisoner. And some privacy would be nice.

Kurt nodded. "Just give it a try. If having him there feels

too intrusive after tonight, I'll pull him, okay?"

"Okay." He knew what he was doing, after all. Speaking of which... "How do I pay you for this? It has to be expensive."

"It's already been taken care of."

How was that possible? "I know you owe Mick and all, but I don't want to be a charity case. I don't have a lot of money right now, but after Rob's accounts go through probate, I'll be able pay you."

Kurt gave her a quick glance before responding. "No, I am getting paid. Mick is picking up the bill."

Her blood warmed, even as her jaw slackened. Either Mick cared, or he was eager to get rid of her. Probably a bit of both.

Kurt drove the rest of the way in silence, and after ten minutes Todd turned into a short driveway of a split-level home with green shutters and white siding. The small front lawn could use a trim, but the house was otherwise neat, and the neighborhood looked safe.

An instant sense of welcome and comfort hit Jenna as she walked through the front door and up a short wooden staircase into an overstuffed living room just big enough for the full-sized couch that lined one wall. The frilly, flowery upholstery and knickknacks above the fireplace reminded her of Tara's place.

Worry sliced through her again. If only there were more she could do to help her friend. *God, please let her be okay.*

Kurt locked the door behind them and closed all of the blinds. "It's getting dark out," he explained. "You don't want to be a sitting duck once all of the lights are on."

No. She most definitely did not. He'd pointed out his men on the street before they parked in the garage. One was hiding in the woods behind the house. Another sat in a van that was parked in a neighbor's driveway. How they'd pulled that off, she wasn't sure.

"Todd installed a wireless alarm system." He looked around the living room and kitchen area, his jaw tight. "Say hello to the inside guy while I check the sensors."

Jenna jumped in surprise when an overweight man with dark hair and glasses stepped out of the shadows from the hallway. Kurt disappeared down the stairs without even introducing them.

"Hey," the stranger said softly, his eyes serious. "Is it okay if I stay?"

Her stomach took a dive when she realized it was Mick. "You're the inside man?" she asked. Of course, Kurt had been in on it. Mick must have asked him to keep her out of the loop.

He nodded, still watching her warily.

How did she feel? Relieved, angry, elated, in love. "What'll we do if the police come here to talk to me?"

"We'll have advance warning." He moved closer.

"You just walked out of your building dressed like that?" She took a step forward and pushed his padded belly.

"It was close. A cop actually stopped me, but he didn't recognize me. He just wanted to show me my own picture and ask if I'd seen myself." He chuckled. "It was surreal."

She pressed on his chubby cheeks, amazed by his transformation. "How did you do this?"

"Cotton balls." He turned to pull them out and throw them away. Instantly, his strong jaw and the hard planes of his cheekbones reappeared.

She lifted her hand to remove the glasses that were distorting and dimming his eyes, and placed them on the counter. "I like you with dark hair," she said, running her hands through the soft strands, unable to keep herself from touching him.

He caught her hands in his own and brought them to his mouth for a tender kiss. "I'm sorry I couldn't tell you the plan. I didn't want you to have to lie for me if the police intercepted you."

The residual anger she'd been feeling drained away. This man protected her with his every move. "Rob must have told you what a terrible liar I am. I never got away with anything in high school."

"He might have mentioned it once or twice." Mick shifted away and released her hands. "I didn't think you were even capable of dishonesty until this morning."

She hated the pain in his eyes and the fact that she'd put it there. Pressing his cheeks with her palms, she held his gaze. "The only reason it worked is because I've always wanted to be with you. I just had more than one motive. But"—she cut in quickly before he could say anything—"I hated myself for using you like that. *That's* why I backed off." Couldn't he see? Couldn't he understand?

His jaw hardened, but he didn't pull away. He cradled her head and studied her mouth, sending little jolts of desire through her veins. "I wish we didn't have these lies between us, Jenna." His arms bundled her tightly to his chest and he sighed, resting his cheek against her hair. "You're the one who could have changed everything for me."

What did he mean by that? Her mind and heart raced, and she had a sudden sinking feeling. If she had any tears left, she would have cried.

Tara sat on a rickety easy chair and put a hand to her jumpy stomach as she watched Colin pace. They'd arrived at the "safe house" just before sunrise after traveling over rutted roads that wound through the rolling hills of horse country about twenty miles northwest of her townhome. The single-story farmhouse would have been quaint, but the large wraparound porch sagged, the wood siding had lost most of its once-white paint, and the roof shingles were curled and cracked.

The interior didn't inspire any more confidence. The scuffed wood floors were covered with fraying area rugs and worn furnishings. Dusty oil paintings of forests and rivers hung on the walls. The entire place must have been decorated with yard-sale or thrift-store finds.

She wanted to believe Colin was trying to protect her, but could she trust him? He hadn't tied her up or anything, but he also hadn't left her side since he'd caught her listening in on his phone call. They had immediately packed overnight bags and hit the road.

He'd told her to lie to Jenna about where they were, but she hoped her friend had gotten the message.

"It's to keep you safe," he'd said. "I don't know who's listening. The boss knows you overheard me talking to him, and he doesn't like loose ends."

She'd trembled at the thought, suddenly cold and scared. He'd hugged her close and apologized for getting her involved in this mess, but his touch no longer had the ability to thaw her.

"Why'd we come *here*?" she asked now, pulling her knees up to her chest.

"I wanted to get out of D.C. but stay close. I'm supposed to make sure you don't talk," Colin said. "The boss meant something more final, I'm sure, but if I can keep you off the radar until this blows over, you should be safe."

*Final* sounded ominous, and a shiver ran through Tara's already cold limbs. But the look on Colin's face was sincere. She wanted so badly to believe him and go back to the way things were before last night. But he was obviously tied in with some bad men, and didn't that make him one of them? "Why were you keeping tabs on Mick and Jenna?" she asked.

He sighed and rubbed his lips before meeting her eye. "At first it was just a job. One that would keep me home from the desert for a while. After I met you, I wasn't so eager to leave town."

Her stomach dipped, and for a split second the pull she'd felt toward him from the moment they met was back. Shaking off her foolishness, she asked, "I mean, why does someone want them watched? Why did Jenna's house get ransacked and blown to smithereens?" Her voice had risen in frustration, and she realized she was standing now, looking down at Colin, who was sitting on the ugly brown couch next to her chair.

"You know I can't talk to you about any of that. Besides, the less you know, the better." He took her hands, scowling when she pulled them away. "I don't want you to get hurt too." Reaching out, he skimmed his fingers along her cheeks with a feather-light touch before letting his hand drop away, dejected. "I'm falling in love with you, Tara, and I hate that this is coming between us. But I can't let you go until I'm sure you're safe."

Oh my God, were those tears in his eyes? "You're falling in love with me?" Yesterday she had felt the same way. He'd had her thinking crazy thoughts about weddings and babies and buying a house together. She'd started playing with the name Tara Di Ferio like some silly teenager with a crush. "You'll have to forgive me if I find that difficult to believe right now."

She crossed her arms and stepped out of the column of warmth he created just by being near. It was hard to think, hard to hold onto her anger, when her body kept dredging up memories of their past week together. In bed and out, he'd been everything she had ever wanted in a man. Was he too perfect? Was he just playing a game? But if he loved her, didn't that change everything?

He was the protective type by nature. That was part of what had drawn her to him in the first place. His methods might be a bit Neanderthal, but what if his heart was in the right place?

Colin leaned back on the sofa, holding the edge in a death grip. "Can't we just pretend we're on a vacation? I promise when this is all over, I'll take you home." He pinned her with a look of raw pain that tore at her heart. "I'd never hurt you, baby. *Please*. I'm trying to protect you."

Some of the ice around her heart cracked at the sight of her big grizzly bear begging for her to believe in him. Maybe he was honestly trying to do the right thing by her. If he had stolen her away for an impromptu holiday, wouldn't she have considered it the most romantic thing in the world?

Honestly, she wanted to trust him. Because as much as she tried to convince herself that she didn't really love him, she did.

In answer to his plea, she pulled her shirt over her head and slid off her pants.

His breath caught in his throat as he watched in shock. Then he lunged for her.

Mick inhaled Jenna's sweet scent, his body tightening in response to their embrace. What was it about her that reduced him to a lovesick fool? If he had any sense of self-preservation, he'd back away now, but instead he tightened his embrace, bringing them as close together as possible.

"I knew you were quick, but…" Kurt stood at the top of the stairs smirking.

"Damn it, Steele." Mick glared at his friend. "Try pounding your stumps next time."

Jenna inhaled sharply, as if she were worried about how Kurt would react to the comment, but he just chuckled. "Sorry, man. I'm programmed for stealth."

Mick rolled his eyes and pulled away from Jenna.

She looked bewildered and ready to cry, her beautiful eyes wide and glassy. Her betrayal had built a wall between them, but his secret was what had started it all. Guilt gnawed at him.

"Okay, the lower level is secure. I'll get out of your hair if you check this floor," Kurt said, giving him a quick questioning glance.

"Sounds good," Mick said, getting to work.

Kurt left after giving Mick an untraceable prepaid phone with all of his team members' numbers programmed into it. Thank God for the man. After Rob, he and Dan were Mick's closest friends. Mick could trust him to take care of Jenna for him and to shelter them both from the law.

But, he couldn't hide out forever. Someone wanted them silenced. He needed to end this game, and he had a bad feeling that he might have to tell Jenna—and a lot more people—the whole truth in order to make it happen.

Maybe Rob shouldn't have asked him to keep what had happened to himself. If he'd known what Mick and Jenna would go through, would he have acted differently? But while revealing everything to her might heal the rift between them, it wouldn't keep her safe. The only way to do that was to make sure the whole world knew what had happened.

Dreading his decision, but certain of his course, Mick finished checking the sensors. Then he discarded the baggy pants and sweatshirt and changed, glad to be back in his own jeans.

A few minutes later, Kurt brought them pizza under the

guise of a delivery driver, and Mick sat across the ornately carved dining table from Jenna, watching her pick the pepperoni off her piece to save it for last. He could get used to this, eating every dinner with her, sharing a home, talking as if they weren't surrounded by armed guards in a strange house.

She licked her fingers and wiped them on a paper napkin. "Rob once told me the team had nicknamed him Plato because he was such a deep thinker. Did everyone get a nickname?"

"Not everybody," Mick said, "but most of us. It's more common among the contractors than it was in the Air Force. Pilots excepted, of course."

"What was yours?" she asked, peering up at him with a hint of a smile.

Damn. Was she flirting with him? He shook his head. "Uh-uh. Not telling."

"Always the secrets," she said with a mock pout. "Tell me some of the others."

What was her game? Was she trying to get him to think about his team—about Afghanistan and Rob—or was she just making conversation? "Well, we called Colin Grizz or Grizzly, because, you know, he's built like a bear, and kind of gruff." Two could play this game.

She frowned and studied him for a minute, then apparently chose to ignore his attempt to stall the topic. "What about Dan?"

"Someone tried to call him Molly, since his last name's Molina." Mick smiled at the memory. "Uh, that didn't go over too well, so they started calling him Jumper because he started out as a PJ like us."

She leaned toward him, looking more relaxed than he'd seen her all day. "Who else?"

He took a bite of pizza and drew the moment out. "Riz because his last name is Rizzoli. Beavis, because he looks like the guy from 'Beavis and Butthead.' Nothing too original." He thought for a minute. "Flipper. Former Navy SEAL. And, yes, Flipper was a dolphin, but it stuck anyway."

She giggled. He liked the sound. Too much. "Come on," she begged. "What's yours?"

"Maybe I don't have one."

"Yes, you do." She popped a slice of pepperoni into her mouth and looked at him over the box. "What if I guess?" Her eyes glittered with heat. She *was* flirting.

"Go for it. I'm still not telling."

"But what if I guess? Don't I get anything?"

"What do you want?" he asked, cautious but intrigued.

She looked down, suddenly serious. "You know what I really want."

"I assume you're not talking about another roll in the sack."

A blush stained her cheeks, but she pursed her lips in distaste. "You sure know how to make a girl feel special. I'll give you that."

"It takes two, Jay."

Slouching in her seat, she crossed her arms and stared at the pizza crust she'd left behind. "Touché."

He decided to throw her a lifeline. After all, he'd made a decision. Not an easy one, but he hoped it was the right one. He took a deep breath. "Fine. If you guess correctly, I'll tell you everything."

"Seriously?" She narrowed her eyes at him and straightened in her chair, balling her napkin in one fist.

Okay, this probably wasn't the best way to go about it, but he wasn't ready to just release something he'd clung to so tightly. He needed to work up to it. "Yes."

She gave him an incredulous look, followed quickly by a sad shake of the head. "Well, obviously you don't think I'm going to get it then." The napkin unfolded and she pulled it into little strips, the sound loud in the otherwise silent house. "Earlier in the week you said you didn't want me to know the whole truth of what happened, and now you're willing to give it up in a game?"

"You know me, baby. I'm all about the fun." The playful tone he was going for never quite made it to his voice.

A look of determination crossed her face, and maybe even a quick flash of understanding, but that was probably just wishful thinking. After a long minute of playing with the strips of napkin, she scooped them up and let them fall like confetti into the empty pizza box. "All right. What do I have to lose?" Maybe she didn't even believe him, but she seemed like she was willing to play along.

"Whenever you're ready," he said.

Tapping her lip, she looked at the ceiling thoughtfully. "Fury. Heck, they could just call you that. The Fury. Or Furious." She glanced at him and pressed her lips together when he didn't respond. Then, as if she'd forgotten about the stakes of the game, her face grew more animated. She was enjoying this. "Mad Mick. Mickey Mouse?"

In spite of himself, he laughed, finding her good humor contagious. They both needed a break from the tension. "Nope."

"Fury. Fury. Furry?"

He shook his head.

"Mick Fury. Mick Fury." She glanced at him. "It's starting to sound weird. You know, like when you say 'orange' too many times and it loses all meaning?"

"Whatever." He raised his eyebrows and circled his finger around his temple in the universal sign for crazy.

She kicked him lightly under the table. "Jerk."

He grinned. How could he be enjoying himself this much?

Mumbling his name over and over again, she *did* sound kind of crazy, though he liked hearing his name on her lips. But, whoa, boy. Don't go there.

"Mick Jagger. Lips. Rooney. McDonald's?" She leaned forward and pressed her hands to the table. "Mickey D."

A little jolt of adrenaline shot through him. She was getting close. He shook his head.

"Big Mick." She tapped her finger on the table and gazed intently at it, her brow furrowed in concentration. "Mick Fury," she mumbled again.

His name had started to lose its meaning to him too.

She sat up and snapped her fingers, smiling. "McFlurry!"

His face heated and his heart gave an extra thump of alarm. "I always knew you were a smart girl."

Jenna gave a surprised laugh. "McFlurry? That's really it?"

He nodded. "Super badass, huh?" What could he say? Being nicknamed after an ice cream treat sucked.

She covered her mouth with her hands, but her smile shone in her eyes. "It's cute."

"Oh, God," he groaned. "Cute is the complete opposite of badass. You're killing me here, honey."

As if a switch had been flipped, the mood in the room suddenly changed, and her smile faded. "Are you really going to hold up your end of the deal?"

He sobered. "Of course."

"Right now?"

The longer he put it off, the worse he felt. Might as well get it over with. "If you're ready."

"I have a feeling that the rest of the story can't be worse than what I'm imagining," she said.

"I hope so," he said, standing. "Let's move to the couch."

He cleared the pizza mess and found a comfortable spot on the sofa, then turned out the light. With all the blinds closed and the sun long gone, the house was dark but for the faint glow of the porch light through the blinds.

"We're going to do this in the dark?" she asked. "Why?"

"Because I don't want to see your face when I tell you what I have to say."

# CHAPTER SIXTEEN

JENNA STUDIED MICK'S SHADOW FROM the opposite end of the couch, hugging a throw pillow to her chest as her eyes adjusted to the sudden darkness. "If you're trying to scare me, it's working." God, what could be so horrible? She wasn't even sure she wanted to know anymore. Stupid, after all she'd put him through to get to this point, but watching him now, seeing the emotional toll it was taking on him…

She didn't want to hurt him anymore.

"Good. Then maybe it won't seem so bad in comparison." In the dim glow of the streetlight that filtered through the window shades, his shadow shifted. He rested his forearms on his knees and stared at the floor.

"How about you start by telling me why you've changed your mind?"

He took a deep breath and met her gaze. "Okay. But to be clear, I still don't *want* to tell you. For so many reasons."

A crack split the night, and the living room window shattered, shards of glass hitting the wood floor with a musical crash. Mick grunted and leaped on top of Jenna, pulling her down onto to the deep-pile area rug and covering her with his body. "Are you okay?" His arms cradled her back and head as he used his elbows to keep his full weight off of her.

Her blood pressure was probably off the charts, but she didn't think she'd been hit. Maybe a few pieces of glass, because her face and arm felt wet, but nothing serious. "I think so. What about you?"

"I'm fine." A bullet tore into the couch with a muted thud. "Shit. Let's move." He dragged her toward the far end of the sleeper sofa, away from the window, but halfway there, his left arm gave out.

"Are you hit?" she asked, helping him scramble the rest of the way. Later she'd be scared out of her freaking mind, but right now, she was too hopped up on adrenaline.

"Not sure. It doesn't matter. We need to get to the powder room pronto."

More shots cut through the air outside, but they didn't seem to be aimed at the house. Were there two guns now?

"I think our guys are on him," Mick said. "Let's run for it. Stay low." He tugged her down to a crouching position and gave her a push. "Go!"

She ran bent over as if sprinting toward a helicopter and slid into the windowless half bath. Mick slid in right behind her.

"Don't you want to shut the door?" she asked.

"No. I need to be able to see them if they get into the house. Otherwise I won't be able to take them out."

"Do you have a gun?" She hadn't noticed one on him.

"Of course."

*Of course. Silly me.* She sat on the toilet, sandwiched between the vanity and a shower curtain covered in yellow roses, while Mick squeezed himself between the counter and the doorway. He supported his left arm against the wall, the sound of his uneven breathing filling the room.

"Let me look at your arm," she said. "If you bleed to death, you won't be any good to me."

"I'm fine. We can deal with it later." He pulled out the cell phone Kurt had left him and pressed a few buttons, the screen bathing the tiny room in blue light. The deep shadows on his face gave him a sinister look.

"Kurt, what the hell is going on?"

There were no more shots outside, but angry voices and sirens could be heard through the broken windows.

"Yeah, I got a bit of a scratch, but I can take care of it."

A scratch. Like hell. When he turned for a better look out of the door, she could clearly see the blood covering his arm and the side of his shirt. He'd been hit.

"Okay. Thanks, man." He stuffed the phone back into his pocket with a scowl. "The shooter ran off, so we don't know who it was. And now the police are on their way. I have to go. Now."

Her stomach dropped. She couldn't let him leave her again. She popped to her feet and grabbed his uninjured arm. "Take me with you."

"No. You're not safe with me."

"I'm not safe without you." And damn it all, she loved him.

"Kurt's guys can protect you better than I can, especially injured and on the run."

"Yeah, they've done a great job so far," she said, not bothering to hide her sarcasm. For God's sake, they'd only been there for two hours before someone had managed to get shots in through the window. "Besides, if I don't go with you, you won't take care of that arm." She held his gaze, determined to change his mind. "Please," she whispered.

"Jenna." He sighed and beat his head against the wall a couple times before he straightened. "*Fuck.* I'll get your bag. Check under the sink for anything useful. Then we'll get the hell out of here."

She pulled open the cupboard while he crawled down the short hallway and snatched her oversized purse from its spot on the living room floor.

"Here," he said, handing her the bag. "Pull the battery out of your phone. Until we know what's going on, I don't trust anyone."

She did as he asked, and then found a first aid kit under the sink and tossed it in too.

He called Kurt to let him know Jenna was coming with him, then removed his own battery, stuffing it and the phone into his front pocket.

"Basement door," he said. Before leading her downstairs, he scooped a blanket off the back of the couch as they passed it and snagged his baseball cap off the counter.

The sirens were closer now, probably just down the street, when they slipped out the sliding door, triggering a shrill beep. Jenna jumped at the sound. "That would have been a good warning if someone had tried to get in."

"Yeah."

Swirling red and blue lights blinked on the grass at the edge of the building. The wet ground glistened under an almost-full moon as Mick grabbed her hand and they raced for the trees.


Twenty minutes later, Mick bit back a curse as Jenna cleaned the wound on his triceps. Luckily the bullet had gone through without hitting the bone. But that also meant that he had two holes in his arm and his muscle was damaged.

He was going to be doing one-armed pushups for a while.

In the sickly light of the gas station bathroom, she bit her lip, her expression shaded by the baseball cap she'd tucked her hair into. "I'm sorry. I wish I could numb it for you."

"Kiss me. I won't feel a thing."

She gave him a get-real look. "Are you saying I make you numb?"

"No." He removed Damon's baseball cap from her head and slipped his good arm around her waist, reveling in the feel of her curves beneath his palm. "I'm saying that when I kiss you, everything else fades away. Pain, worry, everything. Kiss me, Jenna."

Her gaze softened, and her lips parted. He took that as a "yes" and moved in. The touch of her lips was pure bliss, and he couldn't stop himself from nibbling and tasting at will. Damn the situation. She sighed and leaned into him, letting him take the kiss deeper.

How could she doubt her effect on him? When their tongues met, he soared. She was his greatest rush. He would never need Afghanistan or fast cars if he could keep her.

When she stepped back, he groaned in protest and tightened his grip on her waist.

"Hold that thought," she said, fumbling for the antibiotic cream.

The kiss had worked like a charm. His arm still hurt like hell, but he didn't feel like complaining anymore. Too many endorphins buzzing in his brain.

She applied a large adhesive bandage to each wound and then leaned in, her fingers skittering across his tattoo. Her hand stilled suddenly and she sucked in a breath. "Does that say RJR?" Rob's initials.

Their eyes met and he nodded. "I had it added that night you picked me up from the bar." Jesus, had it only been a week ago?

As she rubbed the stylized letters that blended with the tribal pattern ringing his biceps, her eyes welled with tears. She blinked them back and cleared her throat. "That's a nice way to memorialize him," she said, averting her eyes as she rummaged through a brown paper sack of food and drinks that she'd purchased in the gas station's market. She handed him two ibuprofen and a bottled water, along with a clean T-shirt that read "Washington D.C." in blue and red block letters.

"We need to get moving," he said, trying to ignore the thrill of her touch as she helped him pull on the ridiculous shirt. Too bad they couldn't hole up there for the night, but the place was disgusting. Plus, the cops might find them, especially if Jenna's photo made the news and the clerk was sharper than he looked.

They had been working under the assumption that while Mick's photo had been broadcast on the news during the day, Jenna wouldn't be recognized. Yet. And if the baseball cap did its job, the cashier might never be the wiser.

Mick's hair was currently black and wouldn't match his photo, but the police might have already found the bank teller. They could modify his image accordingly. Oh yeah, and he was bleeding. That wasn't suspicious or anything.

"I bought a local map and grabbed a real estate guide from the rack near the entrance," she said. "What if we looked for a vacant house to hide out in?"

Smart woman. "That's a great idea, but we'd be breaking and entering. I don't want to get you into more trouble."

She shrugged. "What the hell, I'm already aiding a fugitive. How much worse could it be?" The way she chewed her lower lip belied her brave words, but he didn't call her on it.

Jenna found three empty homes for sale nearby. Two were

within a mile of the gas station.

They set out, sticking to the side streets, eventually switching over to a bike path that ran behind a large neighborhood. The trail crisscrossed Fairfax County, cutting through the forested areas. It would allow them to stay off the main roads for a while.

The moon shone through the mostly bare trees, making it easy to follow the trail, but they periodically tripped over roots and stones that were hidden in the shadows of the path. Mick held Jenna's hand so they could support each other. And because he liked touching her.

"If I didn't know better, I'd think the whole shooting incident was an elaborate ruse to keep you from telling me anything," she said.

"That may not be as far-fetched as it sounds. Someone could have found a way to listen in. A parabolic dish, a bug… who knows?"

She slowed, as if digesting the information, then turned to face him. "But how could they see in the dark to shoot?"

"I don't know. There are radar devices that use Wi-Fi and have pretty good fidelity through walls. Or maybe they were shooting blind. Anyway, they're clearly willing to go to any extreme to take us out at this point." He came to a full stop. "What's really bugging me is how they found the house in the first place."

"They must have been trailing me and Kurt. You should have him check his car for a tracking device."

Or an inside man. Mick sighed. What a fuck-up. Not that he could do anything about it now. He just needed to keep Jenna safe.

He tugged her off the path and they walked along the sidewalk in silence—just a couple out for a late-night stroll— until they reached the first house. Lights shone brightly through the windows, and a car sat in the driveway, so this one was a no-go. A few more minutes brought them to the second home, and that was when they hit pay dirt.

No lights were on inside or out, and a colorful flyer was wedged between the screen door and the doorjamb. Blinds covered the windows, which meant that he and Jenna would have more freedom to roam the house once they got inside.

Seeing no potential witnesses in the area, Mick waved her toward the backyard. There were no alarm company signs or window stickers. A vacant house was less likely to be wired to a dispatcher even if a system was in place, but he didn't want to take any chances.

Sticking to the shadows, he found a basement window that looked just big enough for Jenna to squeeze through. Preferring not to break the glass if possible, he used his pocket knife to jimmy the old latch until it popped free, and then slid the window back slowly in case it squeaked.

"Are you okay with going in?" he asked.

She stuck her head inside and peered into the dark room. Looking back at him, she said, "No problem. It's a finished basement."

Without another glance, she slipped in feet first and landed with a light thud on the carpeted floor. She slid the window shut and, moments later, appeared behind a curtain at the fake French doors to let him in.

The musty odor of damp earth invaded his nostrils, but the house was at least ten degrees warmer than outside. They'd be comfortable on the dry floor, and they'd be hidden from prying eyes. Better yet, no one would think to look for them here.

"Stay here." Ignoring his throbbing arm, he jogged through the house before returning to the basement. "It's clear. And the utilities are still on. It smells better upstairs, and all the windows are covered." But there was enough light leaking in through the blinds from the street lamps that they could see to move around.

They settled in the living room, where there was easy access to at least a couple of exits, and spread the blanket from the not-so-safe house over what smelled—and looked —like new carpet.

Jenna sat to his right, her back propped against the wall. "How's your arm?" she asked.

Pretty much on fire, but there was no point in whining about it. "It'll be fine. I think the meds are kicking in." He grabbed her hand in the semidarkness. "How are you holding up?"

"Hey, this dangerous life is old hat now." She gave a shaky laugh. "If we survive, I don't think anything will scare me anymore."

"We'll make it. I think I have a plan."

"Does it include telling me the rest of your story?"

*Like a dog with a bone, this woman.* He sighed. "Yes."

She took a deep breath and squeezed his hand. "I don't think you should."

He frowned. "What do you mean? You've done nothing but hound me over this for days, and now you don't want to know?" Jesus, wasn't this the one thing that was keeping them apart?

"No." She shook her head. "I *do*. But my love for you is stronger than my need to know the whole truth about that day."

His throat tightened. She loved him? "And last night was —"

She met his gaze in the dim light, a pink blush tinting her cheeks. "I meant what I said earlier. Last night was something I've dreamed about for years."

She wasn't the only one.

"I'm so sorry about this morning," she continued. "I was only thinking of myself. If I could take it all back, I would. In a heartbeat."

His own heartbeat raced. Jenna Ryan loved him. *Him*. The unreliable, womanizing, adrenaline junky. He slumped against the wall. No. She only thought she loved him. She didn't know there was blood on his hands.

She was in love with some idealized, heroic version of him that didn't really exist. Better for her to know the truth. Better for her to realize her mistake before she had him believing that a woman like her could love a man like him.

"I want to tell you anyway," he said. "I'm planning to release it to the press, but you should hear it from me first."

Her eyes widened. "Are you sure?"

He nodded, releasing Jenna's hand to rest his forearm on one knee.

Where to start?

She watched him intently, knees pulled to her chest.

"As you know, all of this went down the day after we called you. I'm pretty sure it's when Rob mailed you the pictures too, because he sent off an envelope on our way to meet the other guys." Maybe he should stand. He needed to move while he talked.

"We were in a convoy on our way to meet up with some local police troops we were supposed to train. The road was always dangerous, and we rolled hard down the highway, guns out, looking for IEDs, snipers, and ambushes. We were driving aggressively, ready to shoot at the slightest hint of a threat."

Jenna watched him with rapt attention, eyes wide. Rob had probably never talked to her about what they did. Or, more specifically, how they did it.

He cleared his throat and paced the room, images swamping him as he got closer to the heart of the incident. "Just outside a little village area, the lead truck hit an IED. A small crowd of locals gathered while Rob and I raced for the burning truck." God, he could *smell* it like he was still there. That awful, distinct scent of burning tires and plastic. And flesh.

He wiped his sweaty forehead with a shaking hand and took a deep breath. "We're always leery about villagers who linger near the road, because the insurgents will use women, children, even dogs to blow us up. The other guys had their rifles trained on the group, itchy with fear."

The movie in his head took over, and he was there again, barely aware of the words as they tumbled from his mouth.

*He and Rob met Dan at the smoking hull of the truck and pulled the injured men out. Two of them had died instantly, and Olszewski looked beyond repair. When someone on the team yelled, "Guns!" Mick started firing along with the rest of the team, covering Dan, who was applying a pressure bandage to Olszewski's stomach.*

*As he replaced an empty magazine, a sick realization quickly struck him. The locals had no weapons.*

*He watched in horror as the Afghans tried to run. One by one they were mowed down, red blood staining the dirt and the victims' clothes. "Hold your fire, goddammit!" he cried.*

*A small boy dropped to the ground, writhing as he held his gut, screaming for his father. Mick started toward him, but another bullet hit the boy's temple and he went silent. Bile rose up in Mick's throat and he crouched low, spit onto the damp earth, and squeezed his eyes shut.*

*What the hell were his teammates doing? Couldn't they see these people were unarmed?*

*Rising again, he ran toward Rob, who had stopped shooting and was sprinting toward the nearest armored vehicle. Thank God not all of the men had lost their fucking minds. Rob pointed to the Claymore shooter lying behind the tires of a black SUV. "You take him and Grizz. I'll get Smitty." He jerked his thumb toward the truck from which Smitty was cutting the frightened civilians down with a fifty-cal. "Someone has to stop this shit."*

*"Roger that." Mick raced for the gunner at the end, yelling at the khaki-clad contractors who were scattered about looking for targets but not shooting. "Hold your fire, they're unarmed. Hold your fire, goddammit!"*

*They were in such deep shit. And he couldn't even begin to let himself think of the dead or their families. They would come to him in his nightmares, but right now he had to focus. He reached the truck and leaped onto the hood. "Di Ferio! Hold your fucking fire. No one's shooting back."*

*"Smitty said they had weapons." Di Ferio glared at him, but stopped shooting and looked around, his face registering neither shock nor disgust. If anything, he looked disappointed.*

*"Come on, help me stop it."*

*The big man hesitated, but then nodded and climbed down after Mick.*

*A cry came from the middle gunner and Mick looked up just in time to see Rob jerk back as a dark blot spread across his chest. Mick faltered mid-step, unable to comprehend what he'd seen. Had Smitty really just shot Rob?*

*"No!" Mick yelled as his best friend tumbled to the ground, where he lay in a crumpled heap. He raced to Rob's side and covered the gaping hole in his chest, but blood seeped between his fingers, insidious and unrelenting.*

*Rob knew he was going to die, and with his last breath, he asked Mick to spare Jenna the knowledge of what the team had done and how he'd died. When Rob's heart stopped and the tension left his body, Mick felt his own rage bubble up through his veins like fire.*

*He sprinted toward the middle truck, his strength almost superhuman as he sprang onto the armored vehicle and reached for*

*Smitty.*

*"I'm going to fucking kill you!" he yelled, catching the man by surprise and pulling him away from his gun. Without another thought, he swung Smitty around and smashed his fist into the man's face again and again until someone pulled him back. He struggled against the hands that gripped his arms.*

*"Mick, stop. He's out, man," Dan said in a low voice. "I get it, but he's out. Killing him will only make things worse."*

*Mick unclenched his fists and breathed heavily as his vision cleared and his pulse slowed. Smitty lay unconscious across the windshield, his face swollen and red, blood trickling from beneath his right eye. Had he done that?*

*High-pitched cries and low groans filtered through the dust and smoke, nearly drowned out by the ringing in Mick's ears. The civilians lay scattered in an arc alongside the road, many of them dead.*

*Just like Rob was.*

*Mick tore out of Dan's grasp and stumbled off the truck, nearly taking a header into the mud, and ran from the carnage.*

*Oh, God. Tremors shook his body uncontrollably. All those innocent people. How many had he killed? He let out a guttural yell and dropped onto his hands and knees as his stomach rebelled. He puked until he was dry and then rolled onto his back, closing his eyes against the relentless sun and the heinous evidence of what he and his teammates had done.*

*He wanted the desert to swallow him whole. How could he live with what he'd done?*

Jenna sat riveted to the floor, watching Mick pace as if in a trance, seemingly unaware that tears were streaming down his cheeks. Her heart pumped wildly as the story played out in her mind's eye. So much agony and pain crossed Mick's face that she wanted to reach out and touch him, but instead she could only sit in horror as the realization of what he and Rob and their team had done sunk in.

There had to be some mistake. Rob would never hurt anyone. That's why he'd worked so hard to be a PJ. He wanted his part in the war to be saving people. But Mick had no reason to lie about it now. God, what had they been thinking? Weren't they supposed to wait until they were fired on before shooting?

Easier said than done, though.

She pressed the heels of her hands to her eyes, dizzy from the barrage of emotions. If only she had been able to convince Rob to come home sooner. She'd give anything to bring him back.

Her own tears splashed onto her shirt and wouldn't stop flowing. Rob, her beautiful, honorable brother had been gunned down by his own teammate, and the wound of his loss was as fresh as if she were hearing about it for the first time.

At the time, Mick had thought it was a horrible accident. A misunderstanding in the heat of battle. But after Jenna found the pictures, he must have realized that it could have been murder. A cover-up. But he and Rob hadn't wanted her to know that they had innocent blood on their hands, even though they'd tried to stop the massacre as soon as they realized what was going on.

The worst part was that she *didn't* want to know the truth anymore. The horror of it had overwhelmed her senses. She could almost hear her mother saying, "I told you so."

"Jenna?" Mick stopped pacing and crouched in front of her, keeping his distance as if afraid of her reaction.

She watched his hands as he watched her. He'd brought her to ecstasy with those hands. And he'd killed with them. Her gut clenched and she sprang to her feet. She raced into the bathroom and shut the door, hovering over the toilet bowl that gleamed blue in the glow of a nightlight that had been left behind.

Her breath came in staggered gasps, and she swayed on her knees, but her dinner didn't force its way up, so she sagged against the wall, the cold from the tile floor seeping through her pants and making her shiver.

Rationally, she knew that Mick deserved her sympathy. Rob too. They'd screwed up, but their mistake was understandable given the circumstances. And they'd ultimately done the right thing. Rob had given his life to save innocent civilians.

Mick had made his promise to Rob out of loyalty and fear. Could he really be blamed for trying to keep it?

She respected him for honoring his oath for so long, and she understood why he hadn't wanted to tell her the rest of the story. But that was logic, and right now her emotions ruled. She couldn't stop picturing the blood and hearing the screams and watching her brother fall to the ground, over and over again.

And after all of it, Mick was here. Alive.

And she didn't know if she could forgive him.

# CHAPTER SEVENTEEN

MICK WIPED HIS FACE AND slid down the wall to the floor. He sat with his elbows propped on his knees, hands dangling, head leaned back against the cool surface. Retelling the story had been like reliving it. The fear and horror had come back in full force, wringing him dry like a sponge. Fatigue weighed him down and he closed his eyes, desperate for sleep.

How would Rob judge him now? Had he done the right thing by telling Jenna? She had been determined to get the whole story, but would she blame him for letting her have it? He ached to hold her, give her comfort, and take some for himself. But she'd cut herself off from him.

Her sobs echoed in the tiny bathroom and seeped under the door, each one like a knife through his heart. By giving her what she'd wanted from the very beginning, he'd likely pushed her away for good.

That was better for her anyway, but selfishly, he'd started to think they might have a future together. With her, he could be a better man. The kind of man she deserved. But that was before she found out how screwed-up he really was. Before she saw the demons that haunted his nightmares.

Mick's father wouldn't have been surprised by the mess he had made of his life. It seemed as if everything Mick had done or said as a kid had brought the sharp pain of his dad's fist to his stomach or kidneys. Places where bruises were more easily hidden. At some point, he'd learned to hide his goals, thoughts, and true feelings. His mom, his teachers, and the girls at school had never bothered to look deeper. For most of his life, he'd preferred it that way.

But Jenna saw through him somehow. Or at least he thought she did…

Would she still love him now that she knew everything?

This pain and confusion was the reason why he'd never opened himself up to a woman before. But though he'd avoided getting involved with Jenna for years, looking back on it, she'd gotten under his skin right from the start. Rob's warning, and his own fears, had kept him from admitting the truth, but that didn't change it.

He loved her.

What a damn shitty time to figure it out.

When this ordeal was over, he could do what was best for Jenna. He could leave again. Until then, though, he had to keep her safe. And the only way he knew how to do that was to shine a light on what had happened—all of it—no matter how painful it was for everyone involved.

He must have fallen asleep at some point because when he opened his eyes, Jenna was lying on the blanket in the center of the room. Facing away from him, she had wrapped herself into a ball.

Crawling over to the blanket, he stretched out next to her, careful not to violate her personal space. Her back stiffened, but she didn't turn or speak. He longed to mold himself to her, warm her with his heat, run his hands along her curves.

There were so many things he wanted to say, so many things he couldn't even begin to express. But nothing was adequate. Nothing could make this better. And without all his charm, he had nothing to offer.

Still, he had to try to comfort her. "I'm sorry," he said. "I wanted to protect you. I wanted your memories of Rob to be untarnished, because no matter what happened, he was the best of men. I would have given anything for it to have been me instead."

She sat up and faced him then. "Don't say that."

He stayed on his side, worried she might bolt if he moved. "Tell me you haven't thought it."

Her eyes dropped and she stared at her hands.

Wow. That hurt even more than he'd expected. "It's okay. I figured as much."

She shook her head. "I've been lying here thinking about everything that happened, and I'm glad you're alive. It's not fair to blame you." She pulled her knees up to her chest and looped her arms around them. "I did at first. I was angry. At you, at Smitty, at Rob for putting himself in danger. Rob was all I had left, Mick, and he knew it, but he still kept going back to that place to dodge bullets and IEDs and suicide bombers.

"After Jimmy died, I needed my brother more than ever, but he left anyway. Why couldn't I be enough for him?"

He wanted to hold her, but he didn't dare. "We're flawed, Jenna. Guys like us don't know how to have normal lives anymore. When we're over there, we hate it. When we're home, we think we're going to die if we don't go back. When you're used to every day being life and death, the peace and normalcy of home feels false. Meaningless. The rush of war is like a drug. I don't know how else to explain it."

She rested her chin on her knees and studied him, her

features drawn in sadness. "When you and Rob were in the Air Force, I worried all the time, but I was proud of what you did. There's honor in putting yourself in harm's way to rescue others. I told anyone who would listen that my brother was a PJ. One of the elite."

Mick didn't want to hear it, but he didn't stop her. Hell, this was no more than what he deserved.

A tear slid down her cheek, but she let it go. "I'm sure working for Claymore gave Rob the adventure and adrenaline rush he craved, but it was all about the money. Where's the honor in that?"

"He did it for Jimmy," Mick reminded her. And to take the burden off her. But the decision had haunted Rob. He'd admitted as much to Mick once after a few drinks, but he'd never regretted doing what he thought was the right thing for his family.

"You think I don't know that?" she asked. "We both felt helpless watching Jimmy waste away in that coma. And if he'd lived, the expenses would have been staggering. But after he died, Rob could have come home. He *should* have."

"He tried over and over after Jimmy died. Hell, you know that. But by then, it was too late," Mick said. "He didn't know any other way of life. He was hooked."

"Like you," she said.

He nodded. "Like me."

"I know why Rob joined Claymore, but why did you do it? You could have stayed with the PJs."

Mick rolled onto his back and stared at the ceiling. "Why does anybody go private? Money. I figured, hey, same thrill and quadruple the pay? What's not to like?"

"I'm sensing a 'but.'"

If he opened himself up to her, would it change anything? He'd still be a murderer. He'd still be a wreck. "In the military, the camaraderie, the sense of team and brotherhood can't be matched. We're all in it together, none of us can walk away no matter how bad it gets, and any of us would die to save the other. You can do anything knowing the guys have your back.

"Contractors, not so much. It's every man for himself. We're there for the rush and the money, and that's it. It's kill or be killed, and there were only a few men I trusted enough to risk my life for."

"It sounds awful," she said, rubbing her face and switching to a cross-legged position. "The job doesn't seem worth it just for a flashy car and upscale condo that you hardly get to use. Are you saving up for something?"

His mouth twisted into a bitter smile. "You know those bumper stickers that say 'my son and my money go to MIT'? It's like that, only it's my brother."

She leaned forward, a questioning look on her face. "You have a brother?"

"Two actually, but Adam's a prodigy. He got into MIT, but couldn't get enough financial aid to go, so my mom asked if I could help." Had he managed to keep the resentment out of his voice? He hoped so. If anyone deserved a hand out of the trailer park, it was Adam. What torqued Mick off was that his mother had never advocated for him or Doug. Maybe if he'd had an off-the-charts IQ, she would have cared more.

"And that's when you quit the Air Force."

"Yeah. My service commitment was up. The timing was perfect." He'd given up his dream for his brother's dream. Because Adam still had the chance to be a whole person, a productive member of the population. He'd only suffered their father's presence until the age of seven. He probably barely remembered the man.

Lucky kid.

Jenna looked sad. "I'm sorry I never asked about your family before. I don't even know where you grew up."

"Dayton. And it's not your fault. Family's not my favorite subject."

She studied him for a few seconds, then yawned and lay back down. "We should get some sleep." Slowly, wordlessly, she scooted back until she was pressed against the length of him. "It's cold in here."

He took that as a hint, but not an outright invitation, and rolled onto his side, pulling her tightly to him. God, she was tempting, but he didn't want to scare her away, so he left his arm slung over her waist but rested his hand on the blanket in front of her stomach.

"Thank you," she whispered.

In the dark, he listened to her breathing. If his heart stopped right now, he'd die happy. Unfortunately, morning would intrude soon enough. And after he set the rest of his plan into motion tomorrow, nothing would ever be the same again.

Jenna woke on Thursday morning encapsulated by Mick. His heat, his scent, his warm breath on her neck. Sometime during the night, his carefully neutral hand had tucked under her hip and pulled her closer.

It would be so easy to roll over and kiss him. She desperately wanted to. She'd had several hours of restless sleep after their talk last night. She couldn't stop thinking about what she would have done in their shoes.

How scary it must be working in a foreign country where it feels like everyone wants to kill you. She didn't condone what happened, but maybe she could understand it. And now that her emotions had cooled, she wasn't so eager to blame Mick. For being involved or for coming home alive.

She was glad he hadn't died alongside her brother. Her anger and grief over Rob's choices and their ultimate outcome had found a handy target in Mick, but she loved him too much to wish things had turned out differently.

Besides, it wasn't his fault that Rob had stayed too long. And, according to Mick, it wasn't her fault either. She loved him for saying so, even if she didn't quite believe it.

And she loved him for protecting her, despite the risk to himself. He had become the dependable, honorable man she'd always suspected he was capable of being.

Sure, he had a few problems. A few rough edges to smooth out. And he probably needed some counseling. She could help with all of that. Once they were safe again, she could return his loyalty by sticking with him through the aftermath, no matter what happened.

Never mind that they were currently running for their lives. This wouldn't last forever, and she had nothing but possibilities ahead of her. She would go wherever Mick wanted to be. She only needed to convince him to let someone else do the dirty work in the Middle East. He'd done his fair share.

Flipping to face him in the pale light of dawn, she stroked the stubble on his cheek, letting the rough hair tickle her palm. His eyes opened and he stared at her, the question clear on his face. Without giving him time to speak, she kissed him.

His muscles tensed, and he pulled back. "Jenna, you don't —"

"Shh." She captured his mouth again and fitted her body against his, snuggling into his warmth and sending shivers of delight along her skin.

And then it was as if someone had flipped a switch. He rolled onto his back and pulled her on top of him, his hands roaming everywhere. They were under her shirt and over her jeans, cupping her buttocks. His hand pressed her into his erection and his mouth left a hot trail along her jaw and down her neck.

Little noises of delight escaped her lips as her whole body lit up with desire. He grasped her under the arms and lifted her higher, pushing her shirt over her head. She'd removed her bra to sleep, and when he encountered her bare breast, he groaned and latched on.

A current zinged straight from his mouth to her groin. *More, more, more.* The things he was doing with his tongue and hands were driving her insane. She wanted to mesh with him completely, become one body, one soul, one mind.

"Take your pants off," he commanded in a hoarse whisper, yanking at her zipper.

She stood over him and pulled them down, watching him watch her. He reached up and snagged her panties, and she stood there bare, trapped by his gaze. The only thing that saved her from dying of embarrassment was his groan.

He whipped his shirt off and tugged her down onto her knees, circling his arms around her thighs, moving her in toward his mouth. Both shocked and titillated, she placed her hands on his chest for support and closed her eyes.

"Yum," he murmured, putting his mouth on her, stirring additional sensations with his fingers as he expertly teased her to new heights.

He used his tongue and lips relentlessly, pulling her higher until she almost couldn't bear it. Then his fingers slipped inside her, unleashing wave after wave of pleasure that pulsed from her core and out along her limbs. She bit back a cry and tried to collapse onto his chest.

"Uh-uh. I'm not done with you yet," he said, giving her a wicked smile. "Not by a long shot."

* * *

Mick loved watching Jenna unravel under his touch. He hadn't expected her to ever want his touch again. And he still couldn't shake the belief that when this was all over she was going to change her mind. Just in case this was the last time he had her naked in his arms, he'd make damn sure she never forgot it.

He brought her to climax so many times he lost count, and when she finally slid limply to his chest, he was in danger of coming at the slightest contact. Which might be a good thing, because he didn't have any condoms. She sprawled across him, her breath slowing along with her heartbeat. He trailed his fingers down her back and tried to conjure calming images.

After a few minutes she pushed up onto her knees and patted his hip. "Let me see it."

"What?" But he knew.

She wanted to see his pararescue tattoo. The tradition that dated back to Vietnam, when the helicopters the PJs took to rescue downed pilots had been dubbed Jolly Green Giants.

Mick stripped out of his pants and boxers, and flipped onto his stomach to show her the small pair of green footprints inked on his butt cheek.

She kissed the back of his neck and then covered the artwork with her palm. "You're still that man. The one who earned this."

Tears burned behind his eyes and he rolled over to take her in his arms. "Thank you," he whispered.

She gave him a long, slow, exploratory kiss, rubbing her body along his, quickly rekindling his desire. At that moment he would have killed for a condom. "Jenna, honey," his voice cracked. "I don't have any—"

Her finger touched his lips. "Your turn," she said, scooting down his torso, planting wet kisses on his chest and stomach.

His cock pulsed in anticipation. *Calm, calm, ice water, cold showers, Mrs. Burkowicz from third grade…*

Her mouth closed over him and he almost lost it right then. She was wicked, licking, sucking, and stroking until he passed the point of no return. He didn't want to lose control with her. "Ah, baby. I can't—" He half-heartedly pushed her away.

Ignoring his protest, she sucked him from base to tip and then back again. He trembled with the effort to hold back, but then she cupped his balls and gave them a gentle squeeze. The move was so unexpected that he let go with a cry, his body exploding into pure light. Jenna took everything he had to give without complaint, and rose above him with a shy smile.

He came back to himself lazily, suspended in a haze of pure pleasure. His head buzzed, his fingers tingled, and his limbs were too heavy to move, so he just watched her. She was so beautiful in the dawn glow, her face still flushed. He wanted to see her like this every morning of his life.

She planted a kiss on his stomach and he jerked his hips, laughing, suddenly sensitive and ticklish.

"Sorry," she said, stretching out on top of him to rest her head on his chest.

"I'm not."

"That's not what I meant," she said, giving his hip a playful slap.

"I know." He stroked her hair, sifting the silken curls through his fingers. "That was…You're…"

She lifted her head to look at him.

"I love you."

The words tumbled out before he realized what he was going to say. Telling her hadn't been part of his plan, but he wanted her to know that she was more than just good sex, more than a fling to him.

He didn't know how else to express all that.

Her lips parted and she smiled as if he'd given her a gift. "I love you too," she said, planting a quick kiss on him before dropping her head to his chest again and squeezing him tight.

*I'm sorry.*

# CHAPTER EIGHTEEN

A WARM GLOW SPREAD THROUGH Jenna's body as she lay in Mick's arms. The arms of the man she loved. The arms of the man who loved her back. Jenna could face anything now that she knew that. For the first time in days, she felt hopeful.

She and Mick rinsed off in the shower, using the cleaner side of the blanket to dry off before putting their old clothes back on. She changed his bandages, and they ate the energy bars she'd bought the previous night. Some coffee to wash down the food would have been fantastic, but she settled for bottled water. What she really needed was to forget everything they'd done on the floor this morning. The happy memories were messing with her focus. "Okay, last night you said your plan included telling me about Rob. So, what's the rest of this great idea of yours?"

"I'm not sure great is the right word, but I was thinking that the reason we're being chased is to keep us from telling anyone what we know, right?"

"Presumably, yes," she said. "Both about the smuggling and how Rob died." She had a good idea where he was going with this, but she let him get there in his own way.

He nodded. "So it makes sense to me that if we take everything public there'd be no reason for them to shut us up. The damage would be done. Like you said before, the police or the FBI might not do anything with the evidence, but what if we take it to that reporter you contacted?"

"Why are you suddenly so ready to go to the media with this after all the effort you've put into keeping me quiet?"

He looked down at his hands, absently rubbing the calluses and small scars he'd earned over the years. "I'm not ready. I'll never be ready." His gaze met hers. "But I don't see another way to get these guys off our backs. They've already made it clear they'll do anything to keep us quiet."

Her heart broke for him. "You and the other guys will take a lot of heat from the media and anyone else who gets involved. And the State Department might not be able to sweep the incident under the rug if you do this." Jenna's stomach dipped. He could go to jail. After all that they'd been through, she could lose him anyway.

His jaw tightened. "I know, but I'm all out of ideas."

"I can't think of anything better either." She took his hand and squeezed it. "But I'll be with you the whole way."

"This means going out. We have to assume our pictures are everywhere now." He took a bottle from the pocket of his pullover. "How do you feel about going red?"

Good question. She'd never dyed her hair before. "It beats getting caught, right?" But red? Talk about standing out in a crowd.

Since they had no towels, Mick applied the dye while she kneeled over the tub. "What about your eyebrows?" he asked.

"I don't want to get that stuff too close to my eyes. I have a light brown eyeliner pencil in my tote bag. I think it'll be close enough." The hair color wasn't bright red anyway, more like an auburn.

"Should I leave it in for the full ten minutes?" he asked.

"I don't know. According to the stylist, my hair is very porous. Apparently that's why it used to turn green from the swimming pool. How about eight?"

"Green, huh?" He grinned and set the timer on his watch. "I'll bet you looked like a mermaid."

More like a sea monster. The kids had teased her mercilessly.

When his watch beeped, he rinsed her hair until the water ran clear. The feel of his fingers massaging her scalp sent warm tingles down her spine. If only they had more time together.

Pushing her disappointment aside, she squeezed her hair over the tub and let it drip for a few minutes before finger combing it and wringing it out again.

When she sat up, Mick smiled. "Wow. I don't think we need to worry about anyone recognizing you now."

She glanced in the mirror at the stranger with the chestnut strands. He was right. She wouldn't even have recognized herself. And after a few strokes with the eyeliner pencil, her eyebrows were a decent match. Redheads often had pale brows anyway, so hers didn't look weird. She rimmed her lashes with the eye pencil for good measure and stood back. "What do you think?"

He gave her a quick, hard kiss, his eyes sparkling. "I think we're home free."

"All right. Let's go call James Longstreet." Her pulse quickened. Whatever happened, they were going to finish this today. Then they'd finally be free to plan their future.

Maybe he sensed the change in her mood, because he cupped her face and moved in for the longest, slowest, sweetest kiss he'd ever given her. He left her breathless and ready for more, her heart bursting with joy.

After packing up their meager belongings, Jenna went through the house and cleaned up the evidence of their stay as much as possible. With any luck, the owners would never even know they'd had unwelcome visitors.

She locked the basement door behind Mick and crawled out of the same window she'd climbed into the previous night. If anyone saw them now, the game would be up. The sun had risen and people were sure to be getting ready for work. They were hidden from view by trees and the mass of the house, but they had to get to the front without arousing suspicion.

The neighbors to the north still had their blinds drawn, so she and Mick cut between the two homes on that side and stuffed their trash and the blanket into a can at the curb that was waiting for garbage collection.

The morning air was cool, and when Jenna shivered, Mick removed his sweatshirt and handed it to her. "Here. It's huge, but you'll be more comfortable."

Too cold to refuse his chivalrous gesture, she slipped it over her head and covered her damp curls with the hood. "Thanks," she said. "It's still warm." And it smelled like him too. She breathed in deeply. "I could go for some coffee," she said, spying a shopping center at the next corner.

"A coffeehouse would be a good place to test your disguise," he said. "Once we're done there, I'll get Longstreet's number from Information and call him."

Five minutes later they entered a cafe and she removed the hood of the sweatshirt. The delicious scent of coffee and pastries nearly brought her to her knees. Energy bars had nothing on a bacon-cheese croissant. She smiled at the cashier and gave her order.

Moment of truth time. Did he recognize her? Could he

tell she was in disguise? Would he suddenly point and yell, "It's her!" to the small crowd? Maybe she didn't look like a redhead. How did a redhead carry herself? Talk? Dress?

She didn't even know if she was considered a fugitive or a hostage. Her hands started to shake and her knees nearly buckled.

Mick must have picked up on her sudden distress because he leaned over and whispered. "You're rockin' the look. Besides, everyone is absorbed in their own world."

Then he kissed her neck, sending shivers of delight to her toes, and she relaxed. *Quit being stupid.* He was right. Heck, if Hugh Jackman or Brad Pitt passed her on the street she'd probably be none the wiser. Why would anyone notice her?

He paid for their meals and she wound her way through the rustic pine tables to a small round one near the back. No one even looked up as they passed. She waited for the coffee to warm her bones, digging lustily into her food. "This is delicious," she said to Mick between mouthfuls. "Thanks."

He chuckled and pulled his baseball cap lower. His transformation wasn't quite as dramatic as hers, especially now that his killer body was no longer hidden beneath a baggy pullover, but the cap and reading glasses still obscured his features.

After a sip of his own drink, Mick unfolded the copy of the *Washington Post* he'd purchased. "Hmm, look at that." He flipped it around so she could see the headline at the very bottom of the page, accompanied by two grainy black-and-white photos.

*Murder Suspect and Girlfriend Elude Police.* The tiny snapshot of her had been taken at an office party. Her hair was pulled back sharply from her face and she was wearing professional clothing. The photo looked nothing like her, particularly now that she had red hair. Mick's picture rivaled hers for ineffectiveness. The standard Air Force photo showed him standing next to an American flag in uniform. He looked like an ad for the new Aryan nation with his broad shoulders, fair hair, and light eyes, but he certainly didn't look like the man sitting across from her.

She breathed out a sigh of relief and her shoulders relaxed. They would be okay. For now, anyway.

"You ready?" he asked.

"Yes. Let's get this over with."

He nodded and stared at her for a beat before standing, an unexpected frown on his handsome face. "I'll go make the call."


"What the fuck happened this time?" Griffin yelled, barely able to contain his fury. The team's efforts to silence Mick and Jenna were quickly becoming farcical.

He still didn't see the humor.

On the other end of the phone line, Rizzo stammered. "Uh, they got away, sir."

Griffin took a deep breath. For Christ's sake, he was surrounded by imbeciles. "How?" he ground out through clenched teeth.

"Beavis missed and they ran for it."

"Let me guess. You have no idea where they are."

Rizzo cleared his throat. "Actually, sir, we got a break."

"Spill." Partly mollified, Griffin sat back in his leather chair. Maybe things were finally turning around for him.

"Remember those reporters you told us to monitor? Fury called one of them. Longstreet. They're meeting in an hour."

Mick's options were limited. Griffin had figured he'd either go to the police or the press, and he'd taken measures to deal with either scenario. Now he needed to make sure this problem disappeared. He'd spent too much time and money building up Claymore to let a bunch of murderous idiots ruin it.

He'd let the men run the smuggling operation because he had more important things to do, and because he needed to keep his hands clean. But now their attempts to cover their tracks had put his latest bids in jeopardy. Billions of dollars were in danger of being lost because Alan Smith had taken matters into his own hands and noisily erased Rob Ryan from the picture.

There was more on the line than money. Claymore had an important job to do. They helped keep the U.S. safe from terrorists. As the military moved troops out of Afghanistan, contractors were being used in bigger numbers than ever before, and the truth was, they didn't always color inside the lines.

Whether or not anyone was willing to admit it, the U.S. was at war with Islam. Sometimes you had to do whatever it took to get the job done. Screw the media, screw the politicians who spent all day in their cushy digs in D.C. with no concept of what it was like in the desert. They visited sometimes, and after spending a few hours on the dry soil, they acted as if they understood what it was really like. As if they knew the struggle and the frustration of the average man on the ground just from breathing the same dusty, filth-ridden air.

Claymore was doing the work that the military could no longer do, and the fucking American people should love them for it. They should bow down and kiss their feet for saving their fat, lazy asses every single fucking day.

But hey, as long as Griffin and his guys got to keep going over there and doing God's work, the American people and the media could spew all the hate they wanted.

He wouldn't let anyone jeopardize Claymore's mission or

its success. Not Mick and Jenna, not Rizzo and his merry band of fuck-ups, and not James Longstreet either. It was time to get rid of the whole lot of them.

"Sir?" Rizzo said. "How do you want us to handle this?"

Griffin laid out his plan—the part Rizzo needed to know, anyway—in slow, easy-to-understand language that a third grader could handle. "Last chance, Rizzo. Don't fuck it up."

"Yes, sir."

"I'll be at the Leesburg house in two hours. Grizz is already on his way. Once everyone's there, wait for me."

He'd given the dimwits too many chances already. Today was payback time.

Mick stood in the back hallway of the coffee shop and removed the battery from his cell phone, pocketing both. He approached their table and watched Jenna's beautiful profile as she bent over the newspaper he'd left behind. He had one goal. Meet with the reporter, tell him their story, and get the hell away from Virginia.

Okay, so that was two or three goals, but either way he needed to move. Being around Jenna was torture. Even more so after the morning they'd shared.

She had a hopeful gleam in her eye when she looked at him and he couldn't stand it. She'd forgiven him too easily. The next few weeks, maybe even months, of his life were going to be ugly. He didn't want her to suffer for his mistakes. And he couldn't shake the feeling that once the smoke cleared and life returned to normal, she'd realize her mistake and he'd be left wrecked by his foolish love for her.

He wanted his old life back. No attachments, no commitments, no one to care if he went a little nuts.

"How'd it go?" she asked as he approached the table.

Her hair had dried into soft curls that fell to her jaw, and he itched to run his fingers through it. Mainly as a precursor to kissing her. "He was falling all over himself to meet with us," he said in a low voice, forcing himself back into the present moment. "He'll be at the library down the street in an hour."

"The library?"

"Public, but not too busy. And they should have study rooms where we can talk privately. Plus, it's close. I'd prefer to stay out of cabs and off buses until after the story breaks."

"Okay. So, we'll need somewhere nearby to stay the night."

"Let's worry about that later. I want to get over there before he arrives so that we can make sure he comes alone."

She finished her coffee and wiped her mouth with a paper napkin. "Do you trust him?"

One could only trust a reporter so far, but they needed this one. "I think it's in his best interest not to give us away to the police. He'd never get another informant if he did that." Still, Mick would be on the lookout. He always was.

They cleared the table and left, detouring to a discount department store—open twenty-four hours—where Jenna bought a warm pink fleece that clashed with her new hair color. Mick picked out a sporty windbreaker and left the oversized sweatshirt he'd been wearing in one of the dressing rooms.

The walk to the library would take about ten minutes. Jenna slid her hand into his, and they strolled casually along the sidewalk in the gentle morning sun.

"Have you figured out what you'd like to do when the dust settles?" she asked, stroking his thumb distractingly.

This was so not a conversation he wanted to have with her right now. "I'm still thinking about it. I need to get back to work pretty quickly though. My brother has two years left at MIT. I told him he was on his own for grad school." He rubbed her chilly fingers between his palms while they waited to cross the street. "Maybe I'll get a job as a paramedic. The pay won't be as good, but I have the background for it. It's something I could do anywhere. Or, if nothing else, I can go to work for Kurt."

"Where do you want to live?" she asked. The walk symbol popped up and they crossed the road to the library.

*Wherever you're going to be.* But that was crazy talk. He couldn't risk thinking like that. "I'm not sure yet. Maybe near the ocean."

She tucked a strand of hair behind her ear and smiled. "That sounds nice. If I ever got up the nerve to work for myself, I think it would be nice to start over somewhere new."

He didn't—couldn't—respond to the invitation in her statement. Instead, he eyed the parking lot. Four people sat in their cars, presumably waiting like they were, but he'd keep watch, just in case. According to a sign on the door, the library opened at nine. Mick checked his watch. Five more minutes.

"I think you should do it," he said as he leaned against a tree that shaded the front of the brick building. "Rob would be happy."

She put her hands on her hips and studied his face, a frown replacing her pretty smile. "Are you going to leave me when this is over?"

"What do you mean?" Damn. She was too smart, too perceptive. And he needed her to be focused for this meeting. They could argue about the future later. He switched positions, trapping her against the far side of the tree, out of view of the parked cars. Leaning in, he kissed her, drinking in her sweet taste.

Wrapping her arms around his neck, she returned his kiss

with ardor, turning him to putty. If she asked now, he'd agree to almost anything. Even to stay with her. Which scared the hell out of him.

He unclenched his fingers and released the handfuls of her fleece he'd grabbed to pull her closer. Smoothing his palms down her sides, he slowly dialed back the intensity, planting feather-light kisses on her lips in an effort to ease himself away from her. He needed to stop, but Jesus, he didn't want to.

And judging by Jenna's grip on him, she didn't either.

With a low groan of protest, he broke the connection and grabbed both of her hands, scanning the parking lot once again. At the far end of the lot, James Longstreet ambled toward the library, fifteen minutes early. He was wearing a tweed jacket and carrying a red backpack, which was how he'd told Mick to identify him. "He's already here."

Jenna stiffened and looked over her shoulder.

At the same moment, the library doors opened and a short, gray-haired gentleman put out a sign advertising the schedule for the day. Still holding one of Jenna's hands, Mick drew her to the building and through the doors to search out an empty meeting room. He found two down the side hallway and chose the one closest to the exit.

Once inside the room, Mick took a seat facing the door and Jenna sat down next to him, fiddling with the strap on her leather bag. Longstreet peered through the window thirty seconds later and Mick waved him in.

"Mick?" he asked, setting his backpack on the table with a loud *thunk*. He shook hands with him and then pushed back a few strands of graying brown hair that had come loose from his short ponytail. "And Jenna," he said, turning toward her. "A lot of people are looking for you two. I think the police figure that you've skipped town." He squinted, his gaze bouncing between them. "I must say, you've done a good job of disguising yourselves."

"Do you have ID on you?" Mick asked.

Longstreet nodded and held out his press credentials and his driver's license. Both looked legit. And Mick knew that Virginia was now one of the most difficult places to get a license under false pretenses and had one of the hardest cards to counterfeit.

The reporter put away his identification and pulled out a handheld digital recorder and a notepad before settling his bulk into the plastic chair across from Mick's.

Jenna clenched her tote bag until her knuckles turned white. Sensing her nerves, Mick slipped his hand under the table and gave her thigh a quick squeeze. "Did anyone follow you?" he asked Longstreet. "Does anyone know you're here?"

"Not as far as I know. I don't have to tell my editor where I'm going, but I'm not an espionage expert. All I can say is that I didn't see anybody on my tail."

Mick's threat radar pinged madly, but he couldn't explain why. Maybe it was just that he hadn't been able to do his due diligence on the guy. Normally, he would have checked him out online, found some photos, talked to people who knew him. And he'd have backup. They were flying blind, which wasn't a good feeling when everything hinged on this meeting.

The man leaned toward Jenna and pressed the record button on the small device. "When I received your email, I had a feeling you knew something. What made you change your mind?"

She glanced at Mick and he nodded to her even though unease was prickling the back of his neck. He pulled his gun from the holster at his back and set it on his thigh, hidden under the table.

"We hope that our lives won't be in danger any longer if we take the story public," she said.

Longstreet watched her intently and leaned forward even more, his pencil at the ready. "Who exactly are you in danger from?"

"We're not sure how high up it goes, but I think it has to do with these photos that my brother took." She pulled out a sheaf of papers and set them on the table, holding them down with her hand. "They provide evidence of what appears to be arms and drug smuggling by Claymore contractors. Whether or not it's sanctioned by the company, I don't know, but I do think that my brother was killed to keep it quiet."

The reporter scribbled in his notepad, his demeanor tense and excited. "But wasn't he killed in a shootout with insurgents?"

"Not exactly," Mick cut in. "There's a lot more to that story, but the important part is that Alan Smith shot Rob."

Longstreet's jowls sagged in surprise. "Is that why you got into it with Smith the other night?"

Mick looked away. The meeting room had dirty, cracked linoleum floors with multicolored speckles that reminded him of his old high school cafeteria. "Yes." He met the other man's gaze. "But I didn't kill him. Someone else did that. I was with Jenna the entire night."

Her cheeks blazed red and she fiddled with the handle of her bag.

"So Smith shot Ryan in the heat of battle and you saw it happen. Why didn't you report this before now?"

"I reported it to the State Department investigators. And I wasn't the only one. But none of us suspected murder. We thought it was an accident." He took a deep breath. Once he put this out there, there was no going back. "I'm not sure if

Smitty took advantage of the situation, or if he started the shootout so that he'd have an excuse to kill Rob. Either way, unfortunately, Rob made it easy for him."

Jenna sat in the hard plastic library chair and watched the pain cross Mick's face as he described the shooting and massacre to the reporter. It hadn't occurred to her that Smitty might have started shooting with full knowledge that the civilians were unarmed. Her stomach curdled at the thought.

Slowly, Mick walked Longstreet through the entire fiasco, laying it out in much more detail than he'd done for her. She didn't want to hear it. The images were making her ill, and tears let loose long before Mick got to the part where Rob died.

She rubbed the memorial bracelet Mick had given her as he finished his story, ending it by telling the reporter about the attempts that had been made to keep them quiet, as well as Jenna's suspicions about Tara's disappearance.

"I'm not sure if Di Ferio just got involved with her as a means to keep tabs on us or what, but it has to be related," Mick said.

"This is incredible." Longstreet nodded and sat forward, his eyes wide. "It wouldn't surprise me if this goes all the way to Troy Griffin.  Claymore is bidding for two big contracts right now, and this story could kill any chance they have. Without those deals, they could go under. I'd say that's a huge motive for them to shut you down."

"So now you see why I couldn't turn myself in," Mick said. "A company like Claymore has endless resources and plenty of people in their hip pocket. I'm sure the evidence would bury me, and the story we have to tell would be kept under wraps if I took it to the police first."

"Quite so," Longstreet said, his head bobbing up and

down. "I've uncovered a string of inappropriate dealings by Claymore, but this is the first time I've had a witness who's willing to come forward."

"We're hoping that once the information goes public, there'll be no reason to continue targeting us," Jenna said. "The risk of coming after us in retribution would be high. If they're logical about it, they'll see that anything that happens to us after the story breaks would only place more suspicion on them."

"It's a decent theory." He scratched the gray stubble on his chin. "I'd still watch my back if I were you, but they'll have bigger problems on their hands after the story breaks." Longstreet fixed his brown eyes on Mick. "You realize that you're going to need to turn yourself in after this goes public."

Jenna's head whipped around to look at Mick. It was stupid of her not to have realized that.

Mick nodded. "Yeah. I know."

"But you just said that the evidence would probably convict you," she sputtered.

"Not once the story is out." He closed his large hand around hers. "I can't run forever, Jenna."

Her chest tightened, but he was right. If he wanted the police to believe him, he had to be willing to submit to their process. That didn't make her feel any better about it, though.

Longstreet gave her a sympathetic look. "I'm glad to know you're not a hostage. I was worried about that. The police are too."

"I'm here willingly."

Mick gave her hand a squeeze. "How long until you can get the story out?"

"I'll have to validate your story, but I'm hoping to get it in tomorrow or Saturday's edition, maybe even break the news online before that."

"Thank you," Mick said. "We're ready to come out of hiding."

Rising to his feet, Longstreet turned off the recorder and packed up his things, then turned to shake hands with each of them. "Good luck. Obviously, this is a scoop for me, but I hope it gets you the results you need."

"Yeah, thanks. And be careful. Until the story breaks, you're a target too."

"It won't be the first time," Longstreet said with a grin, his excitement radiating from him.

And then he collapsed to the floor.

# CHAPTER NINETEEN

JENNA REACHED FOR LONGSTREET, HER brain not processing what had happened until Mick leaped on top of her and pulled her to the hard floor beneath him. "Roll to the wall!"

She screamed and rolled without thinking, unable to see anything but the blood pooling across the floor, mingling with broken glass from the door. Outside in the hall, more screams joined hers.

Mick reached over and took the reporter's pulse. "He's gone."

Someone had shot him. Panic made her heart race in her chest. How had the bad guys caught up to them? And even more important: The room only had one door. They were out of the shooter's line of sight for now, but there was little to protect them in the room. How were they going to get out? She glanced at Longstreet again. Her stomach roiled, but she fought the nausea. They didn't have time for her to be sick.

"I can't put my full weight on my bad arm, honey. I need your help," Mick said.

She pulled her gaze away from the dead man. "What can I

do?"

"Get ready to jump through that window." He pointed to the far wall, where a tinted window overlooked the main road.

The door burst open and Mick fired his weapon, bringing down a short, stocky, dark-haired man with a shot to the knee. Mick punched him hard enough to knock him out and grabbed his gun. Peeking through the doorway, he sent off two more shots, then turned the new gun on the far window, shattering it with one shot. "Go now."

"What about you?" Jenna asked. She didn't want to go out there on her own.

"I'll be right behind you. Jump out and get behind the bushes."

She pressed a quick kiss to his lips and then ran for her life as Mick put down covering fire. A bullet slammed into the wall next to the window. She screamed but kept moving, launching herself over the broken glass.

Scooting to the side, she crouched into as small a target as possible in the bushes and mulch and examined her bloody hands. She'd caught some sharp edges on her way over, but she would survive. An eternity later, Mick rolled over the window sill, landing on the ground with a thud.

"Were you hit?" she asked, moving toward him.

"I don't think so." He handed her Longstreet's voice recorder and note pad, and the photocopies of Rob's pictures they'd brought to show him. "Here, put these in your bag."

She stuffed them into the tote that was still slung across her shoulders. "Now what?"

"I'm working on it." He waved her toward the back of the building and they crawled along the rough wall of the library, shielded from view by large, leafy azalea bushes that had already lost their spring blooms.

At the corner of the building, he hesitated and took a

quick look. "Shit." He scanned the surrounding buildings and parking lot. From a distance, sirens were making their way closer.

Jenna looked back and saw a man poke his head through the broken window. "Mick, behind us!"

He swung around and fired off a warning shot before pulling the trigger again, but it only clicked. He dropped the empty gun—which he'd taken from the first shooter—and pulled her with him into the bushes. "I'm down to five rounds. Run for that SUV." He pointed to an Escalade about thirty yards away. "I'll hold them off and then follow."

Would he really? She hesitated, afraid that she'd never see him again if she left.

"Jenna, please." He pulled her in for a quick, hard kiss. "Go! Go!"

Head down, she sprinted for the black car, putting it between her and the library as shots pinged into the metal. She'd never been so scared in her life.

Checking first to make sure there were no threats on her side, she lay on her stomach and looked under the SUV. Mick and one of the men from Rob's pictures—it looked like the one he'd called Rizzo—were rolling on the grass, both of them grappling for a gun. Her heart hammered against her ribs. "Come on, Mick."

Behind her, tires squealed and she looked over her shoulder just in time to see a large van pull up to the front of the Escalade. Two men dressed in black cargo pants and T-shirts jumped out and scooped her up before she could scramble to her feet. She started to scream, but one of her captors clamped a hand over her mouth. He shoved her onto the floor of the van and shut the sliding door behind her.

Rizzo had Mick pinned hard, pressing him into the soft, wet

grass, using his strong grip to slowly turn the gun toward Mick. It took all of Mick's strength to keep the weapon pointed away from his body. He was strong, but Rizzo had been on steroids for months, an open secret. Mick couldn't compete with him muscle to muscle.

Squealing tires and a short yelp from the parking lot snagged his attention. He turned his head just in time to see two men throw Jenna into a white van and take off.

Oh, God, *no*. "Jenna!"

Riz took advantage of his distraction and wrenched the gun free. A surge of anger pumped through Mick. He couldn't waste more time wrestling with this bastard. He needed to go after her. Clamping his legs around the other man's, he executed a quick flip. Before he knew what hit him, Riz was on his back with a stunned look on his face. The gun hit the ground and bounced in the short grass, landing just out of reach.

Mick used his elbow to land a powerful blow to Riz's chin. The man's eyes rolled back into his head. *Lights out.*

Scrambling to his feet, Mick grabbed the gun and sprinted to the parking lot where Jenna had been taken. But he was too late. He'd lost her. He slumped against the vehicle with a thud as a hot poker of anguish stabbed him in the gut. He had led them right into a trap, and now she was gone.

Why hadn't they taken him instead? He would gladly have traded his life for hers. If anyone were going to die over this, it should be him. He'd failed her, failed Rob, failed himself.

He bent over, hands on his knees and took several deep breaths. *Fuck.* Why was he still standing here?

Next to the Escalade, Jenna's bag lay splayed open on the ground, its contents spilling out onto the asphalt. Acutely aware of the sirens that could only be a couple of streets away now, he hastily stuffed everything back inside the bag and took off running with it. He could wallow in self-hatred later. Right now he needed to stay alert and alive so he could get her back.

First, he needed to ditch the red leather bag. It made him look like a purse snatcher. Ducking behind a grocery store, he found a plastic sack with the store's bright green-and-blue logo on it. He dumped the contents of the tote inside, careful to get the voice recorder and papers, and left Jenna's bag leaning against a garbage bin.

"Sorry, babe," he muttered. "I'll buy you a new one."

He was familiar enough with the area to know that he was about a mile south of a freeway exit that boasted a busy strip mall. Heading north, he turned into a residential area and started walking. It would probably take the cops a while to figure out what was going on and send helicopters out looking for him, but he wouldn't make it easier for them to spot him by running.

There might be enough witnesses at the library to prove his innocence in Longstreet's murder, but he wouldn't put it past his former teammates to try to implicate him somehow. And dealing with the police would take up precious time that he didn't have.

It took all his willpower to stay calm and focused. Jenna had been wearing her bracelet, which meant he could find her if he could get back to his condo.

Fifteen agonizing minutes later, the street curved and rejoined the road the library was on, leading him straight to another retail plaza with a grocery store, a sporting goods store, a bunch of restaurants, and a gas station.

He slipped into a fast food restaurant through the side entrance so he could skip the front counter area, heading straight for the men's room. With cold water, he washed the blood off his face and hands, carefully dabbing at a cut on his cheekbone. His face would likely turn purple tomorrow, but the swelling wasn't too bad for now.

Digging the ibuprofen Jenna had bought out of the grocery bag, he swallowed several and chased them with some water from the faucet.

Examining himself in the mirror, he realized it was time to make some changes to his appearance. His light brown stubble didn't match his dyed black hair, and too many people had seen him. After the incident at the library, things were really going to heat up.

Tremors racked his body. Whoever was after them was dead serious about keeping them quiet. Mick had warned Longstreet to be careful, but he'd never imagined that Claymore was tracking the man. One more soul on Mick's conscience.

How many more could he take?

Should he turn himself in? The police had the manpower to find Jenna and take down her captors. Mick could quit running.

Tempting, but he couldn't give up. To start, he had to make sure their story was told. Mick couldn't trust that Claymore didn't have someone at the police department in their pocket.

No, for now, he needed to go it alone. Which meant he needed a new look before the cops showed up.

Twenty minutes later, he emerged from the sporting goods store. The notebook and Longstreet's recording—as well as Mick's latest purchases—went into a new black messenger bag before he detoured to the grocery store for a few more supplies.

The store had a single-person men's room, so he locked the door and pulled out a razor and shaving cream and got to work. When he finished, he checked his handiwork in the mirror.

Going bald was definitely a new look for him. The closest he'd ever come was boot camp. Combine that with the goatee he'd carved from a couple days' worth of stubble, and he'd aged himself probably ten years. He ran a hand over his smooth scalp. "Not bad." He'd managed not to nick his skin too many times.

Relying on the tricks that had worked before, Mick changed into brand new khaki pants and a long-sleeved golf shirt, padding his belly. He left his head bare, but placed a pair of square-framed reading glasses on his nose and stuffed his cheeks with cotton balls. Not the most comfortable getup, but it beat being recognized.

If he acted like a man with nothing to hide, people would likely see him that way.

His plan was to go back to his condo. And he'd walk through the front door, much the way he'd walked out the day before.

But first he needed to call in another favor.

Tara approached Colin, who had rushed over to the living-room window to investigate what sounded like an approaching vehicle.

"Shit," he said, letting the curtain drop.

"What's wrong?"

He gave her a distracted look, a deep frown on his face. "They're here."

"Who?"

"The rest of my team." He gripped her arm and pulled her into the bedroom. "Maybe if they don't see you it'll be okay."

"*What?*" She looked at him with alarm.

A crease appeared between his brows. "I don't know what

they're doing, but I need you to stay in here and be quiet until I find out."

Bile rose in her throat. Was he as surprised by his team's sudden appearance as he seemed to be, or had this been his plan all along?

"I'll take care of them, just trust me." He caressed her arms and kissed her hard, nudging her hands behind her. "Stay in the corner behind the door until I come back for you."

She closed her eyes and pressed her lips together, turning her head away. She didn't know what to believe anymore.

"I'm sorry," he said, jerking her attention back to him.

About what?

Before she realized what he meant to do, he slipped a zip tie over her wrists and locked it down. Then he strode to the door and shut it behind him.

Jenna kept her eyes squeezed shut and fought the panic that rose in her chest as she struggled for air. She didn't want to see the mean, ugly faces of the men who'd zip-tied her hands behind her back and taped her mouth shut.

If she could go back and do it again, she never would have left Mick's side. But wishful thinking wasn't getting her anywhere. Neither was the fear that threatened to overwhelm her. Would they kill her? After watching James Longstreet die, she had a sinking suspicion she knew the answer to that question.

So why hadn't they done it yet?

Every time the van hit a bump in the road, something dug into her shoulder, but she welcomed the pain—it kept her alert and angry. The men had jammed her between two rows of seats, and without looking, she knew the older one with the pointy chin had a gun trained on her.

Heavy metal blared from the speakers up front, and the bare floor was cold against her side, but the worst part was that she knew Mick couldn't help her now. Tears threatened, but she held them back. They were nothing but a waste of time, and they'd only make it harder to breathe through her nose.

How could she get out of this? It would be impossible for her to make an escape while the van was speeding down what she assumed was the freeway, but when they stopped she might have a shot. Was there anything in the van she could use as a weapon?

She opened her eyes.

Pointy Chin grinned at her. "How're you feeling, missy? Don't wear yourself out by thinking too hard. The van is clean, and we're pros." He reached out and ran a rough hand down her cheek. "Besides, I have plans for you later."

She flinched and looked away, sickened by his touch. He laughed and sat back, resting his feet on her hip like he owned her.

A quick scan of the van confirmed his words. They'd stripped it of anything useful. Not that she could manage to pick anything up in her trussed hands anyway. She groped in the little bit of space she could reach behind her.

Nothing. Defeated, she closed her eyes again.

"Don't worry, we're almost there," Pointy Chin said. He recrossed his legs, setting his heavy boots on her once again.

If she lived, she'd probably end up with bruises on both hips, one from his feet, and the other from the hard metal floor. To distract herself, she tried to figure out how she could get away. It seemed impossible.

Would no one in her family die of old age? She wanted to live. The desire burned in her chest. And she wanted to see Mick again. Had he gotten away?

What would he do if he were in her situation?

*Think.* She wracked her brain for ideas, but the only plan that came to mind was to kick the guys in the knee or groin and run like hell. She just needed enough of a head start to find help. A lot would depend on where they took her.

The minutes advanced at a sloth-like pace before the van finally lurched to a halt. Jenna's muscles tensed, preparing to take action, but nothing happened. They just sat there, no one moving. After several minutes she heard the sound of another car pulling in next to the van. Two doors slammed and footsteps pounded on gravel.

Pointy Chin trained a gun on her chest and called out, "Open the door."

The wide door slid open, and two men stood in the doorway. She recognized the one holding the large rifle as Rizzo, the man Mick had been fighting outside the library when she was taken. Her stomach turned. If he was here... *No!* She squeezed her eyes shut in a futile attempt to block out the image. She couldn't think like that. Mick had gotten away. She refused to believe otherwise. The rifle-toting scum had been beaten up and he didn't look too smug.

She turned her attention to the other man—a blond who resembled the Russian from the old Rocky movie—who wore a handgun in a holster on his hip. He was the other one from the photos, the one whom Mick had called Dolph. He reached out and grabbed her legs, pulling her toward him.

Then he did something that undermined all of her plans to run. He held her feet while Pointy Chin took out another zip tie and bound her ankles together. Then the blond flung her over his shoulder fireman-style, as if she weighed nothing, and strode away from the van.

She raised her head to look around, but they were surrounded by rolling hills and stands of trees. Probably

somewhere west of D.C., based on the terrain. Maybe
Loudoun or Fauquier County. Not that knowing did her any
good. It just made her realize anew how unlikely her chances
of rescue were.

"Hey, Dolph," Pointy Chin said. "Don't rough her up too
much. I have plans for her."

Dolph laughed and slid a hand up her thigh. "Didn't your
mom ever teach you to share?"

Jenna held back a whimper. She would not let him win.
Trying to ignore the man's groping fingers, she focused on
the pain of his shoulder in her stomach, the blood rushing to
her head, the revenge she'd get if they ever let their guard
down.

Her captor kept walking purposefully forward, and after a
few moments a wooden porch came into view. As he scaled
the steps and entered the house, she lifted her head, catching
a glimpse of a large open room with a small kitchen beyond.

Colin stood next to a dirt-colored sofa, his eyes wide,
mouth open. "What the hell is she doing here?" he asked.

Jenna's chest squeezed. If Colin was here, where was
Tara? She wanted to ask him, but with her captor's shoulder
in her stomach she could barely breathe.

"Ghost's orders, man." Dolph turned into a hallway.

"Wait," Colin called out. "Not in there."

Dolph ignored him, opened a door, and dropped her
onto a musty bed covered with a once-colorful quilt that had
grayed with age. The sudden head rush made her dizzy.
Frantic to get away, she scooted sideways and fell off the bed,
landing on a thin rug beside it. Pain spiked through her
shoulder and the side of her head where she'd collided with
the hardwood floor.

Her captor laughed. "There's nowhere to go." He lifted
her back onto the bed, taking his time getting her situated, his

hands roaming indiscriminately.

The sound of Colin arguing with the other men filtered in from the living room. So there'd be no help from there.

Jenna rolled onto her stomach and Dolph grabbed her arm, his hand driving her metal bracelet into her flesh.

"What's this?" he asked, yanking the jewelry from her wrist. "Aww, isn't that sweet?" He threw the bracelet onto the floor and stomped on it, grinding it into the floor with a sneer. "Your brother was a holier-than-thou bastard."

A sob stuck in her throat, and she squeezed her eyes shut. Fighting could only make things worse.

The muscular blond pushed her onto her back and leaned over her, his foul breath wafting across her face. "Guess we showed him."

That did it. Before good sense could intervene, she brought her feet up between his legs with as much force as she could muster. He cried out and hit the ground, both hands holding his crotch.

"Bitch!"

Pointy Chin appeared in the doorway. "What the hell happened?" He aimed his gun at her chest.

"Damn whore kicked me," he said rising to his feet slowly. "Just shoot her, Beavis. We don't need this shit."

Without warning, Dolph lurched forward and backhanded her across the face. Pain flared across her right cheek and her head snapped to the side. The blow was staggering. If she had been standing she would have tumbled to the floor like a rag doll. God, she had no idea getting hit in the face could hurt this much.

Anger heated her skin, requiring every ounce of discipline she had to stay on the bed. The gun Beavis had pointed her way helped.

"Come on," Beavis said. "Ghost will be here soon. We

have work to do."

Dolph shot her a venomous look and limped from the room. "Screw him. Why can't we just kill her now?"

Jenna's chest constricted. *Not yet.*

"Dude, it won't look like an accident if you shoot her."

Dolph grunted, but followed the other man to the door, limping slightly.

"Patience, man. Patience," Beavis said. Then he gave her a lecherous smile and shut the door.

# CHAPTER TWENTY

"THANKS FOR HELPING ME OUT, man," Mick said as Dan Molina parked on the street in front of his condominium building. "I know this puts you at risk." He'd filled his friend in on the entire fiasco on the way over.

Dan waved off Mick's comment and adjusted his baseball cap. "Come on, this is Rob's sister we're talking about."

Now, Mick stepped out of the Land Rover and shouldered his messenger bag. There was at least one vehicle sitting surveillance about forty yards away, and a suspicious-looking utility van was parked across the street from the building's entrance. Good thing they'd borrowed Dan's neighbor's car and disguised Dan a bit. Anybody from the Claymore team would recognize him. And if that happened, the game would be up.

"I'll meet you in back," Mick said, keeping his head down so no one could read his lips.

Two minutes later he was getting off of the elevator, two floors above his own. Then he took the stairs down and entered his hallway. Empty. He'd still make it quick because someone could be staking out the place from a neighboring unit. Of course, if there was an officer stationed inside, he was screwed.

He stopped one door shy of his own and fumbled with his keys for a long moment, hopefully giving any spies time to relax and turn away. Then he stepped over to his own door. It was boarded over where the police had used the battering ram to open it yesterday, but the lock was intact. He entered his condo, quickly shutting the door behind him.

Within a few seconds, he secured the GPS tracking device. He also snagged a box of ammunition before hightailing it out the door and down the back stairs to where Dan was idling.

"Everything okay out here?" he asked as he slid into the passenger seat.

"Not sure." Dan pulled away from the curb and onto the main street. "The power company van did a drive-by. I'll keep an eye out for a tail. How about on your end?"

"So far so good." Mick checked the tracking device, resting his hand on his knee to keep it from shaking. Thank God the bracelet's transmitter was still working. What would he have done if there'd been no way to find her? "She's just south of Leesburg. Head up to 50." Not knowing whether she was alive, injured, or dead was messing with his head.

He refused to think about it, otherwise he'd have Dan redlining the engine to get there. Unfortunately, they needed to fly under police radar. They rode in silence until Dan merged onto Highway 50.

"You were there when Rob was killed too, but no one's been following you, right?"

Dan nodded and looked back to switch lanes. "If they were, they were invisible."

"I should have warned you before talking to Longstreet,"

Mick said, "but I didn't want to give away my location. I'm sorry."

Dan didn't respond right away, and Mick started to worry. If he did manage to break the story, Dan and the rest of the team would be at the center of a firestorm of reporters, controversy, and outrage.

The silence stretched for a long moment before Dan cleared his throat and gripped the steering wheel. "Look, I'm not proud of what happened out there, but we did the right thing in the end. Frankly, it might be a relief to have it all out in the open." He glanced at Mick. "Secrets eat at you, you know?"

Hell yeah, he knew.

"And," Dan continued, "if Rob's death was part of a cover-up for whatever the hell those guys were doing, then they deserve to be punished for it, even if some of the shit rubs off on us."

What the hell did he say to that? Dan's attitude humbled him. Beyond the window, newer subdivisions of oversized houses and townhomes spread across the old farm fields and forested land, part of the never-ending sprawl of D.C. Around here, people barely blinked at a ninety-minute commute.

"Are you going to call Kurt?" Dan asked, breaking the silence.

Now there was an awkward situation. "I don't want to get him into any more trouble. I'm sure he's already dealing with the fallout from last night."

"My guess is that he'd like to redeem himself after his guys fucked up," Dan put in.

Mick rubbed his forehead. "I don't want him to get more involved. He's put enough on the line for me already." He glanced at Dan, well aware that his friend was also risking charges for helping him out. "I couldn't do this without you," he said. Inadequate, but true enough.

"I'd be pissed if you tried." Dan gestured to the tracker. "Now where do we get off?"

"Highway 15, north. Then it looks like the location is about a mile off the main road." He couldn't think of the dot as Jenna. It needed to be a nameless, faceless red blip. Otherwise his total helplessness and his overactive brain's disturbing imagination would drive him mad.

He stared at the blinking circle that hadn't moved since he pulled it up on the screen, hoping like hell that the bracelet was still attached to Jenna, that she was still breathing.

His jaw already hurt from the teeth-clenching workout he'd been giving it since the moment the van sped away with her. It would be a miracle if he had any molars left by the end of the day.

The blip flashed reassuringly. And again. Mick timed his heartbeat and his breathing to it. Blink. Blink.

And then it disappeared.

Jenna watched the door shut behind Pointy Chin and then gasped.

Tara was curled into a ball in the corner that had been hidden by the open door, staring at her in disbelief. "Jenna!" she whispered, awkwardly pushing to her feet.

Jenna could hardly believe her eyes. Tara was here. For about two seconds, she was ecstatic. But then it registered: Both of them were tied up. It was hardly good news.

She tried to sit up, but her hands were still bound behind her, and the awkward angle hurt her shoulders. Using her stomach muscles—like doing crunches at the gym—she struggled into an upright position. Every part of her ached.

Fear flooded her gut, bringing with it too many

unanswerable questions. What were the men going to do to them? Was Mick alive? Could they escape somehow?

"Let me get that tape off," Tara said quietly. Turning away from her, Tara reached back with her trussed-up hands, grabbed the edge of the tape with her fingertips, and gave it a quick jerk.

"Ouch." Damn, that hurt.

"Free lip wax," Tara quipped without humor as she turned to face her again.

"Tara, I was so worried about you. What are you doing here?"

Her friend gave her a rueful smile. "Have you ever noticed my poor choices when it comes to men?"

Jenna kept her voice low. "Well, now that you mention it…"

"Unfortunately, Colin was no exception. He wants me to trust him, but I don't even trust my own judgment anymore. I really thought he might be the one, and now look at me." Tears shone in Tara's eyes as she recounted what had happened over the last few days and the repeated lies that had brought her to this house. "I want so badly to believe that he really cares about me and has my best interests at heart. But this is pretty damning." She turned and raised her tied-together wrists.

"I'm sorry," Jenna said, wishing she could hug her. "I reported your disappearance to the police, but other than your tip about Leesburg, I didn't know where to start."

"I knew you'd get it!" Tara rose and sat next to Jenna on the bed, snuggling up next to her in an approximation of a hug without arms. "What I don't understand is why you're here. Colin told me they were keeping tabs on you and Mick, but not why."

Jenna's tongue was thick and dry, and her throat hurt, but

it was good to finally be able to share her ordeal. She covered the highlights of the last few days, the photos she'd found, and the basics of Rob's death.

With every sentence, Tara's eyes grew wider and her face paled. "I had no idea," she said in a near whisper. "I wonder if Colin was involved in the smuggling or if keeping tabs on you was just a side job for him?" She stared at the wall. "He already admitted he was using me as an inside source." Her head fell back and she groaned. "I'm such an idiot. Remind me of that when we get out of this. I'm going celibate."

"Speaking of getting out…" Jenna scanned the room. A window looked out onto the tree-covered hills behind the house. Other than the bed, the only furnishings were a small steamer trunk and a yard-sale-quality painting of a waterfall that hung over the bed. "There has to be a way."

No one knew where they were, and she had a sinking feeling that their captors weren't planning on letting them get out of here alive.

Tara stood. "We're both tied up." She glanced at Jenna. "And you can't even walk."

She slowly paced the room, eyes darting everywhere. "I don't see any sharp objects that we can use to cut our bindings." Getting up close, she examined the oil painting hanging crookedly on the wall. "No glass besides the window."

"Any idea how long they'll leave us alone?" Jenna asked.

"Nope. I guess until this Ghost guy arrives."

"All right. Let me see your wrists."

Tara stood with her back to Jenna. Her wrists were red where the zip ties had cut into them. The ties were made of wide, heavy-duty plastic that was notched on one side. Too tough to break, especially without leverage or some sharp object they could use to cut through the material.

But plastic could melt.

Jenna's gaze traveled the room. The light bulb would probably burn her friend's hands before it melted through the plastic. What she needed was friction from something thin but strong. Like—*yes!*—the cord on the mini-blinds.

"Help me hop over to the window," Jenna said. "I have an idea."

The blinds had been pulled all the way up, and three nylon cords hung loose, capped with plastic beads. Jenna swiveled and reached back for one of the cords, glancing out the window first to make sure none of the guys were outside watching them.

"What are you doing?" Tara asked.

"Turn around so I can thread this through your cuffs. I'm going to try to saw through them."

Tara complied. "I think I see where you're going with this," she said, a note of excitement in her voice. "If it works I'm going to start calling you MacGyver."

"I'd say keep your fingers crossed, but they're probably too numb for you to manage it." Jenna fumbled trying to press the bead between the plastic and Tara's skin, especially since she couldn't see what she was doing, and her own fingers were tingling from a lack of circulation.

Finally, she got the cord through and pulled it tight. "Okay," Jenna said. "I need to get this moving quickly, but I don't have a good way to pull it in the other direction, so I need you to get really close. I'll pull it taut, and when I say 'go,' you walk away quickly, keeping tension on the plastic the whole time.

"Got it."

"Go."

Tara took four quick steps, but when they came up against the end of the string nothing happened. She walked in front of Jenna, her back facing her. "Did it even make a dent?"

Jenna examined the white plastic. "Yes!" she hissed, her heart giving a small leap of triumph. A small portion of the tie had worn away. "Let's try again."

It took three more tries before Tara's hands flew apart and she stumbled into the bed. She pumped her fist and covered her mouth, presumably to hold back a whoop of joy. Then she signaled to Jenna to turn around too. "Your turn," she said quietly, a small smile playing on her lips as she rubbed her shoulders and wrists.

With Tara sawing the cord back and forth, Jenna's hands came free in less than a minute. Ignoring the painful prickling in her shoulders and hands, she immediately set to work on the plastic binding her ankles. With free hands, she had so many more options. The plastic cuffs didn't have any metal reinforcement in the clasp, so they'd be easy to defeat.

With the tip of one of her broken hand restraints, Jenna pushed against the tiny burr that prevented the notches from slipping loose. While holding that down, she managed to pull the loop free. She could have had Tara use that method on her wrists, but it didn't matter now. They were free.

Unfortunately, that was the easy part. Now they had to somehow get out the window and away from the house without being detected.

Tara bent over Jenna and grabbed her right hand, turning it palm up. "What happened?" she asked, staring at the red, crusted blood.

"That's a souvenir from the last time I jumped out a window. Maybe an hour ago. Or two?" She'd forgotten about her damaged palms in their hurry to free themselves, but now the pain slammed home again and she sucked in a deep breath. "How many guys were here when you arrived?"

"None, it was just me and Colin."

"So, there are five total. Which means we can't go out the door."

Tara nodded her agreement. "But the window's going to make noise even if we manage to open it instead of breaking it. We probably won't make it far. They all have guns."

"What if we don't run?" Jenna pointed to the large bed with its draping spread.

"I don't have a better idea."

The window frame looked like it was probably painted shut, but there was one lucky break. The glass didn't have mullions like the windows of so many homes in the area did, so they should be able to break it. Jenna took off her fleece jacket and placed it on the floor under the window, then pulled the heavily framed oil painting from the wall, her muscles still protesting. "Get under the bed."

Her friend hesitated. "But—"

"Just do it. There's nothing you can do to help except hide." Jenna would have said she'd never been this scared in her life before, but the last week had brought her through more terror than she'd ever thought possible. At this point, it was a tiny increase in her fear quotient rather than a large spike.

Maybe she was starting to understand how Mick and Rob had operated under stress for all those years.

With a deep breath, she hefted the frame and aimed the corner at the center of the glass pane. Taking three strides, she lunged forward with all her might and shattered the window. It gave way so quickly that she hit the wall and dropped the painting onto the grass outside, grabbing the ledge to stop her momentum.

The guards would be there any second, so she used the jacket to knock out any large shards and laid it across the sill to make it look like they had gone over. The blood she left behind from the cuts on her forearms should be convincing as long as she didn't leave a trail across the floor to the bed.

With any luck, the men would think they'd gone around the side of the house and into the group of trees that ran up the ridge of the nearest hill.

Heart pounding as each second stretched out like an hour, Jenna pushed off the wall and dove under the bed as silently as possible. She huddled next to Tara and reached out to stop the quilt from swaying.

Time sped back up. Two seconds later, the door burst open, slamming against the far wall. "What the fuck?" one of the men yelled. "She's out!" His feet pounded away and a brief cacophony of shouts and scraping chairs came from the front room. "Go, go!"

Tara and Jenna looked at each other, neither daring to breathe or move until the house was silent. Jenna pressed her cheek to the floor to look into the room.

She had to bite her tongue not to cry out.

In the doorway, she could just make out a pair of tan combat boots.

*Please, please go away.*

"You two are even smarter than I thought," Colin said, dashing her hopes.

# CHAPTER TWENTY-ONE

"Come on out," Colin commanded.

Tara slid out from under the bed and balled her hands into fists so he wouldn't see how much she was shaking. She and Jenna had come so close to escaping. Everyone else had fallen for their plan. Why did Colin, of all people, have to be the one to catch them?

She glared at the man who'd made her so happy. Thanks to him, she'd betrayed Jenna and Mick and given her body and heart to a criminal.

He lowered the rifle that crossed his chest, but kept one finger near the trigger. "If you go out the front, you might have a chance, but you have to hurry. The guys will circle back around once they realize you're not in the trees."

His words didn't make sense. Why was he telling them how to get away?

"Quickly," he said, impatience threading his deep voice. He pulled Tara toward the door, gesturing for Jenna to follow them.

"Let go of me." She tugged back. "What are you doing?"

He stared at her. "I'm sorry. I screwed everything up. I know you're confused, but you have to trust me. I'm trying to help."

She wanted to believe him, but he'd burned her before. Badly.

"Tara." Jenna touched her arm. "We don't have a choice. He's our only chance now."

Good point. Tara nodded and followed Colin from the bedroom.

"Let me check the area first." He pointed to the wall just inside the front door and went out onto the porch.

Tara's heart thundered in her chest, three beats for every second he was outside.

Thirty beats later, he popped his head back in. "Head down the driveway toward the road and find a house or passing car. I'll cover you until you get around the bend. When the others come back this way, I'll try to keep them off your trail."

As she passed through the door, he grabbed her arm and pulled her close.

"I wasn't lying about my feelings, Tara. I wish things could have been different between us."

Tears burned against her eyelids, but she refused to let them fall. "Me too," she replied, without meeting his gaze. She shook her arm and he released her without further protest.

She ran after Jenna and didn't look back.

Mick tapped the screen of the GPS unit. Where was the dot? He closed his eyes. No more dot meant the bracelet wasn't transmitting anymore. That was all. But damn if his heart wasn't going haywire. He sat forward in his seat, peering through the windshield for any signs that might lead him to

Jenna.

She had to be alive. He couldn't contemplate any other option.

He cleared his throat and pointed to the turn. "According to where I last saw the dot, she should be at the end of this driveway coming up. Let's stop here."

Dan pulled off the road and parked behind a group of overgrown bushes. Maple trees and tall hedges lined the curving drive. They checked their weapons as they left the Land Rover and jogged in silence, partially hidden by the untended growth. A tractor droned in the distance and the air smelled of cut hay and manure.

When they rounded the bend, Mick spotted a dilapidated roof through the newly green and still mostly bare branches of a maple. They slowed and walked low with guns drawn, darting from bush to bush, constantly looking back—checking their six—for threats.

The rumble of an engine alerted them to an approaching vehicle on the road. Mick dove for cover, Dan beside him, just as a flurry of motion erupted at the front of the house. His breathing stopped when Jenna and Tara ran down the porch steps and took off down the driveway.

Jenna was alive! His heart thudded against his chest as if trying to escape. Sweet mother of God, she was alive. But Colin stood in the doorway with his rifle raised. Mick got a bead on him, but eased off the trigger at the last second. Colin wasn't aiming at the women, he was covering for them. What the hell?

Mick would have to figure it out later, though, because Jenna and her friend were heading straight for the black Yukon that was now advancing up the drive.

"Get Tara," he said to Dan before launching himself toward Jenna. He grabbed her and yanked her through the scratchy branches, out of the way of the approaching SUV, as shots cracked like thunder behind them. She screamed and tried to pull away, and he remembered his new look. In her panic, she hadn't recognized him. He gripped her tighter and kept running. "It's me."

She focused on him then, her mouth gaping with surprise. "Mick."

Behind them gears crunched and gravel sprayed as the driver of the SUV attempted to turn the vehicle. Without stopping to look back, Mick dragged Jenna on a parallel path toward the Land Rover. When they reached it, he squatted down behind the front tire, hoping the engine block would provide some protection if anyone else shot at them.

"Are you okay?" he asked, his blood boiling at the sight of her reddened, swelling cheek.

She nodded, reaching out for him. "How did you find me?"

He held her to him tightly, stroking her hair, afraid she wasn't real. "The bracelet. I should have told you about it, but I was afraid you wouldn't wear it if you knew."

She stroked his cheek before pulling him in for a hard kiss. "Thank you." Her shaky breaths puffed along his chin and he longed to take her home and comfort her all night—hell, for the rest of their lives—but he couldn't let down his guard yet.

"I would never have stopped looking. You know that, right?"

She nodded, her eyes shining, and gave him a weak smile.

Footsteps hurried toward them from the house and Mick put a finger to his lips before peeking around the wheel. Dan and Tara were racing in their direction.

"Thank God." Mick leaned his back against the front quarter panel and scanned the road and the brush beyond.

Clear, as far as he could tell. He swung around and rested his arms on the hood, covering Dan and Tara's approach with his gun.

When he was ten feet away, Dan tossed Mick the keys. "Go!"

"Get in and stay down," he said, shoving Jenna toward the back seat before he hopped in front, using his left hand to keep his gun trained in the direction of the house while he started the engine with his right.

Dan practically threw Tara in the back and dove into the front seat. "Go, go, go," he yelled, swinging his door shut as Mick peeled away. Good thing they'd backed in.

They got twenty yards before the windshield shattered and Mick lost control. The women screamed. Dan swore. Mick groaned as fire bit into the right side of his chest and his arm quit following directions from his brain.

He struggled to keep them on the road, but even the best driving skills were no match for his ebbing consciousness and the rutted asphalt. The last thing Mick heard before a tree branch obliterated what had remained of the windshield was Jenna calling his name.

Jenna screamed and reached for Mick. Blood was everywhere, but luckily the tree branch had plowed right down the center of the car, without hitting anyone. Small round pieces of glass covered the dash, the seats, and both men.

"Stay down!" Dan yelled, pushing himself away from the dashboard as he wiped a trickle of blood from his forehead. Deafening blasts emanated from the gun in his hand as he aimed through the shattered windshield. "How many were in the house?" he asked.

"Five," Tara answered, taking hold of Jenna's hand and urging her under the tree branch to her side of the seat. "But don't count Colin. He helped us get away."

"So with the one in the Yukon, that's five." He popped the magazine on his weapon and shoved in a new one. "Keep an eye out on your side, but try to be stealthy about it. The tinted windows should help."

While part of her mind marveled at Tara's uncharacteristic calm, Jenna squeezed herself under the invading branch and climbed into Mick's seat. He had to be okay. Had to. She was not going to lose anyone else. Not now. "Mick?"

He groaned.

Maybe he hadn't been shot. Maybe he'd just been injured by the broken branch.

Dan glanced back at her sitting on Mick's lap. "What are you doing?"

"I have to help him."

"Shit," Dan said as he reclined his seat and crouched down, positioning his head behind the door frame. "Tara, get into the cargo area and stay down. Jenna, when she's out of the way, lower Mick's seat so that you're both out of sight."

Tara folded the center rear seat down and scrambled into the back. She crouched low and watched through the side window.

Jenna found the switch on the driver's seat and levered Mick back, using her elbows to support herself above him on the leather captain's chair. A bullet slammed into the back door panel on the passenger side, and she jumped in surprise, biting back a scream.

Mick needed her to stay calm. She'd be no good to him otherwise. Still, her hands trembled as she examined his wounds. While he wasn't dead—thank God—he was badly hurt. She peeled back his shirt, gasping at the gooey mess around the hole in his flesh. Passing out was not an option, but holy crap.

There was a reason she had studied computers instead of medicine in college. Machines didn't bleed. The last time she'd had blood drawn, she'd nearly taken a dive off the phlebotomist's chair.

The boom of Dan's gun brought her around.

Taking a deep breath, she removed her own shirt and folded it into a square. Pressing the makeshift bandage flat over the wound, she applied as much pressure as she could with her injured hands. It had to be enough. It *had* to be. "Stay with me, Mick. I love you." Her green shirt slowly turned red, despite her best efforts, and tears dropped from her cheeks onto his bare skin. "Don't you leave me too. Don't you dare."

Mick moaned and flinched under her touch, but he didn't pull away.

She finally understood what it had been like for him after Rob was shot. Watching the life leak out of someone you loved, knowing all along you were helpless to stop it. God, please, not Mick too. She'd do anything to keep him alive.

"Dan! Someone's coming," Tara hissed.

"Jenna, give her Mick's gun."

Where was it? She scooted back, keeping one hand on his chest, and scrambled around with her other hand. She found it between his legs on the seat beneath her.

Tara crawled forward and took it from her. "Now what?" she asked Dan.

He swore and kicked the glove box. Then he took a deep breath and let it out slowly. "The safety should be off, just aim and shoot. Aim a little low because it'll buck back on you. And watch out for breaking glass."

Tara stared at the gun for several seconds before catching Jenna's gaze. "I can do this." Her body disappeared into the cargo hold again.

Jenna pressed on Mick's chest with both hands and rested her forehead on the padded edge of the seat. No matter what, she had to keep him alive until they could get help. Still, no matter what she did, the blood kept coming in a slow but steady stream.

Maybe it was hopeless. They were sitting ducks in the SUV. They couldn't move Mick without possibly killing him, and the bad guys—who had the tactical advantage—were closing in on them. She and Tara were just as trapped as they'd been in that bedroom.

The back driver's-side window cracked and Tara's surprised yelp was drowned out by the deafening sound of gunfire from the back of the Land Rover.

"I got him!" Tara yelled.

"Make sure he stays down, and stay alert. There are still four more out there," Dan said.

Would the neighbors call the police or were the nearest homes too far away for anyone to realize that the racket was actually gunfire? And maybe people were allowed to hunt on their land around here anyway. Jenna had no idea. "Dan, do you have a cell phone?"

"Yes. I tried to call for backup, but I can't get any service." He twisted up and looked through the window, before quickly ducking down again. "See if you can find Mick's phone."

Jenna searched his clothes with one hand and found the cell and battery in the front pocket of his khakis. The angle was awkward, but she pulled them out.

She snapped the battery back in and powered on the phone. Why was it taking so damn long to start up? Two eternal minutes later, the cell phone chimed that it was ready. Jenna held it out and checked the signal strength.

All she needed was one bar. One tiny freaking bar. Was that too much to ask?

She got nothing.

Mick awoke groggy and disoriented. The bitter smell of gun smoke tickled his throat, and his chest hurt like hell. He opened his eyes a crack. Jenna was lying on top of him, wearing only her cotton bra, her red, puffy eyes focused on something to his right.

"Hey, babe."

Her head snapped back to him. "Oh my God. Mick, you're awake."

She showered his face with kisses, and he caught her mouth, using his working left arm to pull her closer. Like always, his pain faded into the background when she kissed him.

Much too soon, she broke away and looked at him, almost smiling. "Slow down there, cowboy. You've been shot and I need to keep pressure on the wound. Not to mention the fact that people are still shooting at us."

Shot? No wonder he hurt like hell. He took in the blown-out windshield and the invading tree branch as his memories slammed home. He couldn't have been out long. "Dan, I don't think your neighbor's going to be too happy about her car."

"That's okay. I was looking for a way to break up with her," he shot back, his muscles tense as he crouched behind the center beam, his gun at the ready. "We're in a bit of a standoff here. We have four guys pinned in the trees, but we can't hold out here forever. It's Rizzo, Beavis, Dolph, and whoever was in the SUV. I couldn't make him out behind the tinted windows."

"Me either," Mick said. He tightened his grip on Jenna.

"Why are you still in here anyway? This is a death trap."

She shook her head. "I'm not leaving you."

Foolish woman. He wasn't worth her life. "If you care about me at all, you'll save yourself."

"I love you. And I'm not going to lose you too," she said, her chin set at an obstinate angle.

"Damn it, Dan, tell her I'm right."

"He's right," Dan said, the reluctance clear in his voice. "We have a better chance on our feet, and if we're lucky, we can find help down the road. There might even be a phone in the house."

"Then you and Tara go," Jenna said. "I'm staying here with Mick."

"Jenna, please, do it for me," he said. He couldn't even sit up, let alone walk, but she appeared to be unharmed. For now. He wanted her to stay that way. Skimming his knuckles along her chin, he locked his gaze with hers. Why did he have to hurt her to save her life? "Even if I make it out of this, I can't be with you."

Her face flushed red and her eyes narrowed. "You said you loved me."

"Good timing, lover boy," Dan muttered.

"Shut your trap, Molina." He'd prefer to do this without an audience, for Jenna's sake, but he didn't have much of a choice right now. He needed to get her the hell out of the car so she'd have a chance. "I do love you. I probably have since we first met. But I'd be hell to live with. You know that. I can't do happily ever after with two-point-four kids and a nine-to-five job. I can't be that guy for you. It's never going to happen."

Jenna frowned and searched his face, the seconds ticking away with agonizing slowness. "I don't believe you," she said, breaking the thick silence as she looked over his shoulder.

"Tara, give me your gun and go with Dan."

"*No*," Mick protested.

She ignored him, taking the weapon from Tara while keeping pressure on his chest. "Be careful."

"You too," Tara said. "We'll get help."

The rear passenger door opened and Dan slid under the tree branch and into the back seat. "Hang in there, man. We'll be back for you."

Mick didn't even have the energy to fight anymore. He was fading fast, losing his ability to focus on Jenna's pretty face as she watched Dan and Tara over the edge of the window frame.

"Rob taught me how to shoot," she said without looking at him.

He reached up and slid his hand under the hair at the nape of her neck. "I love you, stubborn woman," he whispered.

She rested her forehead against his. "I love you too."

A loud crack split the air and something thudded into the car. Jenna did a quick recon out the window and ducked. "Crap. Dan and Tara are under fire." Resting the gun barrel on the top of the window ledge, she aimed and pulled the trigger.

The kickback jolted her against the console and she released the pressure on his wound as pieces of safety glass rained down on him. Holy hell, his chest hurt. He fought a rising rush of nausea and blinked away the dots that swam in front of his eyes.

"Sorry," Jenna cried, scrambling to push the bandage back into place.

"Did you get him?"

"No," she frowned. "I don't know what happened."

Outside the car, gun shots popped loudly. "What's going

on?"

"Dan and Tara are pinned down," she took aim and fired again, bracing herself this time. "Got him!" she shouted with a triumphant smile. "In the arm, but his gun went flying and he's down for now."

Jenna's hair drifted in the cool breeze as she watched the scene through the broken window, still holding his makeshift bandage in place. He'd give anything to get her out of this alive.

Motion from the far side of the car caught his eye and he turned his head.

Troy Griffin—CEO of Claymore, known to his guys as Ghost—stood at the window, his rifle aimed at the back of Jenna's head.

# CHAPTER TWENTY-TWO

JENNA WATCHED IN SHOCK AS Colin took out the man shooting at Tara with a quick twist to the neck. The shooter —Dolph—dropped like a stone at his feet.

She squeezed her eyes shut to block out the image, but it was already imprinted on her retinas. Tara's yell made her look again. Rizzo, the man Jenna had shot earlier, was back on his feet, his right arm hanging limply at his side, the gun in his other hand pointed at Colin now.

Dan was on the other side of the clearing, grappling with Beavis, so Jenna was the only one who could save him.

Sighting along the barrel, she let out a breath and pressed on the trigger. Her shot went wild as Mick yanked her down to his chest. What was he doing? She was about to ask him when something zinged so close to her head that she could feel the disturbance in the air. The percussive boom echoed through the Land Rover, obliterating all sound but the high-pitched ringing in her ears.

She felt herself screaming, but couldn't hear it.

Before she realized what he was doing, Mick had wrapped

his hand around hers, rolled her to the right, and pressed her finger on the trigger. Only then did she see the man standing in the window with an enormous rifle. In a flash she remembered the revulsion that had rolled through her when his rough, dry hands gripped hers at Rob's funeral. Troy Griffin, CEO of Claymore. She barely registered who he was before the bullet pierced his thick neck.

He dropped his weapon and clutched his throat as blood gushed through his fingers. After a couple of stumbles, he fell to the ground.

Mick's hand fell away from hers and he started to gasp for air.

Trembling, Jenna flipped back over, careful not to put her weight on his chest. His wound had started bleeding in earnest again, and his eyes were clenched shut.

"No, no, no! Do not die on me, damn it. You owe me, Mick." She leaned hard on his chest, fighting back the insidious, sticky fluid that cared nothing for love. "Please, I love you so much. We're so close to the end of this."

"Are you okay?" Dan appeared at her window, his voice tight. "I think we got them all."

"Hurry, please. He's fading on me." She pleaded with her eyes. "Don't let him die, Dan. I need him."

"Shit. I'm going." He raced away from the car.

Outside, she could see Tara running around Rizzo—had Griffin's shot hit him, or had Dan taken him out?—to kneel over Colin. He lay motionless on the ground, blood spreading into the dirt around him in a pool. Jenna had probably failed to save him too. So much blood, so many deaths. And for what?

She wanted to rave and scream and pound her fists. Instead, she held both hands over Mick's wound and put all of her weight into it, watching his chest rise and fall with each shaky breath.

"You saved me. Again," she said between sobs. "You've done right by your promise to Rob."

Minutes ticked by as she watched the life leak out of him, helpless to stop it. "When you get better, we can live anywhere you want, but I'm not letting you go without me. Alaska, Hawaii, Florida, the Mojave Desert. I don't care as long as we're together."

Maybe if she kept talking, it would give him something to focus on. Maybe it would keep him from drifting away. "I'm going to take Rob's savings and start working for myself. I've lived in fear for too long, but I realized I was so worried to take a risk that I wasn't living. Not really. I'm ready to live now, Mick. And I want you there too. You think you're a risky proposition for me, but I think you're the safest bet I've ever made.

"The first time I met you, I thought you were an arrogant, reckless, playboy. You set off so many alarm bells in my head, it irked me that I couldn't stop thinking about you. I hated watching you with those other women…" Those parties had been hell, but like a crowd drawn to an accident, she hadn't been able to look away. "But underneath it all, you were always a man of honor.

"If you stayed away from me that whole time because you thought it was the right thing to do, then I want you to realize that now the right thing is for you to stay *with* me. After all we've been through, I know Rob would approve."

Were those sirens? Her ears were still ringing, but she could swear she heard their telltale wailing coming steadily closer. Her heart rate picked up. "They're coming, honey. Hold on just a little longer for me." She kissed his lips. "Just hang on."

* * *

Jenna's efforts to ride to the hospital with Mick were thwarted by the police, who insisted she and the others stick around the scene for questioning and to be looked over by the paramedics. At least they found a spare T-shirt for her.

Afterward, Dan drove her and Tara to the medical center and got them situated in the waiting room, where Kurt was already pacing like one of the big cats at the zoo.

Once Jenna was seated, Dan leaned down to give her a hug. Numbness seeped into her limbs as the adrenaline wore off, and fear clung to her like a stink she couldn't wash away. "Thank you," she said. "For everything."

"You don't even have to say it."

He let her go and knelt in front of Tara, who was sitting in the chair next to her. "Are you all right?"

Without looking up, she nodded, hiding behind a veil of disheveled hair. "Fine."

"Can I get you anything?"

She shook her head, still staring at the floor, her face oddly blank.

With a sigh, Dan gave up; he took a seat across from them, watching Tara with a frown.

Kurt stopped pacing and patted Jenna's shoulder with one hand. "He's hanging in there. The doctor told Mick's mom the bullet didn't hit anything critical."

Maybe not, but he still wasn't in good shape. She sucked in a quick breath. "His mom!" She sat up as shame rushed through her. "I hadn't even thought—"

"I called her." Kurt held up his cell phone. "She's heading to the Columbus airport for the next flight out."

Jenna sagged with relief. "Thank you. I'm not thinking straight yet." Mick was a lucky man to have such good friends.

His eyes filled with concern. "What about you? No

injuries?"

"Nothing serious." Just her heart. "I'm fine."

Kurt shoved his hands in his pockets and pressed his lips together. "Look, I owe you an apology for last night. My team screwed up." His face flushed red. Was he embarrassed or angry? Probably both, given that his reputation was on the line.

She waved aside his concern. "It's over now. Are your guys all okay?"

"Everyone's good. At least physically."

"Well, it's over."

"Yeah, but—"

Jenna put her hand on his arm. "You can't change what happened. Just learn from it and move on."

He nodded and squared his shoulders, taking a seat beside Dan.

Jenna turned toward Tara and hugged her trembling friend. "What did the nurse say about Colin?" she asked quietly.

"They won't tell me anything because I'm not family, but she did say they expect him to pull through." Tara dissolved into tears, her whole body convulsing with sobs. "He saved me." She looked up, her face a mask of misery. "He saved *us*. I didn't trust him, even after he let us go, but he almost died to help us. He still might." She hugged her knees to her chest. "How do I live with that?"

"He'll make it." Jenna rubbed her friend's back.

"I love him, but he's going to jail if he recovers." Tara threw her hand out in an angry gesture. "Jail! I finally meet the man of my dreams and he's a freaking criminal. I'm so confused. I don't know if I could ever trust him again, or if I even want to try."

Dan glanced over as Tara's voice rose. He looked tired

and miserable.

Jenna squeezed her friend's hand. She didn't trust Colin. He was mixed up with the smuggling ring and Rob's killer, and he'd lied to Tara. But he'd also come through for them in the end. That was undeniable. "You can't choose who you love." She should know. "But you don't have to decide right now either."

Tara nodded. "I wouldn't trust myself to make that kind of decision right now anyway."

"I wish you hadn't been roped up in this, but I'm grateful you were there with me." Jenna squeezed her friend's shoulder. "I don't think we would have made it without your help."

"Except that you might not have been there in the first place if it weren't for me," Tara said, her eyes downcast.

"Tara." Jenna waited for her to look up. "The rest of those guys were already watching us. You had nothing to do with that."

Tara gave a slight nod. "Okay," she said, and then excused herself to use the restroom.

Jenna sighed. Her friend had already been a mess. Who knew how this experience would affect her in the long term? Or how it would affect any of them?

They spent the night on the uncomfortable chairs, dozing, talking, and drinking coffee. The air smelled like old food, stale coffee, and ammonia when Jenna awoke, stiff and sore from the previous day's beating. Hushed footsteps, faraway wails, and muffled conversation broke the heavy silence of despair that filled the halls in the early morning.

A doctor eventually alerted them that Mick's condition had been upgraded, and Jenna could breathe freely for the first time since he'd been shot. She was finally allowed to visit after the police were done talking to him, sometime around ten.

"All charges against me have been dropped," he said, his eyes never leaving her face. "Beavis and Colin are somewhere in the hospital under police guard. No one else made it." He grimaced and tugged at the white sheet as machines clicked and beeped ominously around him.

She understood. More blood, more death, some of it at his hands. Men he'd known and worked with, which had to chafe even after what they'd done.

But they were finally free. The police hadn't pieced together all of Troy Griffin's plan yet, but based on the explosives found in the Yukon, it wouldn't have been pretty.

Her stomach turned when she thought about how close Griffin had come to succeeding. She pulled in a deep breath to calm her nerves. Now that he and the others involved were dead or under arrest, she and Mick were no longer targets. The story would get out to the press, of course, but the worst was over.

The fear that had weighed her down for weeks had finally lifted, but there was still a vise around her heart. She held Mick's cool hand and leaned against the bed rail. Could he sense how anxious it made her to see him hooked up to monitors and IVs, wires and tubes? The sight reminded her so much of Jimmy's last horrible months.

As if reading her thoughts, Mick said, "I'm okay. I'll be fine." He squeezed her fingers. "Thanks to you."

She swallowed and nodded. If the bullet had hit him any further to the left, it wouldn't have mattered what she did.

"Thank *you*," she said. "For protecting me. For saving us."

"I wish I'd done a better job. When I saw them pull you into that van…" He looked away.

"But you found me. We're both safe now." She tightened her grip on his hand, afraid that he'd slip away somehow if she let go. "It's over."

"Yeah," he said slowly, rubbing his free hand across the stubble on his shaved head. "It's over."

Her focus strayed to the oak tree outside his window before seeking him out again. Dare she ask? "What about us?"

"Jenna..." How could he make her understand that he loved her? The problem was that he was scared...more scared than he'd ever been in his life. What if she wised up and decided she could do better? What if she left after realizing how messed up he was? But then, she already knew that, didn't she? And he was already living without her. Could it get any worse?

"You wouldn't be hell to live with," she said, invoking their conversation in the Land Rover, as if reading his mind. "Not when you're being yourself. The old playboy Mick—the one who hid behind charm and false smiles—he would be hard to live with. But not you," she finished softly.

She took a step back, releasing his hand and crossing her arms over her chest. "How is that you'll jump out of an airplane, or run into a firefight, but you're afraid to be with me?" Her pretty blue-gray eyes narrowed.

She was right. He was a fucking coward. She'd lost so many loved ones, and yet she was willing to take a chance on him. And he was supposed to be the one who lived for risk?

He held her gaze, hoping she could read the sincerity in his face. "Rob warned me off the first time I saw you. He wanted something...someone better for you. I figured that I could stay away, that I could find someone else, but I was wrong." God knows he'd tried to find someone to replace her, but those other women had all been poor substitutes for the one he couldn't have. He'd paraded them in front of

Jenna, dead set on proving to himself and Rob that he had no interest in her. But for some reason she was still here, still in love with him.

He let out a long, slow breath. "I couldn't get you out of my head. Every time I came home, I'd think, 'Maybe this is the time you'll be over Jenna.' The reality couldn't possibly compare to the way I'd built you up in my mind.

"And then I'd see you again and it was like a shock to the system. If anything, you were more beautiful than I remembered, more irresistible." His voice was tight with frustration. "The only way I could deal with it was to go away again."

Tears glistened on her cheeks, and when he held out his hand, she took it and moved to his side.

"Loving you is not what scares me," he whispered. "It's far too late for that." Releasing her hand, he cupped her face with his palm and caught her gaze. "I'm afraid of loving you too much. I'm afraid of driving you away with my craziness." He wiped her tears with the pad of his thumb. "But I don't want to live without you. I probably don't deserve you, Jenna, but I'm feeling pretty selfish. I want to be with you anyway."

She smiled and his heart soared. "You're not going to drive me away," she said. "If you were capable of that, I would have moved on years ago."

He closed his eyes and exhaled the last vestiges of his fear. *I'll be good to her, Rob. I promise.* Then he looked into Jenna's beautiful face, the face of his future. "Will you marry me?"

She turned her head to the side and kissed his palm, then cradled his hand in her own. "Yes. Just name the date."

"What's today?"

She laughed and warmth spread through his body. "How about we wait until you can stand?"

"Standing's overrated." He pulled her in for a kiss, wishing he was in shape to do more. "Besides, you said you'd like to be on top, and since I'm stuck on my back…"

She straightened and shook her head, but couldn't hide her smile. "You're incorrigible."

"You love me anyway."

"I do," she said, giving his hand a squeeze. Then she leaned down and kissed him.

And for the first time in a long time, all was right with his world.

# ABOUT THE AUTHOR

GWEN HERNANDEZ was a manufacturing engineer and programmer before she turned to writing romantic suspense. She's also the author of *Scrivener For Dummies* and teaches Scrivener (writing software) to writers all over the world.

She loves to travel, read, jog, practice Kung Fu, and hang out in northern Virginia with her Air Force husband, two teenage boys, and a remarkably lazy golden retriever named Zoe.

You can find her on Facebook at www.facebook.com/GwenHernandezAuthor or Twitter at @Gwen_Hernandez. To learn more, visit her website at www.gwenhernandez.com.

30392589R00182

Made in the USA
Lexington, KY
01 March 2014